The Treasure Seeker

The Treasure Seeker

A Melody Meeks Mystery

By Suzanne Hope

The Treasure Seeker: A Melody Meeks Mystery

Content Editor: Katie Schmeisser
Copy Editor: Kevin J Topolovec
Cover Art: Myriam Wares
Editor-in-Chief: Kristi King-Morgan
Formatting: Kristi King-Morgan
Assistant Editor: Maddy Drake

ISBN- 978-1-947381-40-7

www.dreamingbigpublications.com

I am dedicating this novel to my sister Diane, whose independence and spirit for adventure inspired me from an early age, and still does.

Acknowledgements

I would like to thank my beta readers Andrea, Deanna, Tessa, ML, Megan and Sandra for all their thoughtful feedback and advice. Also, thanks to others who have read the manuscript or encouraged me along the way including Andy, Paul, Claire and Steve. Thanks to my friend Jemma whose unique funky style helped me develop the character Melody and finally to my husband Francesco for his constant support and great Italian cooking (especially his *'Caponata'*) which was always welcome after many hours spent working on the manuscript at weekends.

PROLOGUE

The Caribbean Ocean
Somewhere off the coast of Panama
1665 ca.

Buccaneer Bates had a bad feeling about it from the start.

The call came just before midnight. Eight able-bodied men to go ashore with the captain and Wicks his second in command. It would be a small landing party, but a recent skirmish with the Spaniard Marquez had taken its toll on both the men and their ship "The Satisfaction" so, no surprises there.

Marquez's frigate was swift, its cannons hefty, and its aim straight. They'd chased The Satisfaction to a windswept Panamanian archipelago then blown a hole in her stern. It was only by luck she hadn't gone down. She still could.

Once they'd shaken Marquez's from their tail they found a cove and sunk anchor. Closer inspection showed a breach in the hull, large and low enough to cause alarm in a swell, so with a storm brewing on the horizon, some of the crew attempted repairs while the rest did the best they could to ready the ship. The dead were thrown overboard and the wounded were tended down below. While they worked, Wicks counted the remaining able-bodied men.

They were an even smaller band now but at least the bare skeleton crew they needed to sail the ship.

The attack had come in the dead of night, catching the privateers off guard. Many had suffered cuts, gunshot wounds or both. To make matters worse, a keg of gunpowder had caught alight and blown a cannon to smithereens on the lower deck. Lynch, a young buccaneer from Plymouth, had gotten away with his life but he'd lost a leg below the knee and it wasn't looking good. Mr. Roberts, the closest they had to a ship's surgeon, was with Lynch now. With no formal training, he did what he could for him with his limited supply of lineaments and rags and a few tricks he'd picked up in Port Royal. Mr. Roberts was an enigma to the men. A solitary man and not normally one to mingle, the previous night he had opened up to his fellow buccaneers over a hog's leg and a flask of grog. He'd told the men he'd been a butcher in Southampton, until he got into trouble with the law. Now with a price on his head and no prospect of a return to Southampton anytime soon, he'd taken his chances with Morgan, the captain. The men didn't know what he'd done nor the reason for it. Some said he'd murdered a man. But if truth be told, they really didn't care. They were all cutthroats and outlaws, and in this part of the world, a man could reinvent himself many times over. Most did.

Lynch's chances didn't look good. Gangrene would surely set in and if it did, there was little Mr. Roberts could do. Lynch was going to have a slow, painful death, and the rum cask the captain had given him would only help dull the pain so much.

The captain never visited the injured men, sending Wicks instead. But he was generous to a fault. A limb lost defending the ship gained respect and an extra two bags of silver to drink away in the whore houses back in Port Royal - that is, for the ones lucky enough to survive the ordeal. Most didn't. Nevertheless, the men were reckless, took chances. The lure of some extra pieces of eight enough.

Buccaneer Bates had been on many a venture with Morgan. He was a hard man, cut from rugged Cornish rock and was willing to take the risks a privateer's life entailed, but even he had his limits.

"What's the use of the extra spoils if you ain't around to enjoy them?" he'd said earlier that night to a fellow buccaneer O'Mally.

The call came again and there was no avoiding it this second time around. Bates and O'Mally had been trying to get some shuteye on the main deck where the air was fresh, not feted like below where the stench of goats, manure and the sweat of the crew was overwhelming six weeks in, so rousing himself to avoid a boot in his back, Bates took his musket, some shot, checked the blade of his cutlass on the edge of his thumb and headed with O'Mally for the rowboats, which were moored off the stern of the ship. It was an overcast night, with just a sliver of moon poking out from behind thick ribbons of cloud, but with the torches lit, they could see well enough. The boats were filling up with men as Bates and O'Mally got in line.

Morgan, Wicks, the chest, and a girl were already in one boat as the buccaneers slid down ropes to the second. Bates flinched when he saw the girl was coming too.

"Let's pray we're leaving her ashore" he grunted to O'Mally, as if reading O'Mally's mind.

The girl had been locked in the captain's cabin for over a week and the men didn't like it. Nobody was exactly sure who she was, when she'd boarded the the ship, and why. She'd just appeared one day on deck, dark and disheveled. The crew resented having a woman aboard. It was against their code. Some even said the captain loved this wench, despite having a wife back in Jamaica. Others said she was some kind of witch and he was under her spell. Two nights ago, when the captain had retired to his cabin the men had gathered on the lower deck and agreed to call the captain to account for his strange cargos: the chest and the girl. But the Spanish frigate on their tail had put an end to the matter, for the time being.

The row boats set off with the strongest men taking the oars in a slow and steady pull away from the ship. A shiver went down Bates' spine as, looking up, he took in The Satisfaction. She'd taken a battering in this last encounter for sure. From here you could see the hole clear in her side. It wouldn't take much of a swell to breach it, but with a bit of luck she could still get them back to Port Royal, repairs and weather permitting.

He'd already decided this would be his last mission with Morgan. He'd enjoyed the freedom buccaneering allowed, the plunder and spoils. But deep down he knew it was better to settle down and buy a small plot of land; not spend all his loot whoring and drinking like he normally did once back on 'terra ferma.' He enjoyed the fun while it lasted, but the trouble was the spoils were often spent within a month. Then he was forced to set sail again, whether the mood took him or not. By all accounts instead, Morgan had been spending his gold and silver wisely; buying plantations and slaves and investing in the sugar cane trade. Bates wanted to follow the captain's example. He knew with the silver from this last venture he'd have enough to buy something small, perhaps even a modest plot of land on the south side of the island where land was still cheap. Yes, his mind was made up. The drinking and his favourite whore Molly would have to wait. Not only was he getting long in the tooth for this game, but this last skirmish with the Marquez had been too close to call and it looked like it wasn't over yet. It had left him spooked for the first time in years. Even now, the Spanish were still on their tail, close behind, somewhere out there in the night and, he couldn't shake the creeping sensation that his luck might be running out. Morgan had something they wanted, and they weren't giving up. It was different this time. All the buccaneers sensed it, even if they weren't saying as much.

The row boats ploughed on and soon the sound of surf broke through the night's breeze; a signal that a reef was close by. Then the clouds cleared, a slice of moon came into focus and the island appeared: a silhouette, flat and low on the horizon. Bates waited his turn to look through the spy glass that was being passed around the boat. It was indeed an island like many others; familiar yet lonely, remote and windswept. A thin strip of sand formed a pale ribbon of beach and behind, a dense, tangle of jungle was pushing down, encroaching on it. Bates passed the eyeglass on. He didn't like it. He didn't like it one bit. He'd be glad when he was back on The Satisfaction with the main sail up and this god forsaken, windswept archipelago far behind him.

Landing the boats in a cove the men heaved their wooden bulks up onto the beach. Under Wicks' instructions, six men struggled under the chest's weight but managed to manhandle it down onto the sand. It was a heavy, cumbersome solid oak chest and getting it off the boat was no mean feat. Meanwhile, the captain, deep in thought, studied a small, scraggy parchment by the light of an oil lantern as best he could. Then, without a word, he headed to the top of the beach, and fixed his gaze into the jungle. Turning, he nodded at Wicks.

"This'll do!"

"Men, in a line behind the captain, and take one of these," Wicks shouted, taking a bunch of rusty spades from a boat and passing them around.

"What's this all about?" Bates asked Spragge under his breath. Spragge was a young lad and had only just turned seventeen, but he was known for his quick eye and had a quick tongue to match. No stranger to midnight raids, they were both used to the secrecy surrounding some landings. Morgan had proven his worth to the men before and Bates knew that not all was revealed at the outset, but even so, something wasn't sitting well in his stomach tonight.

"Satan'll tell us for sure" grinned Spragge, wiping beads of sweat from his brow and showing the gap in his front teeth where his passion for sugared ginger and the addition of one too many punches in the face had already taken their toll.

The strange procession started up, almost religious like, with the chest held shoulder high by four of the strongest men. Wicks led the way with a lantern while two men cleared the path with cutlasses as best they could. The air was humid, the atmosphere thick, and the going slow through the tangled chaos of the forest, but it wasn't long before the sound of surf receded and those of the jungle grew.

Pressing on, they broke into a shallow clearing. A rock face on the left was covered in a curtain of green. The sound of a stream on the right trickled through the night's air. The captain shouted halt and instructed the men to pause and the chest hit the ground with a thump.

"Take a rest and a swig of rum for your spirits," Morgan said, throwing over a flask and scanning the men who took their turns to pass it around.

The captain paced back and forth, and consulted with Wicks, while the men grumbled and mumbled and drained the remains of the rum.

"Men. Take your spades and dig here!" shouted Wicks, after the captain who, marking the parchment he still had in his grasp, gave a nod. More mumbling and semi grumbling came from the men who were dirty, weary and by now in need of more than just the one flask to keep their spirits up and get them back on their feet.

The captain knew well how things could turn with a crew of tired, dispirited buccaneers. They'd voted him captain, but loyalty needed to be won day by day, and he needed their loyalty now. So, he held up his hand to stop the men before the grumbling turned nasty.

"Men, I know this has been a long hard week. You're right to grumble, but you've done yourselves proud. You've outmaneuvered Marquez and lived to tell the tale. And I promise you that for a job well done here, there'll be an extra cask of rum, a pair of hog legs, and an extra bag of silver for every seaman who digs good and hard tonight."

The men stood up now, the mention of an extra bag of silver sinking in.

"When do we sail for Port Royal?" shouted one of the men, Spice, at the back of the group. He was a good ten years older than the average buccaneer and probably felt that he had earned his silver and whoring more than the rest. His skin was nut brown, battered and weathered by the sun and sea of many a year. It glistened with the sweat and grime of a lifetime of hard living and even harder drinking. "You promised a one month venture with six bags of silver each. But we've been a' sailin n'marauding now for over six weeks, and we've done a fair bit o fightn' too. That last tussle with Marquez was one I hadn't bargain for. When I joined this buccaneer boat, 'twas on different grounds." The men looked around at each other and murmured in agreement. Spice, as he was known to them all for his uncanny ability to identify not only a spice but which island it came from, was always one to speak up, sometimes too much for his own good.

"Tonight, we set sail for Port Royal. The Satisfaction permitting, you'll be home within the week. You have my word. I lay my life on it and you know I have a reputation for keeping my word," said the captain, looking each and every man in the eye as best he could by the flickering flame of the oil lamps which were now nestling on the dank forest floor.

"An' given the plunder we've made, by my count there should be at least nine bags of silver per head, extras for bravery...and as I said an extra bag just for a job well done here tonight. So, what do ya say men? The quicker you get to work the quicker you'll be back on board with that keg of rum and some hog!"

Another more upbeat mumble passed through the men, then Bates spoke up. "And the girl? Is she to Port Royal with us? You know what they say about having a whore onboard. We might not make it back with our hides intact if she's with us. She'll bring us no luck. The Satisfaction's taken a battering. All it'll take is a storm and her witchcraft and we're done for!"

Until now the girl had been absent from the scene. She'd been by the captain's side along the jungle path, but in the clearing, she'd stepped back and had almost disappeared from view. Some of the men now turned to find her, searching the gloom. But she couldn't easily be seen. Her dark skin, hair and black satin dress melted into the forest like a shadow. Then, stepping forward from beneath a banyan tree, the yellow light from the oil lamps flickered across her face. She had a wild look in her eye and a strange, crocked smile broke out over her heavily tattooed cheeks. The men weren't easily spooked but this woman did just that, and some of them flinched.

"I'll decide what fate awaits her," said Morgan stepping forward between the men and the woman, blocking their view. "And don't you worry lads. Whatever I do will be in the best interest of The Satisfaction and you men. Now, what do you say? Shall we get a diggin'? Marquez is on our trail and close behind at that. We need to make haste. Come on men. Let's be off this god forsaken island!"

Chalk Farm, London

Now

If I had to pinpoint the moment when my life changed, I'd probably say it was on a regular Tuesday afternoon last July, the day I had the meeting with Jake, editor of *Zenith* magazine.

I remember the day was bright and sunny, perhaps the first of the summer, but I wasn't in an upbeat mood as I hurried through the streets of Soho late for my meeting. You see, Jake had told me my latest *Melody Talkin'* feature wasn't up to scratch and had asked me to pass by the office to discuss it.

An hour later, stepping back onto the bustling Soho streets after our meeting, I knew I had to face facts. Things were not looking good. A far worse scenario than a feature re-write was upon me. Jake had been clear.

Zenith was under new management and my freelance contract hung in the balance. I went home feeling despondent and depressed.

It was the reason why later that night, alone and distracted, with no friends around for a pint at my local pub, 'The Crown,' I logged onto Facebook…

Sitting at my kitchen table now, looking down to the dark, dank garden below, rain is softly pattering onto the window outside. I take a sip of coffee and watch large drops run down the pane and waterlog the plant pots on the windowsill. I know the plants will die if I leave them out much longer, submerged in water with the cold fingers of winter starting to poke them, but I don't have the energy for windowsill gardening today and in any case, it's far too wet to open the window right now. Instead I savor the hot, aromatic steam drifting up from my favorite yellow mug, take another sip of coffee and reflect on all that's happened since that day last July.

I cast my mind back to the person I was. In many respects I'm still the same Melody Meeks with cropped red hair, a wardrobe of charity shop clothes and a weakness for shiny new Dr. Marten boots. To my mum's distress, I'm still a tomboy at heart, a struggling journalist, and an occasional smoker of roll-ups. But the hair, clothes and tobacco habit are a superficial layer. Underneath I'm a different individual, a different Melody to the one standing on that Soho Street last July.

I've certainly learned so much: How little we really know each other; especially friends and acquaintances from years gone by. How poorly we know ourselves despite living and breathing the part each day. And maybe most important of all, how our destiny is not always ours to control. How it can be set spinning by the most inconsequential act: a turn of events here, an unexpected encounter there. Or as in my case, with an unassuming and casual click of a computer mouse through which murder entered my world and change my life, forever.

Chapter One

I'd been a freelance writer at *Zenith* for three years and regularly came by the *Zenith* office for meetings. Back then *Zenith* was in its fourth year and still struggling. A monthly mix of in-depth features, history, culture, fashion, science. And then there was my *Melody Talkin'* page. It was supposed to be the light-hearted, cutting-edge, female, commentary piece. Supposed to be. In reality, it was a bit Bridget Jones without the originality, the wit, or the following.

Waving me into his office on the fifth floor, Jake told me it'd been a crazy week. He certainly looked worn around the edges, even for him. His dark brown eyes were tired, his skin grey and sallow. Sitting behind a chaotic desk full of papers and layouts he leant back, sighed and glanced over the draft of the August edition of my page with a concentrated frown. While I waited, I listened to the noise drifting up from the street below through the open window behind his desk. The muffled sounds of Soho on a warm summer's day filtered through the noise of London traffic while I waited, studying his face trying to gauge a reaction. But I already knew. These days Jake only ever asked me to come into the office when he didn't like a draft. I wouldn't say I only ever saw him in person when there was a problem, but almost, to the point where these days my heart always sank when I saw his name blinking at me on my phone. You see, fact was I'd hit an inspiration dry patch these last few months and I was worried that this, the August edition, was missing the mark too. It lacked that certain spark. I knew it, and judging by the expression on Jake's face, he knew it too.

"Look Mels...and thanks for coming in at short notice but I have to be honest, we could run it but... well, it does feel a bit...tired," he said, tossing my draft down on the desk, rubbing his eyes and yawning.

"Sorry," he apologized between the yawns, "It's been a long week. I was here till gone midnight last night. Look, is there anything you can do to...I don't know, spice it up a bit? I'm finding this topic a little bit...well, dry to be frank. Coffee?" he asked getting up and going over to a Nespresso machine on the side, popping in a capsule and turning to me.

"No thanks, I'm fine." I tried to smile back. "Just had one."

"I think you've forgotten who your audience is." He continued with another frown as he watched the black, bitter smelling coffee drain into the small paper cup. "Look I know it's supposed to be a final draft but...do you think you could have a go at re-working it a bit? It'll mean more work for you but...I'm thinking that maybe you could add in that story you told me about...you know, the one about the dinner party?"

Jake was old school and still worked on hard copies and, to make matters worse, while he waited for his cup to fill, I sneaked a glance at the draft sitting on his desk. I could see in a flash it had scribbles all over it, in angry red ink. My heart sank some more.

"I guess I can put some more time into it. Adding the dinner party won't be too hard," I said, trying to sound nonchalant while my mind flashed back to the red pen, scribbled all over the draft. I was trying to keep my calm, but underneath I was annoyed. I'd already spent a lot of time on the piece, had another stack of small articles to finish for another client and 'spicing it up,' as he put it, wasn't going to be so easy. Not only that, but given Jake's reaction and all the red pen, it was clear that it wasn't so much a re-working, more a complete re-write. Damn.

"When do you need the final version?" I asked trying to keep calm, getting out my phone and flicking through to find my schedule for the following week.

"How would next Tuesday be?" he asked, taking a sip of coffee, going back to his desk and putting his feet up.

Jake was OK. There had even been times in the beginning when I'd thought he was good looking. With a mop of messy hair, a scrawny frame and just enough stubble to light a match he had that grungy, trendy, Brit-pop thing going on. We'd done a fair bit of flirting in the first few months too. The office gossips had been all over that. There'd been a couple of jokes about us down '*The Goose & Stump*' pub for a leaving do just last week. People can get lippy after a few beers and without any food to soak them up. Jake had shrugged it off, even found it funny, but I was livid. The last thing I wanted was people thinking I'd bagged a freelance contract because we were an item, but I knew they did. Worse even, that they thought it was thanks to my mum. She'd been working at The Times in the early eighties with Jake's dad. They'd hardly been in touch since but when I'd come out of the post grad on Journalism, she'd given him a call. I don't know how far strings had been pulled, but a few weeks later I'd had an interview and got a contract at *Zenith*. I'd tried to put it to the back of my mind ever since. I'd never asked mum about it, but I'd always wondered if the office gossips knew. Then one afternoon I'd heard a couple of assistants from the design studio chatting outside the disabled toilet on the second floor. The general gist had been: *"Was Melody getting her contract renewed next year? Of course, she's shagging the boss…and her mum had shagged his dad too."*

"OK, no problem. Tuesday it is." I said making a note in my calendar and trying to sound positive. I needed inspiration, that was for sure, but from where was I going to get it? My energy levels for my *Melody Talkin'* page were at an all-time low, my boredom at an all-time high. The reality of my 'going nowhere fast' career in journalism suddenly came into sharp focus and I felt weary. Putting down my phone, it must've shown.

"Look Mels, sorry to be a bit, you know, down on this draft," Jake said draining his coffee and flippantly indicating at the semi-butchered draft on his desk "but you know we've got problems with circulation. I'm under a lot of pressure to get it up and now Mac's breathing down my neck too. Numbers from last month weren't great either, and to be frank, I need to find a way to boost sales. I'm working on some big-name celeb interviews for the start of next year with Kate but if that doesn't work, we may have to go for a complete re-launch." He paused. "Look, and as I mentioned on the phone, that's the other thing I wanted to chat to you about today. I know it's early to talk about next year's contracts and well, I want to give you the work, but..." he continued with a frown "... Mac's going to be looking for something a bit more current, a bit more edgy for next year, especially with the new focus on digital sales. I hope you don't think I'm passing my stress to you, but there's only so much I can do. And, look, nobody's safe around here right now. We're all under scrutiny, even me. You know, with Mac sinking a lot of his own money into *Zenith*, he's all over it…if any contracts get the chop, it'll be the freelance ones first. You know how these things go and..."

"Don't worry Jake, I get it." I smiled weakly, trying to keep a mounting sense of panic under control. This was bad news for me. I needed my *Zenith* contract and Jake was giving me a heads-up, a warning, loud and clear. I had to raise my game. This wasn't just a blow for my current contract, but for my entire future at *Zenith,* and my career too. Fact was I'd had my sights on more than my *Melody Talkin'* page, and I'd been planning to broach it with Jake next week. A while back he'd told me that Sam the current feature writer was leaving at the end of the year and since hearing the news my heart was set on getting the contract. It was the type of journalism I'd wanted to get into for years, more serious investigative stuff, and now it was up for grabs. Not only this but the thought of a proper contract, not a shitty freelancer deal, was too good to be true. But the writing was on the wall. To stand any chance I'd have to do better. Jake leaned over the desk and looked at me earnestly.

"Can I be frank, Mels? Word in the office is that that you're keen on getting Sam's contract when it comes up next year. Is that true?"

"What?! Who did you hear that from?" I exclaimed, blushing and wondering if Jake could read minds.

"Well, people talk." He said shuffling a bunch of papers on his desk and looking up again. "Look, in the end, who I heard it from doesn't matter. Is it true? I'd like you to be candid with me, Mels. I can't help out if I don't know what you want. And you know that there's going to be a lot of competition for that contract. Jennifer, for one."

Jennifer was another freelance writer. She was good, too.

"Having said that, fact is, as much as I'd like, I can't promise anything," he continued. "It's not going to be my decision. You know how Mac is with these things and, well, now we're under pressure to get circulation up, he's going to be worse than before. I can't take a shit right now without his permission."

Mac. He was the new chair of the board and a complete control freak. He'd only been around six months and was meddling in everything, according to Jake. Word was he wanted a big shake up at *Zenith*. I'd only met Mac a couple of times and we hadn't really hit it off. It was clear he had his sights on cutting my *Melody Talkin'* page and there was only so long Jake could hold him off with my contract coming to an end at the end of the year. All things considered, especially with Mac throwing his weight around, things were not looking good. Still, Jake had raised the issue, so I seized the moment and pressed on.

"Look, *Melody Talkin'* is great. It was a fantastic start for a young writer but, you know, I've been doing it for almost three years now and well, we've talked about this before....I..."

"...want to get into more serious, investigative stuff?" he finished for me with a smile.

"See, you know me so well," I admitted with a shrug. "I'm still just looking for that break," I continued. "and when I heard Sam might be leaving, I was hoping the feature contract could be mine..."

"OK Mels. It's good to know you're still looking to make that move." Jake cut in, leaning forward in his chair and looking mildly uncomfortable for the first time. "I can understand, really. But, look, we can be straight with each other, right?"

I nodded.

"Well I do have the sense that you've been, well, let's say...struggling a bit recently. Your page is ... 'samey' these days. Are you finding things hard right now? Writer's block? You know you can be honest with me..."

Jake was right. It wasn't just the August edition either. I had to admit it. These last couple of months I'd lost my va-va-voom. I was lacking inspiration, lacking ideas and lackluster. I'd felt it myself and now Jake had noticed too.

"You're right. I've been finding it a bit hard of late," I admitted, thinking on my feet. "But I probably just need a holiday or something. A break, a weekend away, whatever...and then I'm sure I'll get my mojo back and look, don't worry. You can count on me. I'll tighten up this month's page, make it more upbeat." Taking Jake's glance at the clock on the wall as sign that the meeting was over, I got up and started shoving my things back into my bag to leave.

"Cool!" he said smiling, jumping up and stretching. For a moment he looked more relaxed.

"I know you can turn it around Mels. And then, once you've got your *Melody Talkin'* page back on track, let's see about that feature contract. OK?" Stopping to pause, he looked thoughtful then went on.

"Listen, why don't we try something. I'm meeting with Mac next week and if you could already have a list of potential feature ideas to show him, well that might be a good start. I know Mac and first you've gotta win him over on your ideas and way of thinking. And if you can show him that you can deliver on those, he's going to be easier to convince later. Then, if he likes them, I may ask you to write something up to show him what you can do. I mean, he only knows you for *Melody Talkin'*. If you can show him what else you're capable of, that might be a good start. How does that sound?"

"OK!" I grinned back. Suddenly I felt flushed with hope. It was a slim hope, but better than nothing.

"I won't let you down Jake. I'll get the *Melody Talkin'* page and the list of ideas to you by early next week."

"Great." He grinned, scratching his head. "And that's a great idea, I mean, the holiday," he said jumping up to walk me to the door. "You haven't been anywhere in a while, no? Why not take a couple of weeks, even a month? I don't care where you are if I get the features we agreed on time. Take yourself off, have some fun and, after all, you're lucky. I mean, you can work from anywhere, right? Wasn't that one of the things you said appealed to you about being a freelancer in the first place?"

Chapter Two

Back home that night, while I was running a bath, I ran through my recent *Melody Talkin'* pages on my laptop and I couldn't get the conversation with Jake out of my mind.

"Shit, shit, and... shit," I muttered to myself as I opened, speed read and closed each file. "I'm losing my touch."

I was my own hardest critic, but I had to face facts. Jake had been right. My page just wasn't working any more. For the first time I was worried I might lose my current *Zenith* contract for *Melody Talkin',* let alone have a hope of the full time feature one. It was true that I was finding it increasing hard to come up with something inspiring for this page. Three years in and the banality of it was getting to me and, worse than that, it was showing.

Suddenly the phone rang.

"Melody, it's your mum."

Mum and I were close, but she could be high maintenance at times. Added to that we didn't always see eye to eye. It didn't help that she always thought she knew best when it came to my career. And then, for the last 5 years she'd been dating Tony.

Tony was a lecturer in the history of art at Goldsmiths University. In his spare time, he also taught a watercolor class at Islington town hall on Tuesday nights and Mum, looking for something new and inspiring to occupy herself one winter, had enrolled and fallen for him hook, line and sinker.

"You should see his series on Lake Windermere in the mist," she'd told everyone repeatedly during the first term. "He's a genius!" But genius or not, Tony was a bit of a flirt and mum was the jealous type and let's say the relationship was 'stormy.' They split up at least three or four times a year and, when they did, I was usually the shoulder she chose to cry on. It was stressful at first having mum blubbing down the phone every few months and then not hearing from her for weeks after when they made up, but over time I began to recognize the pattern and lost less sleep over it.

Mum was a journalist, and a good one at that, but her career had gone off the rails years ago. She blamed my dad, blamed herself, and I sometimes wondered if she blamed me too. At school she had never been the academic type, but she'd loved writing and was an avid news junkie. So, once out of school she'd gone on a journalism course at the local tech and soon landed her first job at The Lavender Times, in South London. She was just 18. It was 1974. After a few years and three local rags later, she got her big break: Sub-editor at The Times. It was no mean feat back in the day when journalism was a male dominated world and women had to work twice as hard to get any breaks at all. She was just starting to make a name for herself as a tough cookie who got the story out no matter what, when she met my dad and got pregnant with me. Night shift subediting wasn't compatible with a baby, and to make matters worse Dad, who turns out wasn't a progressive at all, insisted she stay home and be a 'proper mum' while he carried on with his own career. At the time he was trying to make it big as a musician (jazz guitar) and despite coming from a wealthy family they didn't believe in handouts. Times were tough, musicians don't make much cash and mum was as frustrated as hell. Eventually they split up. Then years later when I was in school, she tried to get her career going again. But the world of journalism had moved on. There were new kids on the block, and the best she could do was editing in the less than prestigious locals. She hated it. She never forgave my dad, and on bad days I wondered if she'd ever forgive me too. I guess it's hard to have almost had the career of your dreams but not quite made it. I knew she was banking on me not making the same mistakes and sometimes the pressure to get my career on track weighed on me.

Thankfully however, today all was calm on the Tony front and she didn't ask about *Zenith*. Instead she launched into an update on

Tony's latest water colour exhibition, some inconsequential gossip from the Croydon Chronicle and the gory details on Auntie Joan's eyelid tuck. Resisting a fleeting temptation to update her on my latest failings on *Melody Talkin'* (she always had an opinion and I was in no mood to hear it today) I was soon back on the sofa settling in for another night of Netflix, surfing the web, and a bowl of microwave noodles. I'd tried messaging a few friends in the neighborhood to see if anyone wanted a quick pint in our local, 'The Crown,' but no luck. Never mind. The sunny weather had already passed and it was raining. No surprises there. Another typical summer evening in London. It was depressing. The British papers didn't help with their *'The Great British Summer'* articles. You know the kind of thing; tips on how to BBQ, where to have the best picnics, 100 summer coastal walks. Really, what reality were they living in?

I knew I had to rework my *Melody Talkin'* page and start planning the list of feature ideas for Mac. I also had a bunch of other short pieces to write; bits and pieces my mum had passed on to me from contacts, knowing that I needed the cash. But the afternoon meeting had left me unsettled, and I kept putting it all off. So, I spent some time on Twitter and updating my Instagram account, then I switched to Facebook. The usual postings appeared on the screen.

'What's it all about?' asked Jeanie in Manchester.

'How the hell do I know?' was one comment in response.

'My kind of paradise' said Monica, *Zenith*'s Art Director with a photo of her private plunge pool in Corsica. *Show-off*, I thought to myself grudgingly.

After 'liking' a few things here and there, and posting a few things of my own, I scrolled over 'People you may know.' I scanned to the right across the list of names and profile pictures, recognizing some, others not. Friends of friends, dinner party acquaintances, a couple of girls I'd been at university with, then one name caught my eye. Spencer Channing. Clicking on the picture to get a better look, and to peak at the profile I couldn't believe my eyes. Spencer Channing. Tall, blond, handsome, charismatic. Was it really him?

It was my last year at Cambridge and the beginning of the Autumn term. With the constant threat of final exams bearing down and the real world outside the confines of the University Halls on the horizon, the stress was already getting the better of me, so I'd arranged to meet up with some friends for a Saturday night drink to decompress. The plan was to start in the students' union bar then head out into the centre of Cambridge for a pub crawl. For the mood I was in, it was likely to end up being a bit of a bender. My friend Alison was running late, so while I waited for her to arrive, I decided to get myself a drink and went up to the bar. I was waiting to be served when Spencer walked in. He was tall, had tousled wavy mid length blond hair, blue eyes and had a confidence that captured the room. I normally went for dark guys, but Spencer was mesmerising. Despite a lack of girlfriends for 'back-up support,' I somehow decided to take matters into my own hands and edge closer to him at the bar. Trying not to be too obvious, I shifted around and positioned myself on his right. The plan worked and it didn't take long before he glanced over, our eyes locked, and he gave me a big, friendly grin.

"Hi, just getting in a round of drinks for my friends," he said, nodding causally to a group of guys sitting over to the right of the bar. "You here on your own? Wanna join? We're just debating which is the best college to be in. I'm in Kings. How about you?"

"Err, Hi. I'm in Queens and OK, would love a pint, thanks. Was just about to get one myself." I blushed, thinking all my Christmases had come at once simply for the fact he was talking to me. I couldn't help wondering who he was and how come I'd never seen him around before, and as if reading my mind, he grinned at me again.

"Give me a hand with these? Oh, and by the way, I'm Spencer, Spencer Channing. Reading Archeology. Nice to meet you..."

"Oh, yes, sure, Hi, and err, I'm Melody Meeks. Reading English."

"Cool name!" He smiled as, grabbing the pints, we walked over to the table where his friends were sitting. "How did your parents come up with that, the name I mean? It's kind of, well, unique!"

"Oh, it's my dad," I smiled back "He was a musician. Wanted to call me all kinds of things apparently. It was crazy, but in the end my mum just gave up and agreed to Melody. I've never liked it. Kind of weird putting Melody with Meeks, but hey I didn't get a vote."

"Dad a musician? What instrument?"

"Jazz guitar. He was in a band for a while, playing small jazz venues in London," I told him, omitting the fact that they'd never made it big.

"Really? I play a bit of guitar myself, more classic rock tunes though. But I'm not great. Never have time to practice."

We sat down and he quickly introduced me to his four friends. A couple I vaguely recognized from around the library, the other two not at all.

"We don't normally come into the Students' union bar," Stephen, on my right, explained, after they'd all been introduced and he'd taken a sip of his pint. "We usually hang out back in Kings or go to The Maypole."

"That's our local," Spencer added, nodding over to a skinny dark-haired guy on the right called Simon. "That's if we can drag Simon away from his PhD, right Simon?" I soon found out that Simon, a real boffin type with the obligatory acne, glasses and M&S sweater, was studying astrophysics. He didn't seem the outgoing type but managed a grin back. It started adding up. That's why I'd not seen this bunch around and about before.

Soon Alison arrived with some friends from Queens, and before long we were one large group heading into town; Spencer, Alison, various friends and two Korean students who nobody knew but had randomly attached to the group on the way out.

"Hey, let's go to The Maypole." Shouted Spencer, as he led the way. "Why break the habit of a lifetime." He laughed.

While walking to the pub, to my delight I started to sense that Spencer was flirting with me. He was often at my side, kept catching my eye, grinning.

"I didn't realise such trendy, cute girls were hanging out in the students' union bar these days. Love your hair too. Very, erm, funky. I've never had a girlfriend with hair shorter than mine. It might be interesting to try." He grinned over, an unashamed, confident, if corny flirt.

"Hey, watch it. This hair takes a lot of styling." I gave him back with a smile.

You see my hair is very short. It's been a crew cut for years. It started when I was at school. I was fourteen and the only redhead in class. All that teasing about being a ginger nut, a Duracell. You know the kind of thing. Well, one day I tried to dye it blond. It was a total disaster and came out looking like straw. The only thing I could do was cut it all off. I'd cried for days, but over time I realised I quite liked it. I'd always been a bit of a tomboy, so the hair just seemed to fit in. It's been cropped short ever since.

We got to The Maypole and soon had a table in the corner at the back. I'd never been in this pub before but could see why they liked it. It was full of character with low ceilings, lots of oak beams, and a fireplace where I guessed they had a log fire going in the winter. A comforting smell of hops and wood smoke hung in the air. The drinks were flowing, and the group seemed to be having fun. Even Simon was coming out of his shell and was in animated conversation with the Koreans. No doubt the beers were helping. Spencer was next to me again and only seemed to have eyes for me. He kept asking me lots of questions and soon, his hand practically touching mine on the table. Then noticing our glasses were close to empty he gave me a wink, jumped up, and in a flash was at the bar ordering another round of drinks for the group. I felt dizzy with excitement. I was getting all his attention and couldn't believe my luck. Then suddenly, a kick came from under the table. It was Alison.

"What?" I asked putting my drink down with surprise.

"Cigarette. Outside. Now" she said under her breath, fixing me back.

In the car park at the back of The Maypole we perched on a low stone wall and she lit a cigarette while I got my tin and papers out and started on a roll-up.

"This guy Spencer, he's flirting with you right?" she asked after taking a drag.

"Seems so. I can't believe it! He's so gorgeous, don't you think?!" I said, balancing the tin on my lap.

"Listen Melody. I think I've heard of this guy. I'm sure he must be the same one. I mean, how many Spencers can there be studying Archeology? Anyway, I think he's a bit of a player. If it's the same Spencer, he's the one who dated Anita Brown for a few weeks last year. She was really into him. Said he was into her. So, she thought. Then he just dumped her. Just like that. No reason. Do you remember?" I shook my head and pretended to concentrate on the roll-up.

"I don't remember that," I mumbled after a few seconds, fiddling with the filter, and licking the paper before closing the edges. Once done, I found my lighter, lit it, and took a long drag. I focused back on Alison and tried to fight a bubbling sense of irritation that Alison might've just ruined my night. She must've sensed my sudden shift in mood.

"Sorry, Melody. Listen, I'm not saying this to be mean. I just want you to be careful of this guy. You're not annoyed with me, are you? I mean for bringing it up? I just don't want to see you hurt and…"

"Alison don't worry! I'm not looking for a relationship if that's what you mean. What'd be the point? It's our last year and with course pressure and exams and all that, I haven't got time for it. I need to focus. And not only that. Who knows where I'll be going come July. I'm not looking to get married, alright? But hey, if he wants to hook up tonight, well, he's so totally gorgeous, what's the harm in that?"

I was trying to sound cool, but I was little stung, and taking another drag of the roll-up, starting to wonder if Alison could be jealous. The thing was Alison was unusually pretty. She was slim with a great figure most women would die for. She had a great personality to match, was witty, clever and great fun too. Result was she was always the one in the group who got the male attention, wherever we went. We were used to it. At times we'd joke about how we could use Alison as bait to reel in men and take her cast-offs. She had one boyfriend after another and at times it was hard keeping up. But tonight it was different. Spencer wasn't given her any attention. He hadn't given her a second glance. He was giving it all to me. I tried not to feel a little smug. It wasn't easy given my track record with men. I could hardly believe my luck and decided there and then that I wasn't going to let Alison ruin the moment.

"Anyway," I finished, putting out the semi smoked roll-up with my boot and looking up "Like I said, I'm not about to fall for a guy just like that. I'm not a fool."

Famous last words indeed.

Spencer and I were soon an item. The last year at Cambridge was stressful with course work stacking up by the day, exams and more exams, but we hung out all the time nevertheless. We studied and revised together, went drinking together, and ate together. Sometimes on weekends we hardly made it out of bed. He was strong, dominating, and seemed to have an endless appetite for me. He told me how much he loved my body. That I was slim and lithe and just what he preferred. Said he even liked my tomboy looks too. I was so flattered as until then I'd never been confident about my appearance but, being with Spencer, I began to get just a little surer of myself. After all, I started thinking, if I could bag a guy like Spencer, perhaps I wasn't so unattractive after all?

We were getting close too. In the early hours one morning after too much Scotch and a couple of joints he told me he was an only child and that both his parents had died in a car accident when he was fifteen but didn't want anyone to know. He didn't need anyone's sympathy, he said. He explained that was why he often hung around the university during the holidays. Said he preferred it to staying with an aunt in Scotland, an aunt he'd never got on with. Said he had to stand on his own two feet as he was all alone in the world. It made me admire him more. And through all of this, at times I still couldn't' believe my luck: That Spencer had chosen me out of all the girls that he could've had.

The weeks and months rolled by and we were inseparable. Christmas and Easter came and went. He stayed in Cambridge refusing invites to stay with my mum in London over the holidays. Then exams, end of term parties, celebrations and life outside the confines of Cambridge started to beckon.

And that's when it all fell apart.

I started prodding him, pushing him slightly, testing the water. Despite what I'd said at the beginning, I realised I wanted more. I wanted to know what he felt for me. Did he see a future for us after Cambridge? A life together in London? Moving in together? Did he love me? Every time I brought it up, he became tense. Then one day right at the end of term - the bombshell.

Spencer asked me to meet him in The Maypole. When I arrived, he was sitting in his favorite corner playing chess on his iPad. He'd almost finished his pint and draining it, banged the empty glass down on the table. He didn't jump up to get me a drink like he normally did but instead switched off the iPad and started talking. He was cool and calm. He looked me directly in the eyes and told me he'd got accepted on an MSc in Bath, and he wanted to go – on his own. He said it wasn't working between us anymore and told me we were over. He didn't look phased, emotional, uncomfortable. He didn't say he was sorry. He didn't try to explain. It took two minutes then he walked out of the pub, and out of my life. I haven't seen or spoken to him since.

In the days and weeks that followed it was like he'd dropped off the face of the earth. I went to his rooms in Kings to try and speak to him, but he was never in or didn't answer the door. I tried calling him, but the phone rang out. Then collage was over, we all moved out, and I headed down to London, broken and bereft. Even there I still couldn't give it up. I tried emailing him again, but he never responded. I tried calling him, but got a message saying the number had been deactivated. I sent letters to him care of Bath University but never got one back. It was four years ago but I still thought about him every single day. Where was he? What was he doing now? Had I really meant nothing to him after being with him almost a year? Why did he end it like that?

Alison never once said I told you so. She should have.

And suddenly here he was again, in profile, grinning and gazing over the side of a boat, a Facebook blast from the past delivered to my living room in Chalk Farm London via my social media news feed. He looked tanned, he looked happy, he looked different from the Spencer I'd known at Cambridge; his thick, messy, blond hair now a crew-cut. He looked good. Was that really him. It had to be him. My stomach lurched.

It was him.

In a flash, I had an unspeakable urge to reconnect with the past. I wanted to hear his voice, see his face, but more than anything, to understand once and for all what had been going through his mind that day, four years ago in The Maypole. It was a bad idea. It was a terrible idea, but despite myself I clicked the 'Friend Request' button and added a short message

'Spencer Channing – from Cambridge Uni? Is that you? If it is, it would be great to hear from you. Melody.' I closed my laptop and went to bed.

I spent the night tossing and turning in bed. What had I done? This was insanity. I'd opened an emotional can of worms and I couldn't go back. Now I was worried he might not respond, but I was also fretting in case he did.

The next morning over toast and espresso I switched on my phone and, to my astonishment, a message from Spencer appeared via Messenger.

'Hi Melody, is that you? Well I never. You look great. (Had a look at your FB page). Still that funky hair! What's it been, 4 years? I'm living in Rome. After Bath I went on to do a PhD in Paris then moved out to Italy shortly after. I'm now a junior lecturer in ancient Roman archaeology here at La Sapienza University. What you up to? Would be great to hear from you – where you live, what you're doing, boyfriend, husband ☺ ? I'm still the bachelor boy I'm afraid - married to my job! If you're ever in the Eternal City let me know, it would always be great to see you.' Spenc. Xxx

I read the message over and over, trying to read between the lines and second guess what he was thinking. He'd practically invited me to Rome. Hadn't he? Or maybe not? He was no doubt just being friendly, sending a polite message back…And that's when I started thinking. My mind latched onto an idea that had been germinating the night before. An idea about the list of features Jake had asked me to write up for Mac. What if I did get back in touch with Spencer and went to visit him in Rome and wrote a feature about it? It might sound crazy but, the more I mulled it over the more I was convinced it could work. I could see the feature in my mind: Something about how in today's world we connect, reconnect, stay in touch, or don't by social media – Facebook, Instagram, Twitter, WhatsApp….The story of two people, Spencer and I, and how we reconnected after years of not being in touch by the mere click of a mouse and what happened. I was sure it had leg. Then my mind went back to the conversation with Jake about holidays and how a writer could work from anywhere. I hadn't had a holiday in years, and I needed one. It occurred to me that I could take advantage of the opportunity and combine meeting Spencer with a holiday in Italy. I could do the next month's *Melody Talkin'* page and the any other small contracts I'd get from my mum while in Italy too. After all, what had I got to lose?

I made myself another espresso and mulled it over. Sitting at my kitchen table and spurred on by an impromptu 'seize the day' spirit, I grabbed a pencil and started sketching out this and a few other ideas for features in my notebook. And as I worked on it, I kept coming back to the Facebook feature. I was convinced it could work.

Later that afternoon I opened my Facebook account and wrote to Spencer:

Hey Spencer! Great to hear from you! Yes, it's me – Melody. Congrats on the PhD! That's really something. You were always such a boffin ☺ Can't believe we haven't been in touch for so long. Just goes to show how time flies. I'm doing well – freelance feature writer for Zenith magazine – you may have seen my Melody Talkin' page? Probably not! ☺ I'd love to see you again and I haven't been to Rome for some time. Were you serious about meeting up? I was thinking of taking some time off work and visiting. Don't panic, I'm not planning on dumping myself on you for two weeks or anything, I might rent a place in Tuscany or on the Amalfi Coast but thought I could add on a weekend in Rome. We could meet up for dinner, drinks, cappuccino or something. Whatever works for you? What do you say?' Melody

The next day Spencer wrote back. He sounded enthusiastic. Said he'd love to meet up. August was good for him too. He told me he was big on scuba diving these days and was about to leave for a trip to the Caribbean and wouldn't be back until the second week of August. But by sheer luck the timing still worked. I was ecstatic. I was panicked. I wondered what the hell I was doing. But I told myself that at least I'd get closure on Spencer once and for all and hopefully if all fell into place, cracking feature out of it too.

Next week as planned I emailed Jake my *Melody Talkin'* re-draft and a list of feature ideas including the Facebook one. I'd worked on the list of feature concepts until the early hours the night before, fleshing them out, tweaking words here and there as we writers can do, and was still as nervous as hell in case, despite my efforts, they still didn't fit the bill. You see, it was an unsettling time in the industry. Things were tough. Every month someone I knew was being laid off as print editions continued to die and free digital content became more available than ever before. Just last week a good friend Annabelle had lost her '*Ask Annabelle'* agony aunt page in a monthly. She'd been distraught. This was her biggest contract and now she was left dangling by a wire, the wire being her less-well paid job on *Underground* a London freebie. Her only other contracts were copy editing, which was tedious work, all us writers dreaded it. I'd spent the night before at hers with a bottle of wine and a selection of M&S nibbles trying to help her make a list of ways to get on top of her impending financial doom. The list included cancelling the gym membership, using *Pond's Cold Cream* instead of *Crem de la Mar*, drinking *Prosecco* not *Moet & Chandon*, this type of thing. Annabelle was used to the finer things in life and was not impressed. She was a world away from my charity shopping and budget make-up lines, but eventually she seemed to come around when I told her that maybe, just maybe, this was the best thing that could've happened to her. After all, I said, now she'd finally have the time she needed to finish the book she'd started three years ago. I'd read the first five chapters. It was a Lord of the Rings type of fantasy novel, not really my thing, but it was good, and she really perked up when I told her that the time was right if she could just get cracking with it. There was a huge appetite for this type of stuff, especially since Game of Thrones had been such a massive hit and with Netflix looking for content she should turn it into a script. So, full of trepidation, with Annabelle's plight on my mind, and the new draft of my *Melody Talkin'* article done, I met with Jake the following day.

"*Melody Talkin'* is looking much better now Mels. I just marked up a few very minor changes and, well, apart from those, it's a goer. I really liked the part about the singleton dinner party. Glad you added that in. Very funny. Job well done, thanks for turning it around."

I was relieved.

"And what about the features list?" I asked, almost holding my breath. I was back in the *Zenith* office; Jake was back on the coffee.

"I read your feature list and outlines, and think...look, I think there's some potential there. Out of the five, the one that stands out is the Facebook idea. Mac was in the office yesterday and I showed him the list and he agreed. Do you think you could work it up into a draft? He was interested to see more on your angles to the Facebook story and your writing style on that type of piece. I can understand. He's only ever seen your *Melody Talkin'* style, you know…"

I nodded barely able to speak. Jake continued.

"We disagreed a little on the other ideas to be honest. I liked them all, thought they were great. Mac was, well a little more critical, said they may need, let's say, a little bit more refining. And he felt a couple had already been done, especially the one on internet porn, although I realize you were trying to do a different take on it." He paused putting the papers down.

"And don't get your hopes to far up Mels. He might decide to go with someone who has more of a track record. Fact is that you don't have one in this type of thing and Mac's nervous about it. Also, you should know that he has someone else in mind as an option - someone who worked for *Culture*, so, look I just wanted to be up front about it. You might put in the hours and still not get a staff contract. I'll put in a word for you, but you know how things are with Mac, I'd hate you to..."

"Look Jake, this is the best chance I've ever had for a staff contract and I'm willing to put in the work and take the chance just in case. No pain no gain!" I said, trying to sound confident.

"Well Mels, you go for it. You know I'm backing you, right? You work on the Facebook feature as a start and I'll work on Mac. You know this week I think Mac's beginning to ease off just a bit...Anyway, agreed?"

"Agreed." I smiled back.

Chapter Three

"I'm so envious right now," said Emma. It was the day before I was leaving for Rome and we were enjoying cappuccino and carrot cake at the South Bank. It was raining, again, and we were taking shelter in the Royal Festival Hall cafe after a walk along the South Bank.

"When I left this afternoon, Josh was having a tantrum and Sophie was screaming the house down at the prospect of being left alone with Dan. She's just not used to it. She only wants to be with me," she continued, tucking into the large wedge of cake on her plate.

Emma was one of my closest friends. We'd met at the journalism post grad and had shared a flat before she met and married Dan. She'd put her career at Vox magazine on hold with the birth of her first child then last year she'd had her second, a beautiful girl Sofia who was normally a darling but seemed to be starting the 'clingy phase.' It was clear; Emma was beginning to suffer from too many days home alone with the kids, a husband who worked all hours and the realization that she wouldn't be getting a relaxing holiday for the next 18 years.

"Maybe I can run off with you to Italy and just dump the kids on Dan for a couple of weeks. What do you think?" she said half laughing, half almost in tears. Studying her face, I couldn't help but notice that she looked tired and worn out, really for the first time since Sofia had been born.

"Any time just say the word," I said smiling and giving her arm an affectionate rub across the table. "You know I'd love to have a holiday with you" I told her truthfully. "Remember when we went to Paris for the weekend? And what about that time in the south of France when we rented that amazing villa and I got sun stroke."

"Oh god, I'd completely forgotten about that," she said. "Seems like a lifetime ago. Apart from you getting ill on the last day, we had such a blast. And remember that night out, you know, when we went to that local bar in the town. What was it called? 'Whisky Ping-Pong Bar' or something really odd like that?"

"Goodness, I completely forgot about that too," I laughed.

"And we ended up drinking Pastis with those two old guys at the bar and the next day we had hangovers from hell. Remember?"

"I certainly do!" I laughed. "I'd rather not!"

"I'd give anything for a night out. Just can't risk even getting close to a hangover with the kids. I never thought I'd miss having a hangover!" She went on, her mood flashing back to miserable all over again.

"Look, this phase will pass, and things will get easier again. You said it yourself. Rremember that woman at the nursery group? You know, the one you told me about. Amanda, wasn't it? Didn't she go through exactly the same thing when she had her second? She pulled through it, right?" Emma smiled wanly but didn't look so reassured. I went on. "Look, when I'm back, why don't I come over in the evenings sometimes when Dan is working late to keep you company? The number 23 bus drops me right at your front door. It's so easy. We can either hang out together on the sofa with a bottle of red, or you can have a break and even get some sleep. I could watch over the kids. Really, its fine for me. I'd make a movie night of it!" I was being kind. Kids weren't really my thing...

Emma smiled knowingly. "You don't want to spend the evenings in with me and the kids," she said.

"Look, it's not like my social life's humming right now anyway," I insisted before she could say no, "and it'd be a good way to spend a bit more time together. And then longer term we could plan a weekend away, you know, like old times? It might even do Dan good to have the kids for a few days. I've always thought we should go to Dublin for a spa weekend, and then there're the pubs…We'd have so much fun."

It wasn't that I didn't like Dan. He was a great guy and the really solid type, but I couldn't help wondering if the late nights in the office were some kind of excuse to not take on more with the kids. Then Emma told me sometimes Dan would come home smelling of beer and he had to admit to stopping in the pub with colleagues for drinks on the way home. Nothing wrong with that, but Emma didn't have the luxury I'd thought more than once.

"Thanks Melody," she said through another mouthful of cake, looking somewhat rueful. "I really appreciate the offer. No doubt I'll be taking you up on it. But hey, I'm even boring myself with all this. Tell me again, what's this feature you're working on and why Rome? Sounds amazing!"

This was the question I'd been dreading if truth be told. She'd never met Spencer, of course, but she knew the story, and had been sympathetic too. I still hadn't gotten over Spencer when we'd met on the post grad course and I'd cried on her sofa a few times about it too. She'd been such a rock. So supportive. But recently over a bottle of wine she'd spoken more frankly and had been firmer with me. Told me that after four years it was time to move on. Said it sounded like I was way too good for him and by the end of the night she'd persuaded me to try Tinder. Some weeks later I'd plucked up the courage, signed up, and even had a few dates, all of them awful. Alessandro from Italy had seemed OK at the start, but then it turned out he was way too politically right wing for me. Rohan the half Sri Lankan web designer was just too into his 'amazing' vinyl collection. It had been like dating a guy from the Nick Hornby book 'Hi-Fidelity.' Then last week the icing on the cake, Simon. He'd had bad breath and had tried to grope me across the table upstairs in The Lamb and Flag Pub in Covent Garden just ten minutes into the date. I'd pretended to go to the loo and scarpered out of the back door, leaving him to pick up the bill. Then on a whim, I'd gone late night shopping instead. It had been way more fun. 'Blame it on Emma' I joked every time another date went horribly wrong.

After explaining the Facebook feature idea and how I'd reconnected with Spencer, she went quiet for a while, a slight frown-line appearing between the eyes, like she was thinking it through. I could already see where this was going, and my defences kicked in.

"Look, I just need to pull a good feature out of the bag…" I tried, slowly stirring my coffee "and this really is the best idea out of the bunch." I continued rather weakly. "And, well, you know, maybe seeing Spencer again isn't such a bad thing if I do find out that he's just not worth it all, then fine. Better for me in the long run. Or I was also thinking…maybe he has some explanation for what happened, you know why he dumped me like that. Something I didn't realize at the time…But whatever happens, if nothing else I think meeting him again will help me draw a line under it one way or the other...."

While I was rambling, she drained the remainder of her cappuccino, and took a spoon to the foam which was resisting gravitational pull at the bottom of the cup.

"OK," she said, after scraping out the last of the froth, putting the spoon down on the saucer and fixing my gaze, "But, just, well… you watch yourself, OK? You know I think you're still more into him than you even know yourself. Remember, he left you after, what was it? Almost a year? Without any explanation, not even a hug, a kiss goodbye and completely disappeared. I mean completely. He just dropped off the face of the earth…until now. I've heard of some bad breakups, but I've never heard of someone doing that before. I mean, normally there's some kind of explanation involved, like – 'I met someone else', or 'This is why it's not working for me' you know…something…"

"Oh, come on Emma," I jumped in, hating myself momentarily. After all I could see where she was coming from but, I was starting to prickle, feel defensive and annoyed.…

"In the end it really was just a college fling. You know, thinking back, and in fairness to him, I realise now that he never actually made any promises to me at all. Nothing. I got in way over my head, I lost all sense over him. So, I share some of the blame. I mean, I built it up in my mind, you know, like it was this big, serious relationship when it wasn't at all and, like I said, OK, he could've handled it better at the end, I think we agree on that, but we were both really young, inexperienced back then..."

"I know Melody, I get all that," she smiled sympathetically cutting me off, "and look, I'm not in your shoes," she said, not looking totally convinced. But then the frown melted away. "Hey, at the end of the day it's really your call. It really is. I mean, with affairs of the heart, who's anyone else to tell you what to do? Not me, that's for sure! You go for it. I guess if you do put some closure on Spencer one way or the other, in the end that's not a bad thing. And at least you'll get to hear his side of the story after all these years. Just one favour. Don't imagine for a minute that you two will get back together again, will you?"

"Of course not!" I jumped in. "No expectation on my side, believe me. Really, good lord!"

"Well, make sure you do a cracking feature at least. Then you'll have this guy Mick, Mac, whatever he's called, at *Zenith* eating out of the palm of your hand. I mean, after all, what can possibly go wrong. Now, how about another cappuccino?"

That evening I perched on the kitchen windowsill and smoked a roll-up out into the garden. It was almost 8 o'clock and there was a pale, soft light descending on the city, a blessing after the intermittent rain of the afternoon. The sound of children playing kept spilling up from the kids next door as they bounced on their garden trampoline. It was a quintessential British city garden sound. As a kid, I'd never had a trampoline, let alone a garden to play in, so I don't know quite why, but it was strangely reassuring. It sounded normal.

I often sat in this spot at the end of the day, weather permitting. My flat was compact, tiny even, but it was mine. Dad for all his failings had given me a small chunk of money some years back. Said he was happy to pass on some of my inheritance early when he knew it could make a difference. It hadn't been much, just something that had come his way from his well-to-do relatives, but the timing had been good, and it'd helped me get a foot on the property ladder at a young age. And I loved it. One of my favorite things about the flat was the location. When I'd bought it, prices had been at a record low and Chalk Farm had edged into my price range. One stop from the buzzing Camden Town and a short walk from the more leafy and upmarket Primrose Hill, it was perfect for me. It had become my sanctuary.

Dad also helped me out every so often with some funds which appeared randomly and in my bank account once or twice a year. I always knew it was him with the Bank of Toronto indicated on my statements. Mum called it 'guilt money.' I wasn't complaining and called it 'extremely gratefully received' money. Then he'd pop up from time to time in my email inbox with news from Canada, his teaching job and family updates.

After he divorced mum, dad had emigrated to Toronto and started a new life teaching music in a high school. He'd remarried and had two kids. They were now fourteen and twelve. I'd never met them and sometimes thought I never would.

One of these transfers had just arrived the week before. It couldn't have been better timed. This would cover my three weeks holiday in Italy and then some. I decided not to mention this to mum. It usually had two effects, the first being a rant about what a terrible husband and father he'd been and the second about how he'd screwed up her career. And apart from that, I think it made mum feel bad. She didn't have much money and couldn't help me out much as a result. The Croydon Chronical didn't pay like a national paper would, which was another thing she remained permanently bitter about. It wasn't an issue now. I was earning enough to get by on, just, and I was determined to stand on my own two feet, but I know it had bothered my mum when I was a student, and I got that.

Putting out the roll-up, I dropped back down to the kitchen table. This was where I did most of my writing. In the summer it caught the best evening light, in the winter it was warm and cozy. After writing dad a thank you email and leaving a saucer of milk out for Simpson, my friendly neighborhood ginger tom who often made it up to the ledge, I slipped into bed, thoughts of Rome, *Zenith* and Spencer spinning in my head.

Chapter Four

The flight to Rome was uneventful and in cattle class with the obligatory hour delay, a pre-packed sandwich, all washed down with a screw-top of warm Chardonnay. But I didn't care. I was on holiday. After grabbing my suitcase from the reclaim belt, I made for the taxi rank and was soon heading into the Eternal City.

As I scooted along the highway, with the passenger seat window down, the warm summer air blew in my face. Given the non-starter summer in London, it was pure joy. Not only, I had three blissful weeks ahead of it ahead; one in Rome, two on the Amalfi coast. I was already dreaming about endless good food, wine, and the extensive list of Kindle best sellers I'd downloaded to read on the trip the night before. Then thoughts flashed to Spencer. It was inevitable. I'd been unable to shake him from my consciousness since we'd been back in touch and with just days to seeing him in the flesh, there he was again, real enough in my mind's eye, standing front and centre. One minute the smiling, warm, affectionate Spencer. The next the cold, distant Spencer; the Spencer from our last encounter in The Maypole.

"It'll be fine," I tried to tell myself. It had become something of a mantra these last few days.

After navigating the chaotic evening rush hour traffic, the taxi slowed down and zig zagged up the *Aventino* hill.

One of the seven hills of Rome *Aventino* was peaceful and leafy, a tranquil oasis a little removed from the frenetic bustle of the surrounding city below. Large terracotta villas, churches and convents with peaceful gardens and leafy courtyards: a collection of quiet streets and lanes set it apart from the more popular, working class quarter called *Testaccio* at the foot of the hill. The hotel was small, understated and set back from the street. Nothing fancy and nicely discreet. I felt right at home.

The receptionist was a short, old, frail looking Italian man who introduced himself as Gianni and had an air of being part of the furniture. Within minutes he'd organised my bags to my room and I was sipping my first chilled, fizzing glass of Prosecco in the shady courtyard garden. The sun was already on its way down, but the warmth of the Mediterranean still clung on, like it had seeped into every brick, every nook and cranny. After the dismally wet summer back in London it felt like heaven.

The next few days passed by with a relaxed routine; a light breakfast in the hotel courtyard garden followed by a leisurely mid-morning walk to *Campo de'Fiori* a *piazza* (square), the heart of the city, which hosted a lively flower, fruit and vegetable market each day. I loved people watching. Even though you could see the city was slowly beginning to empty as locals left the blistering urban heat for holidays on the coast, *Campo de' Fiori,* was still pulsating with life. Then in the afternoons I took in some sights, revisited old favourites; the Pantheon, St Peters, the Vatican followed by a siesta at the hotel before heading out again for an evening stroll and some dinner in one of the many restaurants or *Trattoria.*

Days started to blend in together, evenings drifted one into the next and in no time at all it was Tuesday night and I was meeting Spencer.

I showered, anguished over what to wear and settled for white linin shorts, a T-Shirt and converse sneakers (my Summer Dr Martin boot alternatives). Then, after taking a little extra care over my barely-there make-up, just a dab of mascara and lip gloss, I set off on the 30-minute walk to our agreed meeting place in Trastevere. I'd been to Rome many times and Trastevere was always a favorite, with its narrow, cobbled streets, terra cotta buildings, bars and restaurants. It was always buzzing with life and this evening was no exception. After crossing the river and taking a turn here and there, I emerged onto the noisy main street *Viale* Trastevere. A tram rumbled by, scooters shot here and there, it was frantic compared to quieter backstreets, but I loved its energy. Then once again, into the maze of cobbled lanes, for a moment I lost my sense of direction but, checking my phone, I could see that I was almost there and in just a couple more streets I arrived at our meeting point.

Piazza Santa Maria in Trastevere is a large square with a huge church, tucked into the left-hand corner. I'd been here a couple of times before and seeing it again reminded me why Spencer had picked this spot for us to meet. It was perfect. You just couldn't miss it.

I sat down on a stone bench in front of the church. It was smooth and polished from centuries of use and still warm from the late afternoon sun. Glancing around I began searching for Spencer in the steady stream of people criss-crossing the piazza, the lively throng of people out for the night, enjoying the sites and bustle of the city.

I'd started to feel nervous back at the hotel but now my mind was racing, my thoughts a tangle of panic and anxiety which made my stomach churn. Would we recognize each other? Would it be awkward to see him again or would we pick up like old long-lost friends? Would he explain what had happened all those years ago or not bring it up? Would I have to ask him? And what would he think of me now? Did I look OK? Perhaps the shorts and Converse didn't look elegant enough? OK, elegant wasn't really my style but perhaps I should've made more effort? Looking at the way all the Italian women were dressed up with heels and with their long flowing hair I suddenly felt dowdy, plain and bland. And another thing: I still had to talk to him about the feature. Would he even agree? Taking a deep breath, I tried to calm my nerves but sitting there I just couldn't help but wonder if the whole thing had been a terrible idea.

Time seemed to drag so I pulled out my phone, checking my message inbox, but the screen was blank. For a moment I thought I saw him coming across the square: a tall guy, dark blond hair, sunglasses, a cheeky grin, but as he got nearer I could seehe was too young and I could hear him chatting into his phone in Italian. He walked straight past and greeted a girl to my right. They both walked on hugging and laughing. It wasn't Spencer.

Glancing at my watch, it was almost 9:00. He was 30 minutes late. I checked my phone again, still nothing. I started trying to fight a creeping sense of irritation. I got up and strolled around and then lacking anything better to do sat down again. Looking at my watch, it was 9:10. I started speculating, the reasons why he might be late; a meeting at the University which had overrun, perhaps the infamous Roman traffic. Then another glance at my phone but still no missed calls, no messages. Nothing. By now it was 9:15 and Spencer was 45 minutes late. Why didn't he have the courtesy to send me a message! I was beginning to lose the battle, my fight against a mounting irritation. Then a thought. Could it be that I was waiting in the wrong place? He had my number though so why hadn't he called? I sent him a message and waited. Nothing. I sat there a few minutes more then found his number on my list of contacts, pressed call and waited. A voice mail service kicked in. First something in Italian that I couldn't understand. Then: *"Hi, you've reached the voice mail of Spencer Channing. Please leave a message and I'll get back to you when I can."* I left a message and hung up.

By 9:30 I'd been sitting on the bench for an hour and my bum was turning numb, so I decided to do a circle of the piazza. I was sure Spencer had said to meet in front of the church, but I started to have doubts. Maybe he'd said the opposite and I'd somehow got confused. I checked back on my phone, pulling up his message, but he'd indicated, 'in front of the church,' In any case I did two circles of the piazza but couldn't see anyone who looked remotely like Spencer, and if he were somewhere in the square, he'd see me, wouldn't he? It was now almost 9:45 and on my last circle I'd spotted a nice looking bar where I'd have a good view of the church. Pleased with myself for coming up with 'a plan,' I went over and dropped down at a table with a good view of the entire piazza and church entrance, ordered a Peroni, and put my phone on the table. One eye on the square, one on the phone waited. I tried calling again. Nothing.

By 10:30 it was clear - Spencer wasn't coming. He'd come across as genuinely interested in meeting up, but he'd completely stood me up. I couldn't understand. How dare he treat me like this again, especially given our history, what he'd done at Cambridge?! Irritation turned to anger. I was fuming.

Draining the beer, I left some euros to cover the bill and a tip on the table and wandered off aimlessly for a while before, want of a better plan, dropping down in one of the many pizzerias I ordered a Margherita. Eating my pizza, I kept checking my phone, but nothing. The message screen remained resolutely void. I felt 'stood-up.' I felt deflated. I felt alone.

Glancing around the restaurant all the tables were lively. Groups of Italians out with friends were laughing, joking, having animated conversations. A bunch of students on my right were sharing jokes and laughing loudly together. There were a few couples too, maybe on a first or second date. Spencer not turning up suddenly hit me like a punch in the gut. Another two weeks alone didn't feel like so much fun anymore. The sparkle and excitement of my Italian adventure was fast wearing off. I had to face it. Emma had been right. He'd treated me badly at Cambridge and he'd done exactly the same four years later. All these years I'd been wasting my energy wondering, thinking that maybe there'd been a reason for what had happened. That perhaps there was something to justify his bad behavior. Something I hadn't understood or known about at the time. But no. Fact was he was just a selfish liar. I just hadn't been able to see it at the time. Well I did now.

I pushed aside my half-eaten Margherita and, blinking back the tears, asked for the bill. Back outside, feeling at a loss and alone, I drifted like a minnow in a stream of people heading down to the river. The nightlife of the city was swelling up, getting louder, more raucous. For the first time I noticed how Trastevere seemed more touristy since my last visit, tacky even. It didn't feel so genuine anymore. Many of the menu boards were in English, the neon sign above an ice cream parlor flickering, too gaudy against the quaint 17th century building. A group of half-drunk English girls on a hen night staggered by clutching beer bottles, one of them tripping on the uneven cobbles, the rest squealing and shrieking in response. A bunch of Africans were doing a hard sell on knock-off bags laid out on a cloth on the cobbles. They were asking a fraction of the price of the genuine Prada and Gucci in the stores a stone's throw away, but they looked cheap, plastic and fake. Glancing around in a daze I needed a drink, but not in one of these places with the music pumping, the tables and clients spilling out onto the lane. Turning around, I headed back in the opposite direction trying to get away from the crowds, back to the Santa Maria Square. I crossed it and started looking for a place to drop down in, somewhere to lick my wounds. Then, as luck would have it, a cozy looking bar up ahead caught my eye. Getting closer, the lights were dim, the jazz music soft and there was a space at the bar. I made my way in.

Picking a stool between a young couple on the right and an older man nursing a glass of red on the left I got out my phone, put it on the bar so I could keep an eye on the screen and ordered a Montenegro *'Amaro'* on ice. Bar Samovar was small, slightly shabby but in a bistro, arty kind of way. Old jazz pictures were hanging in a random fashion across one wall, and twisting around from the bar to better take it in, I could see tables dotted around with a mixed clientele, some young, some older. They looked like a cultured arty crowd.

"English?" asked the bar man with a cheeky, twinkling smile as I turned back, and he passed me my drink. "On holiday?"

"Yes, I'm over for a few days from London." I responded taking a sip of the *Amaro* – my first of the holiday. I loved this herbal *digestivo.* It had a strong aroma with hints orange and chocolate. It was intense, had a determined amber colour and was instantly comforting. How fitting. 'Amaro' literally translates to 'bitter' in English, so an ironic way to end what had turned into a bitterly disappointing night.

"First time in Rome?" he asked, resting his elbows on the counter.

"No, I've been here a few times. I love it." I tried to smile back, strangely feeling glad for the conversation.

Alessandro introduced himself and we shook hands over the bar. He was was of average build, had a shaved head with what looked like a week or two of regrowth. He told me he was an artist in his spare time but had to work in the bar to pay the bills. He explained that despite all the tourists he still loved Trastevere and that the bar was not only his place of work but his social focal point. He obviously loved the place and I could understand why. Bar Samovar had the balance right. Both lively and laid back and it was warm and cozy. I was beginning to feel more relaxed. The atmosphere was conducive and the conversation helping. Before long I was telling Alessandro how I'd just been stood up by Spencer, about the feature and how I didn't know what to do next.

"Spencer?!" He said stopping still mid cocktail shake and scrutinizing me closer. "Spencer the English man, from La Sapienza, no?"

I was stunned.

"You know Spencer?" I practically exclaimed, putting my drink down and fixing him across the bar.

"Sure, I know Spencer. He comes here for many years. He lives in Piazza San Cosimato – here." He said putting the cocktail shaker down and gesturing behind him on the right.

Of course! I thought. Why wouldn't this guy Alessandro know Spencer? Spencer had told me he lived in Trastevere, so why wouldn't he come in here? After all, it was probably his local.

"What shall I do?" I asked Alessandro as I drained the remaining drops of Montenegro from the glass while sneaking a look at my phone for the hundredth time to check it for a message.

"Call him tomorrow, see what he says," he said, frowning slightly and looking thoughtful as he started unloading wine glasses from the washer under the counter.

"And what if he doesn't respond?" I asked shoving my empty glass over the counter in his direction. "I've tried him a bunch of times tonight and he hasn't picked up. Why would tomorrow be any different?"

He packed the glass with more ice, poured a second more generous glug of Montenegro over it and passed it back with the vague hint of a smile and a shrug.

"Does he, does he have a girlfriend?" I pressed on, carefully eyeing up Alessandro, trying to see if there were any reaction.

"No, not that I know," he said carefully. "Not that I follow Spencer '*così bene*' you know, I mean not that well, and he has been in here with girls, sometimes, but I never see him with the same one, you know…" he said looking slightly uncomfortable.

"I see," I said, taking a sip of my drink and trying not to look fazed.

"Maybe he lost his phone, or it was stolen, couldn't make it and can't get in touch. Do you have his address?" he asked as he continued to unload the washer and stack the glasses on shelves behind the bar.

"Yes, I do," I said, feeling instantly uplifted at this suggestion, picking up my phone where I'd saved the address as if to show him.

"Then why not go there, tomorrow, see if he's there? Maybe something happened to him. Like I said, his phone was stolen, or, I know he has a Vespa, maybe he had an accident or something. Could be anything."

On my way back to the hotel in the taxi I tried Spencer's number again, but nothing. Just the same voice message. I frowned to myself. Why hadn't he shown up? Had he had a change of heart about meeting up? And if something had come up last minute, why hadn't he called or left a message? Or maybe Alessandro was right. Maybe he'd had his phone stolen and couldn't get a message to me. I didn't know Spencer at all these days but still, it didn't make sense. And what Alessandro had said had started to play on my mind. What if he'd been right and Spencer had been in an accident? The more I thought about it the more I started to worry.

"God you're so bloody selfish," I told myself as the taxi sped over the Tiber back to the Aventino Hill.

Chapter Five

The next morning, I woke with a dull headache between the eyes. I hadn't slept well, and the Montenegro probably hadn't helped. As I lay in the sumptuous king size bed, I tried to focus on anything but Spencer and instead, the unfamiliar sounds of the morning; a dull thud from an adjacent room, the clink of a breakfast tray in the corridor, a distant scooter, but my attempt at mindfulness didn't work and my thoughts kept drifting back to unexpected course of events of the night before even more.

After breakfast, I headed back to Trastevere mulling over the options. I tried Spencer's phone in the taxi. Still no response. It didn't look good. Either Spencer had had a change of heart about meeting up and was avoiding me or worse he was lying in hospital bed somewhere. I didn't buy the stolen phone theory. He could've found a way to email me by now and I'd checked my Hotmail. Nothing. And now the feature was also playing on my mind. Without Spencer there wasn't one. I could phone Jake to see which of the other feature ideas he'd like best, but I had to face facts – it hadn't sounded like Mac had been overly keen on any of them. It was looking like I'd need to come up with a backup plan fast.

Bar Samovar had a different feel in the bright morning light. More a coffee bar by day and friendly bar man Alessandro was nowhere to be seen.

"Alessandro work evenings," an older guy with a goatee beard and glasses told me when I asked. "He here tonight. You wanna leave message?" he almost growled without a smile. Maybe he'd gotten out of bed the wrong side, or maybe he was always like this. It was hard to tell. With a tinge of disappointment, I said no thanks, ordered a cappuccino and picked a table outside. It was stupid but it hadn't occurred to me that Alessandro might not be there, and a friendly face would've been welcome. Drinking my cappuccino, I was lost in thought when suddenly my phone buzzed and, quickly snatching it up from the table, I was certain I'd see Spencer's name on the display, but it was mum. Swallowing my disappointment, I took the call.

"Melody, it's your mum. Just have some time to kill and thought I'd give you a call."

Mum always took August off work when she could, the idea being that Tony had the whole summer off from teaching at Goldsmiths and they could do something fun together, go somewhere nice, but the reality was that she rarely had anything to do and spent most of the month on her own, because Tony was useless and never ended up taking her anywhere. The most she could expect was a trip to the Lake District where he liked to spend time sketching and painting. I knew mum was constantly disappointed but every year she took the time off just in case, every year he failed to deliver, and every year they had a big bust up about it. This year wasn't any different. She'd already told me last week that he'd gone away on a study visit to Venice with his students and mum was home alone again with nothing to do. But thankfully at least mum loved reading and kept herself busy most of the summer with her nose in a book.

"Did I tell you about the latest biography I'm reading?" she started. "It's marvelous – all about..."

"Mum, you know I'm in Rome now, right? This call's probably costing you a fortune, not to mention my roaming charges."

"Rome! Oh, I completely forgot! How's it going? How was it seeing Spencer after all this time? Did he turn into a gentleman after all?"

Mum had never been a Spencer fan. She'd never met him of course, but I'd made the mistake of crying on her shoulder one night. I'd learnt my lesson. Mums never forget. I'd never do it again.

"Well I haven't met him yet but... never mind, it's a long story..."

"A long story? Well make it short one! What's going on?"

I grudgingly filled her in on the basics, finishing with my predicament on the feature now Spencer had gone AWOL. Again.

Mum was always a much better listener when Tony wasn't around and when I'd finished, she was quiet for a moment then –

"Well strikes me you've still got a story there, Melody but only if you go around to his place and see what's going on. If you don't then there's nothing much you can do. But no expectations. Do you hear me?"

As soon as she said it, I knew she was right. By now I was on my second cappuccino and the caffeine fix and mum had helped clear my mind. Why not stick to the original plan? After all, I'm a journalist, I told myself. I can make a story out of this yet. The pep talk had worked.

Saying goodbye to mum I flipped to the notes page on my phone and pulled up Spencer's details. 28, *Piazza San Cosimato*, Trastevere, Roma.

"Excuse me," I said to the surly guy back at the bar as he passed me my bill.

"This is near here, right?" I asked, showing him the phone over the counter and feeling grateful that at least this guy seemed to speak good English. Scrutinizing the address through his reading glasses and eying me up over the top of them he gave me a nod.

"Yes, here," he said pointing in a direction which to my best guess put it right behind the Piazza Santa Maria in Trastevere where I'd been supposed to meet Spencer the night before.

"Piazza San Cosimato. 5 minutes from here," he confirmed before turning to serve the next customer.

I left some euro on the counter for a tip and headed out into the bright, early morning sun. It was already shaping up to be blindingly hot. The next coffee would need to be an iced one.

I made my way back in the direction of Piazza Santa Maria fuelled by the cappuccino and a renewed desire to find out what was going on with Spencer. Trastevere was still waking up. A bunch of women street cleaners were chatting, laughing while they swept away the debris from the night before. Shops were opening, restaurants preparing tables for lunch service, locals were on their way to work.

I soon reached Piazza Santa Maria and pressed on, finding any available shade on route. It was getting hotter by the step and I could feel beads of sweat tracing lines down my back. Then, trying a narrow, cobbled back street, I found it.

Piazza San Cosimato was a large, vibrant piazza with a vegetable market in the middle. It had more of a local vibe than the *'Campo de' Fiori'* and was a hive of activity - women, men, young and old were all busy loading bags with groceries, laughing with the stall holders and getting on with the general task of living. It was a far cry from my metro supermarket in Chalk Farm. Trying not to get distracted with the buzzing scene in front of me, I circled the piazza and soon found number 28. A string of polished brass buzzers on an intercom panel to the right of a huge, dark, cumbersome wooden door announced the inhabitants. Running down the list I quickly found Spencer's name. '*Channing*' jumped out in contrast to the long list of Italian surnames. Taking a breath, I pressed the buzzer and waited, hoping for the best, not knowing what to expect and half expecting nothing. A short while passed and then,

"Hello," came a female voice from the intercom.

"Oh, hello," I said, so surprised I almost lost my train of thought. "Err, yes, err sorry, can I speak to Spencer please?" There was a long silence and then...

"Who is this?" the voice came back rather abruptly. It was hard to tell, impossible to define exactly, but the voice sounded strained, the accent English. Could this be Spencer's girlfriend? Was I making a mistake turning up like this? He'd said in the email he was single, so this didn't compute. Despite my racing mind I pressed on.

"Oh yes, I'm sorry. I'm Melody, Melody Meeks, an old friend of Spencer's from Cambridge. I was supposed to meet him last night, but he didn't turn up, so I just passed by to say hello, to see if everything is alright. Is he home?"

"Oh, I see..." said the voice, then after another extended pause "...well in that case...as you're a friend...look, you'd better come up". The door buzzer sounded, and the door swung off the latch.

"We're on the 6th floor. It's right at the top," came the voice again.

"OK, thanks," I said trying to sound cheery, despite feeling none too cheery at all.

Inside I found a shabby, dank, and musty smelling internal entrance which led to an internal courtyard where I found the elevator. It was one of those antique, open cage types, and looked like it had seen better days. Closing the doors and pressing '6,' it carried me up, creaking and wheezing. At the top, a landing with a small skylight cast some welcome illumination into the pressing gloom. Looking around it took a second to spot '*Channing*' on the third door on the right. It looked heavy, wooden and was veneered in glossy blood red coloured paint. I rang the bell.

A very slim woman of around my height and build opened the door. She had dark brown hair tied back in a tight ponytail and thin, sallow features. She looked like she had a bad cold, an allergy or something. Her nose and eyes looked red and sore. She was holding onto the door, like she was half using it to prop herself up. Now it was open I could see how solid and substantial it was, and it looked like she was glad of it.

"Hello. Melody did you say? I'm Helen. I'm Spencer's sister." Spencer's sister. For a moment the words didn't register but repeated in my mind. Spencer's' sister.

"But, I'm, sorry I…sorry I don't understand," I said, trying to take in her features, see a resemblance. The person on front of me was short, dark, with sharp features. Spencer was tall, blond with blue eyes, with softer features. In fact, there wasn't a resemblance at all.

"Sister? I mean, Spencer doesn't have a sister, well, at least that's what he told me…"

I could see her surprise, almost confusion, and then perhaps some realisation. Not looking me directly in the eyes, she opened the door wider.

"Melody, did you say? I guess you'd better come in."

The apartment was dark, the air feted the atmosphere black. It was such a contrast to the blistering bright day outside, it took my eyes a while to adjust but I started to make out what looked like a nice if compact apartment. Parquet floors, white walls and antique furniture. Nice stuff, not old cast-offs but solid, quality pieces. And slowly more detail came into focus. Statues, pieces of pottery, stone carvings. And there were books, lots of books. In the corner on a table was an old, large, carved wooden chess set. I caught my breath. We'd played chess with that set many times back in Cambridge, often after hours of afternoon sex, always, with a glass of chilled Chardonnay and Puccini for company. He'd said it was his favoured possession. This was Spencer's place.

"Coffee?" She asked, taking me in, sizing me up, her eyes quickly running over my every inch.

"Thanks. Coffee would be great... if it's not too much trouble," I ventured, starting to feel increasingly uncomfortable about turning up like this, although now I was even more curious to know where Spencer was, why on earth he hadn't shown up the night before and not only, but why he appeared to have sister and had told me otherwise.

She made to go over to the kitchen and I suddenly became conscious again of just how dark it was in there, just how gloomy. I realised now. All the shutters were closed. No light was getting in here any time soon.

"It's no trouble. I could do with another myself," she responded, almost to herself. "I'm still in a daze," she said, shaking her head and running her hands over her head. I couldn't help noticing how her hand was shaking.

"These last few days, well, it's been impossible to sleep, you know, we're all still in shock I think...mum's arriving tonight, that's going to be just awful..." She seemed to have already forgotten the coffee and had dropped down, perching limply on the side of the sofa. Suddenly she seemed weak, fragile.

"Mum' I said, slowly. "You mean your mum, like, Spencer's mum?"

I was also sitting on the sofa now. Helen hadn't asked me to sit down but I was beginning to feel quite strange inside.

"Sorry, wait a minute. Spencer doesn't have a mum. He told me at Cambridge his parents had died in a car accident. And, w-what are you talking about? Shock? Shock about what? Where's Spencer?" In an instant my stomach did a turn. Not a good turn, like when you see someone you fancy across a crowded room, but the type you get when you sense something awful might have happened and you won't be able to go back to how it was before you heard it, ever.

"Oh, I'm sorry. What was your name again? Melody? Yes I forgot, I'm sorry, I've never been good with names and well right now, with all this to deal with... you're a friend of Spencer's here in Rome...you said you'd planned to see Spencer last night...?"

"Yes, no, I mean I'm a friend but not from Rome, but I was going to meet him last night – well, it's a bit of story. Actually, we arranged it last month. You see we reconnected on Facebook and... I know he was on holiday until recently but last night we were supposed to meet up and well he didn't show up and you see, he gave me his address, so I just thought I'd come round and see..." I stopped in my tracks. Helen's shoulders were shaking. She looked up at me rubbing her nose, her face screwed in anguish, tears rolling down her cheeks.

"I'm so sorry to have to tell you..." she said pulling a ragged tissue from her pocket and putting it to her nose, talking through it, between the sobs.

"...there's no easy way... you see I'm so sorry but...look Melody, oh god. Spencer's dead."

Chapter Six

In the kitchen, I fumbled around looking for the coffee pot. It was dim in there too, but somehow it didn't seem right to put the light on. Eventually I found it; one of those kinds that comes apart in three pieces; the bottom bit for the water, the middle for the coffee and the top where the brewed coffee comes out. When I'd figured it out, I put it back together, with the coffee in what I hoped was the right bit, lit the gas and started searching the cupboards for cups. Glancing to the living room, through the gloom, I could see Helen crumpled on the sofa, quietly sobbing. I was close to tears and probably in some state of shock myself. Looking in the cupboards I could see that Spencer had been well stocked with what you'd expect: tomato sauce, boxes of pasta, coffee. A jar of marmite stood out against the Italian items. I winced remembering that we'd both been huge marmite fans at Cambridge and moved on to another cupboard. After a while I found two cups and poured in the freshly brewed coffee.

"Here you go," I said back in the lounge, passing Helen one. "I added milk, no sugar. I hope that's OK?"

"Thanks," she said looking up and taking the cup from me with a weak, watery smile. "Sorry about that, it just, just overwhelms you at times. It's not like we were close, I mean, I hardly saw him, especially these last few years, but I can't believe he's…gone," she said, taking a sip of coffee with one hand, while the other clutched a grubby, ragged tissue. I passed her the box of Kleenex from the coffee table, and putting the cup down, she took another.

"Look Helen, I'm so sorry turning up like this. It's probably the last thing you need right now." I said, taking a sip of coffee too, trying to get my head around the fact that I was talking to Spencer's sister, a sister he told me he didn't have.

"No problem," she said, looking at me almost quizzically. I was about to ask her what had happened, how he'd died but she went on…

"Tell me again. You said you'd just met Spencer on Facebook or something?"

So, I told Helen the whole story. How we met at Cambridge and had dated for almost a year. How he'd dumped me, and I'd never heard from him since. I told her how I'd contacted him recently after spotting him on Facebook and about the feature idea too. I finished with how we were supposed to meet the night before in the piazza around the corner and how he'd never shown up…of course.

When I finished there was a short pause. Suddenly I felt overwhelmed with emotion. I couldn't believe that Spencer was dead and that I was face to face with his sister. It was all too much to take in.

"I have to admit I'm a little bit weirded out right now," I confessed, putting the now empty coffee cup down, tears welling up, burning behind my eyes. Helen passed the box of Kleenex over.

"I can't believe it..." I managed, between the tears, the dawning realisation of the situation setting in. Spencer was gone. He was dead. I would never see him again. It was unreal. We sat in silence, for what must've been at least a couple of minutes. I took another tissue, tried to dry my eyes and blew my nose. Helen eventually got up and picked up the empty cups and, taking them to the kitchen, turned back to me.

"Look I don't remember Spencer ever mentioning anything about you to me. Like I said, we weren't at all close, practically estranged these last few year, so, well, I don't really know what he was thinking – I mean about you two meeting up again , but, I'm sure he would've been happy to see you again..." She was trying to be kind, but somehow, they were just empty words and it just didn't seem genuine.

While she was in the kitchen rinsing the cups, I sat thinking about Spencer. Grabbing another tissue, I went over to the kitchen doorway. There was something I had to ask. I didn't want to, but I needed to know.

"Helen, if it's not too painful, can you tell me, how it happened? I mean Spencer... Was it an accident or something? I heard he had a scooter...was it that? And why do you think he told me he didn't have a sister and that that his mum was dead…when she isn't… I just don't get it."

Drying her hands on a tea towel, her back to me I could see how slumped her shoulders were.

"Look, let me freshen up. I'll be back in two minutes, then I'll tell you. Tell you everything."

"It was a freak accident." She took a deep breath. We were back on the sofa and Helen had warmed to me again. Or maybe she just needed company, someone to talk to. It was hard to tell.

"You know how Spencer is passionate, sorry Spencer *was* passionate about scuba diving?" she corrected herself with a visible wince.

"No, I didn't," I admitted. "Well, I gathered it from his Facebook postings and then he said he was going off on holiday to do the scuba thing," I explained.

"Well he was. He just couldn't get enough. Every opportunity he was off somewhere tropical to do scuba. And he loved to combine it with his other passion – pirate history, marine archeology. You see he got into a group, a bunch of people he'd met over the years with a similar interest, you know, people he met at archaeological conferences around the world. They all shared the same passion and organized holidays away together. Well this summer it seems he went to one of his favorite locations in the Caribbean. He'd been there with the same bunch earlier this year, Easter I think it was. Yes, I'm pretty sure it was Easter."

She got up and went over to the corner. On the wall there was a picture in a frame. A photo of a bunch of guys in bathing suits on a boat. The location looked hot and tropical.

"This is him on holiday a couple of years ago. It's in the Caribbean, somewhere off the coast of Panama." I came over to look. There was Spencer. He was centre in the group, short hair, sunglasses and blue trunks. He looked fit, healthy, tanned and muscular. He looked devastatingly handsome. He looked happy.

"Not that I'm an expert, but apparently the diving there is great," she said, pointing at the photo "He told me once, some time back, that there were still loads of wrecks there too." She continued, going to sit back down. "You know from pirate ships from hundreds of years ago. See that piece over there?" she said, indicating to one of the shelves which was festooned with old looking artifacts in wood and metal.

"Well on the right there, see that old coin? Well he found it on a diving holiday there a couple of years. He swore it was gold and from one of Sir Francis Drake's ships. He brought it back last year. I was worried that he'd brought it through customs. You know, there are laws protecting this type of stuff. Spencer just didn't seem to care though. He was so crazy about this pirate thing. I don't think he could bear to hand it over to the authorities. I saw Marco yesterday and he told me that Spenser had been going to get it made into a pendant and wear it as a necklace, like on a piece of leather as a lucky charm." She swallowed again, taking a deep breath.

"Shame he never did it." I let her pause, took the coin, and turned it over in my hand. It was small, solid and clearly from a different era. You could just about make out the bevelled profile of a person on one side when you held it up to the light. Turning back, I studied her face, trying to grasp the tread of the story.

"Marco?" I asked.

"Oh yes, sorry. Marco is a very good friend of his, at the university. He's another one of the lecturers there. Well this summer Spencer went off on one of his holidays with the usual bunch. They'd just arrived and there was a storm coming up. Despite being keen to get in the water the group decided to call it a day and hang out at the hotel. They didn't want to take any chances. They all agreed to stay at the hotel, at the beach, until the storm passed over. A storm can be dangerous when you're diving of course. But Spencer and Bruno, well they decided to charter a boat and go out without telling the others. This is what Marco and Bruno told me at least..."

"Who's Bruno?" I asked.

"Oh, yes, sorry, I'm not explainling all this very well, am I? Bruno Di Franceschi. He's the senior lecturer at La Sapienza where Spencer worked. They went on a couple of these holidays together. Bruno's widowed, in his early sixties I think, and as far as I understand these holidays are a real focus for him. You know, something fun do to with a bunch of like-minded guys. He seems like a lovely man, but I've only met him once, this this week... Anyway, Bruno says they went out diving as Spencer was insistent on getting started. Didn't want to waste any time even though it was clear the others weren't into it. I mean going out to sea on a rough day. Anyway, apparently they headed out super early and the storm didn't look to be developing at all after all. They laid anchor and went in for what they thought would be the first dive of the holiday. After an hour they started to make their way up to the surface. Bruno says that the water got choppy near the surface. It appears that the storm had arrived, suddenly come over while they'd been down. Bruno made it back up to the boat, but after 10 minutes Spencer hadn't surfaced. Bruno got a fresh oxygen tank and went back in telling the boat Captain to keep a look out for him and to send a 'Mayday' to the local coast guard. Actually, that was pretty good of Bruno. The Captain said the storm was whipping up the sea by then. Bruno searched as best he could but couldn't find Spencer. The coast guard took at least a couple of hours to arrive. By that time, it was clear...something had happened to Spencer...." She stopped to wipe away the tears welling in her eyes.

"As you can imagine," she continued after a second, "Bruno was beside himself with guilt. Said he should've never agreed to them going out. Should've talked to the others about it. Should've kept a closer eye on the weather. Should've kept a closer eye on Spencer. Said at the time it didn't occur to them that they might be in real danger, especially Spencer, being the more experienced, the strongest diver out of the group."

"And why didn't they? Tell the others they were going out, I mean?" I asked, curious about this story.

"Well, Bruno says they were the last two in the bar the night before and decided together to take a boat out the next morning. Seems they wanted to set off really early to miss this approaching storm, so they just left a note on reception to tell the others. They didn't want to wake them, I guess. But I suspect the others would've been quite rightly against it. When you understand the sea, you don't take risks when there's been a storm warning. Not that I blame Bruno" she added. "I mean, Spencer can be pretty determined about things. I'm sure if Bruno says Spencer was adamant about going, I'm sure he was." For a moment we were quiet, lost in our thoughts.

"But what about Spencer, I mean, lying to me at Cambridge? He told me that both his parents died in a car accident, that he was the only child. Sorry I don't like to pry but, well, that's odd, no? I mean, why would he do that?" I looked at her face, trying to pick up a reaction. She looked awkward, maybe a little confused. I couldn't read her at all.

"How well did you really know Spencer, Melody? I mean at Cambridge. You said you've not been in touch with him since, right?" I suddenly felt a little cold.

"Well, like I said, we were together almost a year, well let's say 10 months. It was intense but, you know how these things are. At the time I thought we were close but, with hindsight, perhaps not as close I thought."

"Did you never think it was a strange story? Like, him saying he was an orphan?"

"No never, why should I?"

"Look, Spencer was an orphan and was adopted. He's not my real brother, by birth I mean. Mum and Dad so desperately wanted a second child, but after five years of trying, well, let's just say it wasn't happening. Then they decided to adopt. Spencer came from a Scottish orphanage just outside Edinburgh. They didn't know anything about him, apart from him being abandoned there the year before but I think his mother was still alive. That's what we understood a least. He was 5 years old when he came to live with us. Spencer, well he was quite a little character. Right from the beginning."

I was enthralled. Spencer adopted? Quite a character? "What exactly do you mean?"

Helen went on. "Well he was the most charming little boy. Charm, I think it was in his DNA. And mum and dad just couldn't say no. Every ice cream, every toy. He was spoilt rotten. At school too, all the teachers just loved him. All the girls in his class developed an instant crush. He was a stunning little boy, you know those blue eyes, blond hair. Then a few things happened."

"Things?"

"Yes, like we found out that Spencer was quite the little liar. There were lots of small lies, we just put it down to him being a cheeky boy, but sometimes they were bigger. Like mum found out he wasn't in school for weeks. He'd invented a whole pack of lies that checked out – with the teachers, with mum and dad. He'd been bunking off, but unlike most boys who bunk off school and hang out in some place, smoking and drinking and getting up to no good, Spencer had been going to the local library and studying by himself. When we questioned him, he told us that the other kids in the class he was in at school were too stupid and where holding him back. It was peculiar to say the least. Then dad died. He had a massive heart attack. It was terrible and from then on it was just the three of us. That's when Spencer got harder for mum to control, you know without dad being around. Mum started letting him get away with things. Like one day she found out he'd taken money from her purse without asking, that he'd been shoplifting too. Then he stole something from the local church. I think it was the goblet they used for the communion service. Anyway, Mum found it in his room. There was a huge row about that one. For once mum wasn't having it and made him put it back. He had to sneak into the church to do it so that nobody would know it was him. That was the last time mum really got her way. He was difficult to control after that. We just put it down to him being adopted and having a batch patch. You know, teenage stuff."

"Oh, I see," I nodded, taking this all in. Trying to imagine the hard time he must've had growing up, knowing he'd been abandoned. Poor Spencer. Helen went on.

"The other thing about Spencer is that it soon became clear just how bright he was. It was like he didn't really have to study. It was incredible. He was good at everything – Arts, science, history, and maths. You name it, he could do it. He did well in his exams, was particularly good at history, became quite obsessed with it, then did really well in his A levels – straight A's in fact. That's when he got accepted to Cambridge. He'd always loved history, it seemed like the natural thing for him to specialise in, archaeology I mean." She stopped, looked sad.

"But by then we weren't getting on. He seemed to push me away. I tried to be close to him, but it was like…like he never really wanted it. I never understood what I'd done. It was like he didn't really...like me. Perhaps he even resented me, as mum and dad, well they were my biological parents, and not his." She paused.

"Then I found out that Spencer had somehow persuaded mum to change her will, it meant that whenever she died, he'd get everything. We cleared it all up in the end, it was all a big misunderstanding, but well, at the time it put our relationship under even more of a strain. As you can imagine, I was livid, with mum too. But she explained that, at the time, she'd done what she thought was the best, because she'd felt that Spencer needed it more than me."

"Needed it more?" I said, shocked. "How could he do that? I mean try and cut you out? And why did your mum do it? And what do you mean 'he needed it more?'" I searched her face. I felt bad probing but couldn't imagine Spencer doing that. There had to be a reason.

"Oh, I should explain," she said, "By then I'd left university and had just gotten married to Jim. We met at Lancaster University and got married the year after. Jim comes from a pretty wealthy family and not only this, but in his first year working in the city he'd already done very well for himself in banking and, well, it's true I don't need mum's inheritance at all, we have plenty of money, and Jim will eventually have a large inheritance too. You see he's an only child, and well, Spencer, in fact, he had nothing. And let's be honest. You don't become a University lecturer for the money, do you? But anyway, we got the thing sorted out. I spoke to him about it. Well in fact I got angry with him, Spencer I mean, about it, but he said he was sorry. Said he never meant mum to change the will. That she'd done it herself, off her own bat. Swore that he'd never asked her to do it. Mum was mortified and changed her will back. She said sorry to me too and said it wasn't Spencer's fault at all. Said that she was just trying to do the right thing by him but on reflection, well maybe she'd made a mistake as I shouldn't be cut out no matter how well off Jim was. We cleared it all up over time, and in the end, it just seems like it was a huge misunderstanding, but well, we weren't much in touch after that. I don't know, something had shifted between us. I kept trying, but Spencer just wasn't interested to be in touch. We'd see each other occasionally but it was like we were just going through the motions, so to speak. It didn't help either that Jim kind of had it in for Spencer. Said that there was something off about him. Didn't fully trust him. Spencer has always been hugely charming, and Jim just never warmed to him. To be frank, not that I like to admit this, but for a time I used to think he was a bit jealous too. I mean Spencer was always a bit of a girl magnet to be fair. He's had so many girlfriends over the years, and I think Jim found it a bit hard to keep up with him…"

"Look Helen, I really should be going I think." I said standing up and making to leave, the reality of the situation beginning to sink in, hearing all these Spencer details a little hard to swallow. I felt sick. My head was spinning. I needed to get outside. I needed fresh air, space to digest this new dawning reality. I needed sunlight. Fast. I was still trying to make sense of the fact that Spencer was dead let alone why he'd lied about his parents and sister and hearing now that he'd had strings of women, girlfriends…" Helen stood up too, I rambled on.

"I don't want to intrude on you any more than I have. I really appreciate you taking the time to explain what happened. But listen…"

"Sorry Melody," she said, fixing my gaze "I didn't mean to be insensitive. Look I don't know why Spencer told you his mum and dad died in a car accident. Maybe that was him coming to terms with being abandoned. Maybe it was easier for him to frame it like that. And I don't know why he said he was an only child. I guess he was in a way, not counting me as his adoptive sister…And Spencer did tend to stretch reality at times. Sometimes it was hard to separate his fact from fiction. He'd had a troubled childhood…who knows…Like I said, perhaps it was his way of coping with it all, perhaps..."

I went to grab my bag. I wanted to leave, to be on my own.

"And now I seem to remember, I think he did maybe mention something to me. I mean about you. Yes, I remember now, Melody. It's coming back to me, one of the few times I saw him just after Cambridge. He seemed down. Low. Almost depressed. When I asked him what was wrong, he said he'd made a big mistake. Said he'd ended with a girl; someone he'd deeply cared for and that it might've been the biggest mistake of his life. He was down about it and didn't know what to do. Said he'd had his reasons at the time, but I remember being surprised. Like I said, we weren't close at all. He'd never mentioned anything about a girl to me ever before in that way. I think, meeting you now, hearing that you were with him in that last collage year, well, Melody, I think maybe he was talking about you."

I felt numb and electric at the same time. My stomach lurched. He'd mentioned me to Helen. He had cared for me! Spencer. Perhaps. Perhaps. I studied her face. She seemed genuine. Why should she tell me otherwise? A wave of regret and sadness washed over me.

"Look, I'm not due to leave for Amalfi until tomorrow afternoon. I have a train at 3pm. If there is anything I can do in the meantime, I don't know what, but I can leave you my number and if you need anything..."

"Melody, I know that this is all very weird for you. I mean, as you said, even though you were close to Spencer at Cambridge you two haven't even been in touch since then, but as you're here I wonder if you would like to come to the funeral tomorrow? I know that might be strange for you but maybe it would be good for you to come, say goodbye. After all, sounds like even if it were a while back that, for a period, you guys had been close…"

For a second, I didn't know what to say. I think I was still in shock about Spencer being dead. It was just so out of whack to be here now, talking about him in the past tense, when I had been supposed to meet him for a beer a few hours back. And then there was the feature, my article. I'd hardly had time to take any of this in, it was the last thing on my mind, but one of the the reason's I was here, meeting Spencer in the first place was for the feature. What was I going to do about that?

"What time's the funeral?" I asked, uncertain. Thinking on my feet.

"2 p.m., *Isola Tiberina.* It's right in the centre. The next day we'll have the burial at Verano Cemetery – just close family and friends. Strange thing was, even though he was young, he'd left a handwritten will. I found it in the drawer over there in an envelope." She indicated to a desk in the corner. It looked like where he worked at home, it was covered in books, journals, papers, but I was hardly listening by then.

"That's why we're having him buried in Rome. It's what he wanted. It's been a huge hassle to get organised, but … anyway, sorry I'm rambling. About the funeral tomorrow - you're more than welcome, really. After the church were having a small reception nearby. There'll be a lot of Spencer's friends, work colleagues from the University. He'd only been working there just over a year, but well, they all seem fond of him. Look, if you'd like to come you won't feel out of place, I'm sure."

As the words sunk in it struck me that perhaps going to the funeral was the right thing to do. And it sounded like there'd be time, maybe after, to meet his friends, speak with Helen again, even perhaps his mum and figure out more about the Spencer I thought I knew but clearly didn't know at all.

"Sure Helen. I'll come." I said. "It would be strange not to go, seeing as I'm here. Thanks for...well, thanks for inviting me."

"You know, I'm asking you 'cos I think that's what Spencer would've wanted." She smiled weakly.

Outside it was blindingly hot. It was a dry, blistering heat and the sun was directly overhead, but I decided to walk. I needed some time outside, in the bleached brightness of the day to beat off the dark, oppressive atmosphere hanging on my shoulders from Spencer's place, and I needed a cigarette. A lunchtime lethargy was taking over the city, but I wasn't feeling lethargic. I was drained.

Finding some shade in a doorway and my tin with tobacco and papers from the bottom of my bag, hands shaking, I rolled my first cigarette of the day. Lighting it, I took in a long hard drag. The tobacco was strong, the taste in my mouth bitter, the sensation nauseating. But I needed it.

Spencer was dead, the victim of a freak diving accident. Doing something he loved, his life had been cut short. I thought back to the photo – the one in the frame on the wall of his flat. Spencer grinning, with a group of friends. He'd looked so happy, so full of life. Then Helen, the sister I never knew he had. The story he'd told me about being an only child and both his parents being dead in a car accident was just that. A story. Why did he make all that up? Then the bombshell; Helen saying she remembered him talking about me…I needed a drink.

Crossing *Piazza San Cosimato*, I dropped down at one of the many bars that lined the square and ordered myself a glass of white wine. While I waited for my drink to arrive, I took out my tobacco tin, started to make another cigarette and tried to take stock as the world carried on regardless, the bustle of the lunchtime service, oblivious to the pit I'd just fallen into. Spencer's apartment, Spencer's sister and now…Spencer's funeral. Finally, the wine arrived, and I gulped it down, lost in thought and was soon ordering a second. Spencer…

And what about my feature? If I was even capable of doing it now, it would have to take a different tack. Perhaps a piece on modern relationships, of the superficiality of following friends on social media, of connecting too late. I admit that, reflecting on my feature, having just found out Spencer was dead, sounds harsh, exploitative and unethical but, if I wrote the piece well, it could still work for me while at the same time being a nice remembrance of Spencer…

I ordered some pasta but then spent the next hour pushing it around on the plate. It was just 1:30 p.m. but I called it a day, asked for the bill and headed back to hotel.

Chapter Seven

August, and there wasn't a hint of a cloud in the sky. It was blue in the way only the Mediterranean can do it - confident, like it's going to be around for some time.

Instead of catching my train to Amalfi I was speeding along the *Lungo Tevere* in a taxi to the funeral of my old Cambridge flame, Spencer Channing. Spencer, the only man I had ever loved and had never really gotten over. Spencer the enigma that, in an unexpected, sad turn of events, I was getting aquatinted with all over again. Not to say in the hotel bar the night before after a few glasses of red, I'd been tempted to skip the whole thing. Tempted to bypass the funeral and catch my train to Amalfi as planned. Images had starting building in my mind; the stunning view down to the sea, the turquoise pool, a cocktail and a book. I'd been dreaming of it for days, clicking on and off the hotel website in anticipation and didn't want to miss even a day. God knows, the place was expensive enough. And more to the point, I wouldn't have to face Spencer's funeral. But mulling things over back in my room later that night I'd decided to keep my word to Helen and more importantly, to myself. I was going to dig my black linin summer dress out of my suitcase (the only one I had, thank god I'd packed it!), give it an iron, take a deep breath and turn up. I was going to pay my respects…and I was going to show some grit. Not only, if there was any way I could still get a feature story out of the desperately sad situation, without compromising Spencer or my love for him, I was going to do it. And who knows, Jake and Mac might be impressed and my mum (yes, the tough cookie journalist from the seventies') might even be proud of me yet.

The funeral was on *Isola Tiberina*, a tiny island in the middle of the Tiber River in central Rome. Nothing more than a random cluster of buildings; a church, hospital, bar and restaurant, it was linked to the embankment on one side by a foot bridge and on the other by a narrow road. I arrived early, took an expresso in the bar and had a smoke before making my way across the square to the church.

I hadn't been there long before people started gathering. Small groups of mourners in black suits and dresses, huddled together, talking quietly together. Then I spotted Helen getting out of a taxi with an older woman. Spencer's mum. I took a deep breath and went over. Helen grimaced, and nodded.

"Mum, this is Melody, you know the person I told you about last night. Melody this is Margaret, Spencer's mum."

Spencer's mum eyed me up, rather coldly I felt. She was short, painfully thin and had very thick silver-grey hair cut in a neat, tidy bob. She was wearing a black knee length simple dress and little kitten heal shoes. Very classy.

"Well Spencer never mentioned you to me Melody, but then Spencer wasn't much for talking these last years, at least with me," she said, taking me in.

"Oh" I said awkwardly, "I'm sorry to hear that."

"Yes, I didn't mention yesterday Melody," Helen jumped in, "Mum and Spencer hadn't spoken in a long time… I'll explain to you later."

Other people were coming up to Helen and his mum to offer condolences, so I drifted into the church. They hadn't exactly made me feel welcome, more uncomfortable if anything. It stung a bit, but I reminded myself that they were in grief and, after all, it wasn't like I'd been a big part of Spencer's life. In any case, I was glad to slip away and get inside out of the heat.

The church was cool, the mid-afternoon sun soft and multi coloured, the effect of the ancient stained glass windows which filtered the external white light into something more reassuring. The pungent smell and of incense floated down from the altar where Spencer's coffin rested covered in a huge bunch of pure white lilies.

A photo of Spencer was carefully positioned on the top. It looked like one from a holiday somewhere hot. He was tanned and was grinning out, dazzling with a confident, exuberant smile. It made my stomach lurch all over again.

People were quietly drifting in, taking seats. Then Helen appeared, glancing around at the back when she spotted me sitting alone.

"Look why don't you come up here and sit with us?" She said, coming over and indicating to the front of the church.

"Are you sure?" I hesitated "I mean will that be OK with your mum...after all, Spencer and I we were just...."

"Melody don't worry. Don't sit there on your own. Come over. I'll introduce you to Jim. We Brits should sit together, there aren't that many of us here. A lot of his friends from Cambridge and Bath had either lost touch with him over the years or couldn't make it. Most of the people here are from the University in Rome where he was working, *La Sapienza*."

Helen lead me up to the front of the church, indicating the second pew and quickly introduced me to Jim who nodded, shock my hand and went back to checking his phone. Spencer's mum Margaret came in and sat down. She was wiping her eyes but didn't look up. Helen sat down on my left. We waited in silence while more mourners filed in and quietly took their places. Then someone was tapping on Helen's shoulder and she turned around.

"Hi, Marco. Thanks so much for coming."

"Spencer was my special friend. He always will be," said a guy directly behind me, looking for a second like he was chocking back a tear.

"Marco, this is Melody. She's.... she's a… a very old friend of Spencer's…from Cambridge university and just happened to be in Rome."

"Hi Marco," I said leaning over, shaking his hand. Marco had short dark cropped hair with flecks of grey just starting to show at the sides, and very dark brown eyes behind heavy black rimmed glasses.

"*Buon giorno.* Nice to meet you. I wish it could be in...in a better situation."

"Me too," I nodded, feeling the weight of the occasion on my shoulders.

"This is Luca, Fabio and Massimo," said Marco, indicating to the guys to his right and left. We all shock hands over the wooden pew.

"We played five-a-side football together, with Spencer." said one of them, I think it was Luca. I nodded at them all and turned back around as Helen explained in a whisper.

"Marco was Spencer's closest friend here in Rome. As I said, Spencer and I were hardly in touch, especially these last years but a year ago Jim and I were in Rome for a weekend. We met up and he introduced us to Marco. Seems a nice guy. He also works at La Sapienza. He's a lecturer in Roman history. They were very close. From what I remember they met at Bath University...yes, I think I remember right," she explained, looking thoughtful.

"And over there, that's Bruno di Franceschi. Do you remember? He was the man I was telling you about yesterday, the one who was with Spencer when the accident happened."

Over to my left where Helen was looking, I could see an older, distinguished man of around sixty, tall for an Italian with thinning grey hair swept back. He'd probably been quite a 'looker' when he was young. But today he looked pale, gaunt and a little stooped - hard to tell having never met him before if this was his normal posture or more the weight of the occasion. As if reading my thoughts, Helen leant over.

"He's taken Spencer's death really badly. He feels responsible. Of course, we've told him he isn't... but like I said, he's taken it very badly…"

Just then the priest arrived, and the service began. It was all a bit of a blur. Various readings, some hymns or something which sounded like them. More readings. It seemed to go on forever but eventually it ended. Spencer's mum was in a state, crying and had to be held up by Helen and Jim on the way out. A reception was taking place straight after in a local restaurant nearby, Helen reminded me, but looking at her mum, she decided it would be better to take her back to the hotel for some rest.

"Once I get her settled, I'll come back to the reception and see you there," Helen explained before heading off to the taxi that was waiting in front of the church. I watched as Jim helped her inside and the taxi pulled away, slowly across the bridge.

After the service I took some time to myself, down by the river to reflect, collect my thoughts, have a private cry and get myself together and by the time I arrived at the reception, around thirty or so people were already standing in groups quietly chatting, drinking prosecco, no doubt sharing stories and memories of Spencer. A simple restaurant or '*trattoria*' in the ghetto, the Jewish quarter and a stone's throw from *Isola Tiberina*, it was small, had a rustic feel and a pretty, shady courtyard garden with an impressive bright pink bougainvillea in full bloom running along the entire back wall. I was still in half a daze but couldn't help thinking that it added a welcome bright spot of colour to the sombre occasion.

I got myself a drink from a waiter who was circling with a tray of drinks and tried to mingle, but it wasn't easy. They seemed a nice, polite enough bunch but no one seemed so enthusiastic or forthcoming about striking up a conversation with a stranger, especially in English, so feeling at a loose end, I picked a spot outside and sat down to make myself a roll-up. After I'd been out there for a short while smoking, I spotted that Helen had arrived and before long she waved at to me to come over.

"How is she?" I asked, putting out the cigarette and stepping back inside.

"Well, as you can imagine…I gave her a tranquilliser and she's asleep," she grimaced back.

"And how are you bearing up?" I asked.

"I need to mingle, try to say thanks to some of these people who came. Honestly, I don't really know who half of them are, it's all rather awkward," she said, not really answering my question and glancing around the restaurant. For a second, she looked daunted.

"Come with me? We could try and say hello at least?"

She seemed to want my support, so I followed her around, trying to introduce myself again, shaking hands, having half conversations where Spencer's friends and colleagues spoke some English, but it was still hard going, and we soon got separated. Suddenly feeling exhausted and a little hungry for the first time all day, I gave up, wandered over to the buffet, grabbed a plate and was half-heartedly picking up some bits and pieces when Marco appeared next to me.

"Ciao," he said with a gentle smile. "So, remind me, how do you know Spencer? School or was it at University?"

I instantly liked the look of Marco. He seemed warm and friendly, with a nice pinch of reserve. Forgetting the buffet food, I was soon telling him the whole story about how I'd seen Spencer on Facebook, reconnecting after four years, my feature, everything. Marco seemed a good listener, appeared genuinely interested. After a pause I turned the tables.

"Your English is amazing. Where did you pick it up?"

"Oh, thanks," he smiled, "My mother's English, and I've spent quite a bit of time in the UK since I was seventeen actually, studying too. I went to university in Bath, did my MSC there before a PhD in London."

It added up. After all, his English was perfect with only a faint hint of an accent.

"So that's where you first met Spencer?" I asked.

"Yes. We were both on an archaeology masters at the time." He nodded.

"And you're a journalist." he said, looking at me, as if sizing me up. It was more a statement than a question.

"Yes. Well, no....look, I have this page in an English monthly called *Zenith* and it's quite light and fluffy and I'm trying to, to break out, into more investigative journalism. It's not easy though. There's so much competition."

"You mean like, what is that film called, oh yes, All the Presidents Men."

I laughed. "If only!"

"And this feature with Spencer in it, was going to help you do that?" For a second, he sounded skeptical.

"What did Spencer think about it?" He went on, taking another Prosecco from the passing waiter and studying my face again.

"Actually, I didn't get the chance to ask him," I explained sheepishly. "I'd been planning to broach it on Tuesday."

"Must've been a shock," he said.

"Sorry?"

"Hearing about Spencer."

"Oh yes. It was a terrible shock," I admitted with a grimace, also remembering Helen's face, the tears.

"When I heard the news, I couldn't believe it," he said, shaking his head. "In fact, I still don't believe all of it," he continued, taking a sip of prosecco and suddenly looking very serious, a frown appearing between his eyes.

"Sorry, what do you mean, you don't believe '*all of it*?" I asked, wondering if I'd miss-heard. Perhaps it was his English, even though he seemed to speak it so fluently. He looked at me hard, was about to say something then stopped for a second before going on.

"I'm sorry, Melody. I shouldn't have said anything, especially not here, but…" he paused, hesitating, weighing me up before continuing. "Well this whole story doesn't quite add up to me," he said, glancing round quickly to see if anyone was listening. Lowering his voice, he continued.

"Especially after what Spencer told me about that dive location from their last holiday at Easter."

"What do you mean? What about that dive location?" I asked, curiosity pricked. But Marco wasn't listening, he was looking over to the back of the restaurant which led out to the courtyard. Following his gaze, I could see Bruno di Franceschi. Helen was talking to him. He looked distressed. He was listening, staring down at the floor, shaking his head.

"Marco, what is it? What about the dive location from last year?" I asked again, trying to bring him back to our conversation.

"Sorry Melody, I shouldn't really say any more. It's just my theory..." Marco turned back to me.

"What theory?" I asked, pressing him, curiosity really getting me now. Marco glanced around again. I followed his gaze around the room. A group of Spencer's friends, colleagues in the corner were looking over, talking about us, I was sure by the way, they kept glancing over. I suddenly felt vaguely uncomfortable but tried to push the feeling from my mind. Marco seemed to reflect for a second or two before going on.

"Look, are you doing anything tonight?" he asked, putting his half-empty glass of prosecco down and getting out his phone.

"No, I'm not as it happens, I…"

"You want to be a serious journalist, right? So, you must like uncovering things, getting to the truth." Marco asked, cutting in.

"Sure, but I'm not that type of journalist right now, like I said I have a friend who works for *The Times* and she says..."

"Do you want to know what I think? I mean about what really happened to Spencer? How I really think he died?" he said interrupting me. I hesitated. Where the hell was this going? Spencer had died in a freak diving accident. Helen had told me. What was Marco talking about?

"Well... I don't know, I mean..."

"Melody, if you don't have plans, just meet me for one drink. Hear me out. Also, you know I'd love to hear some stories of Spencer, you know from when he was at Cambridge. I'm curious you know, about the Spencer before… and I can tell you more about him too. Could be interesting for your article. The one you're writing about Spencer. On the Facebook encounter you just told me about, no?"

"Oh, well I don't know if I should do that now. I'm not entirely sure if it's a good idea anymore. I came to the funeral with that in mind, but I've been thinking about it today and I'd have to speak to Spencer's mum and sister..."

"Look I think it's a great idea. You should do it. If it's sensitively done it would be a great way of remembering him. Looks like he didn't have much of a relationship with them either, no? Then there's a funny thing too. Spencer told me that both his parents were dead. Said they had died in a plane accident. So I was a bit shocked when his mum turned up today, you know."

Suddenly I went cold. "He told you that, too? Oh boy, that's too weird."

"What do you mean?' Marco fixed on me. "What?"

"Well Spencer told me that as well." I said, feeling like the ground had shifted again.

"Like when we were at Cambridge together. Only he said to me it was a car accident. Why would he do that? His sister said it was perhaps his way of dealing with being an orphan, but not to mention his adopted parents or sister at all?"

"I really don't know." Marco stared back, frowning. For a moment we were silent. Thinking.

"And did he tell you he was an only child?" I quizzed him.

"No, why?"

"That's what he told me," I explained. "You can imagine how surprised I was to meet his sister yesterday…"

"Sounds like we have a lot to talk about," said Marco.

"Ok," I said, tentatively. "I guess I could have a glass of wine. Nothing late though, I'm getting the 9 a.m. train to Amalfi first thing tomorrow morning."

"Ok great." He said, breaking into an almost cheeky smile. "Drinks on me. I think we need them."

Chapter Eight

We met at 9pm in Piazza dell'Immacolata in San Lorenzo, a student part of the city just north of Termini railway station.

"I'm glad you came. I wasn't sure you would," he smiled as I walked up.

"You have my number," I reminded him. "I don't think you would've given up quite so easily, right?"

"Right," he grinned. "I know a quiet place just there." He indicated to a narrow street on the opposite side of the square. "We can get a drink. We can talk. I can explain."

The bar was small, dark, cavernous, and empty, except for a couple of young guys at the bar with a bottle of red. They looked like they'd been there for a while. And not a tourist in sight. Marco had chosen well.

"Ciao, Mario," Marco greeted the young bar man. With no customers to serve, Mario was slouching on the bar, his face illuminated by his phone, flicking through what looked like his Facebook account.

"Ciao Marco. '*Come va*?'" Mario responded nonchalantly, looking up with a nod. Marco was clearly a regular in here.

Marco chose a table at the back set in one of three wooden booths. Looking around in the dim light I could see that the place suffered from a little damp and could do with a coat or two of paint. Or maybe it was charming like this. I couldn't decide. There were old dusty black and white photos in frames on the walls; shots of Rome from the 50s. Some of them had damp spots, were brown and aging like they'd been there since the 50s themselves. On the wall on the right there was football memorabilia; a football scarf for AS Roma hung above a door, signed photos of players here and there. A couple of small flat screen TVs bolted on brackets higher up suggested that this was sometimes a sports bar, maybe crowded and buzzing then.

The barman Mario sloped over with a couple of wine menus and dropped them on the table. He chatted to Marco in Italian, I heard Spencer's name a couple of times. Mario patted Marco on the shoulder affectionately and Marco passed the menus back without even looking at them.

"Red or white?" he asked me.

"Red, thanks." A bottle of wine and a bowl of some of the largest green olives I'd ever seen soon appeared with two glasses. They smelled amazing, like a Mediterranean summer on a plate. Marco poured the wine and took a sip, looking thoughtful.

"So, tell me about Spencer. You met him at Cambridge, right?"

For the next hour I told Marco all I could remember about Spencer. About how we met in the student union bar. How charming he'd been and how I'd had a huge crush on him from day one. How we'd been inseparable for months and how I'd practically moved into his rooms. How we'd revised together, played chess together, listened to every classical music CD in his collection together, alphabetically, then had started back at the beginning to listen to them all over again. How he loved drinking Cambridge Pale Ale, G&T and port after dinner, but loved Pimm's and Lemonade more in the summer. How he smoked roll-ups out of his window at two in the morning, just to keep me company, even though he didn't really smoke. How one time he'd woken up the students in the dorm rooms upstairs, as he was laughing so loudly. He'd got a bucket of water over his head that night, but he'd laughed it off and they forgave him instantly the next day. How he'd light up the room as he walked in and always had time for everyone. And how, sometimes to my dismay, he was an unabashed flirt; women, men, old, young, lecturers, girls at the supermarket check-out, store assistants, barmen, whoever he met... but how in a strange way I was fascinated to watch him in action. It was his way of getting what he wanted; that sneaky discount, an extra 20% off, the best table in a restaurant even though it was already reserved and another round of drinks after time had been called. Not that I didn't sometimes get incredibly jealous and insecure of course… And most of all, how he was the brightest star of the faculty. How the lecturers loved him, almost like he was one of them. How effortlessly he passed every exam with the highest score, and thinking back now, how amazing it was, as I never saw him revise for more than ten minutes in one go.

Then I told Marco about the breakup, how lost I'd been. How from one day to the next he disappeared from my life and I'd never seen him again. Until Facebook. About how he told me he was an only child and how both his parents had died in a car accident. That he told me he'd been orphaned but that I had no idea that his adoptive mother, father, and sister even existed. That the only relative he'd ever mentioned was an aunt he hated.

When I finished, we were both silent for a while.

"So, Marco, you've heard about Spencer from me, the Spencer at Cambridge. Tell me a little about the Spencer *you* know."

"What do you want to know?" he asked, putting his glass down.

"Well, anything."

Marco looked thoughtful for a while. "Spencer was my closest friend at *La Sapienza*, but we first met about four years ago at Bath University. I always remember seeing Spencer when I arrived on the first day of term. You know he looked...very English. Well I guess he did to an Italian. Blond, tall, very blue eyes. He came right over and shock my hand and we became friends, almost instantly. I can't explain why we hit it off so well, but I guess we just enjoyed each other's company.

"We soon found out we shared a very similar sense of humor. He was kind of quirky and liked to, how do you say? 'Take the piss' out of everything, himself too. He was very dedicated to the course. He seemed to find it all so easy. I kind of looked up to him. Then when the course finished, I went off to London and did my PhD. We lost touch a bit then. I found out after that he went to France, but I'll get to that in a bit." He took a sip of wine before carrying on.

"I finished the PhD and started looking for a job, and I got a lucky break here at La Sapienza. They were looking for a junior lecturer, I applied and got the job. Then one day out of the blue, I hadn't been there for long, Spencer phoned me up. Said he'd done a PhD in France, and was looking for a job, had found me on LinkedIn and fancied Italy. As luck would have it, they'd just advertised for another junior lecturer here and, well I gave him a good character reference, put in a good word for him and he got the job.

"He started here, well must be a couple of years ago now. We celebrated that alright. We couldn't believe how lucky we'd both been, to get such good jobs straight out of PhDs. It's quite unheard of you know. Anyway, we both lectured in ancient Roman History, he specialized more in Republican Rome and I more Imperial, but it was great having him around again. Like I said, we'd lost touch a bit over the PhDs, when he'd been in France. He told me he'd been in Paris, at the university there. Came out fluent in French too. Spencer, well sometimes I think he was a genius you know. I mean, trust him! A PhD just wasn't enough for him, he had to learn a language while he was at it! But anyway, we soon picked up again where we'd left off. We spent hours in the lecturer's room at La Sapienza discussing theories, papers he was writing and the like. We often met up after work, played five-a-side football and at the weekends went out for drinks, dinner, whatever. We went to the stadium to watch AS Roma play on Saturdays or Sundays or came here when we couldn't get tickets.

"We did a couple of holidays together too, skiing last year to the Dolomites, although Spencer didn't like skiing. Oh, he was good at it, don't get me wrong. But he wanted to try snowboarding and took to it quickly. We even went on a couple of double dates," he said, smiling almost to himself. "That was fun. It was early on when his Italian wasn't so fluent, so his date didn't go as well as mine. I can remember him now the Monday after, back in the lecturer's room. I'd managed to get a second date, but his date, I remember she was called Ilaria. Well Ilaria hadn't been too keen it seemed. He was pretty sulky about that I remember. First time I'd seen Spencer not his happy-go-lucky self. At the time I thought that maybe he was lonelier than he let on and wasn't so 'relationship phobic' as he'd once described himself. Then when I talked to Francesca, my date, the next week she said that Spencer's date had been bored senseless by Spencer, who just insisted on talking about the Romans all night. It wasn't his Italian at all. I had words with him about that, but he just didn't get it. Back then he thought that everyone should be as into ancient Roman history as he was." Marco paused to take a sip of wine before going on.

"That doesn't sound like Spencer at all!" I exclaimed. "The Spencer I knew would have charmed this Ilaria off her feet, Italian or no Italian." Marco took another sip of wine, thinking it over, then he went on.

"But that was in the beginning. Despite the date not going well, that was back when Spencer was, well, like I said, 'happy-go-lucky.' That was in the first years I knew him. You know, at Bath and in the beginning in Rome," he said, looking more serious now.

"But Spencer really changed these last few months. It probably started even longer ago," he said, frowning, trying to remember, trying to piece together something that would make sense. Something maybe not so easy to define. He carried on.

"Yes, even six months ago. How can I explain?" he said, searching for some examples to illustrate his point. "Well, when he first arrived in Rome, he kind of accepted everything. La Sapienza can be a bit frustrating sometimes. You know, typical Italian bureaucracy? Well, at first Spencer seemed to laugh it off but then over the last few months he seemed to find it more and more frustrating. You might think that's quite normal, but he started getting angry about it, you know, shouting at the admin staff, causing a scene. It would take quite a few drinks on a Friday for him to shake off his annoyance. Then he started getting really picky about the students he was teaching and was super critical of those he didn't think were up to the mark. He had a huge fight with one of the admissions tutors one week. I remember it so well. He was hauled into the principal's office and told to calm down, but he stormed out. He got a warning for that."

"Did you talk to him about it?" I asked, curious to know more.

"Sure, we went out for drinks that very night. He was furious about the management, but I felt there was something else behind it. So, I tried to get to the bottom of it. At first, he closed up, said he wasn't interested in talking about it anymore. He was drinking straight rum that night. I remember it well as I'd never seen him drinking rum before. After a few glasses he started opening up. It all started coming out. I don't know how much of it was the rum talking but, well, we never talked about it again, not after that. Anyway, as I said, he started opening up. We talked about his fight with the principle. He said he thought the guy was a complete idiot. But the more we talked, the more it came out that it wasn't really about the principle. It was more like he was tired, frustrated with lecturing. Always having to teach such 'substandard' students as he described them. He kept pouring himself more rum. He'd ordered a bottle of Captain Morgans. We were in here as it happens sitting over there." Marco gestured to one of the other booths behind me.

"Anyway, as the night went on, he opened up more and more. He said he was tired of archeology, full stop. Said that he'd been wrestling with this dissatisfaction for a while. Felt that he'd given it his all, his life, and for too long and he couldn't stand it anymore."

I was shocked. Spencer, tired with archeology? I said as much, Marco listened and then continued.

"I know. I was surprised too. I used to call him Indiana Jones, he was so into it, but he said it was a combination of things. All the 'crusty' professors just whiling away the time writing nonsensical papers and waiting for retirement. All the detail, the painstaking work involved. Months pouring over one small artifact. Said he just didn't have the energy or patience for it any more especially considering how he'd realized that people just weren't interested really. He said he was tired of how when you met someone their eyes just glazed over when he started talking about it. I think that might've been a reference to that girl he'd had the date with," said Marco almost with a smile. "Said he was boring himself even and wanted out. He confessed that he'd thought about to going to the principal's office a couple of times to hand in his notice, but he never did. He said he didn't know what else to do, where he'd go. He said he had no savings. Said he'd spent everything these last years on the diving holidays and that was what he loved. That and being by the ocean. Said that each time he had to leave the Caribbean to come back to Rome he wanted to just phone up, resign and never come back." Marco took a large gulp of wine and looked at me hard.

"Melody, he was depressed. He was looking for the next thing but didn't seem to know what exactly it was or how to do it. He was a bit lost, but at the time I took his talk about the Caribbean as a bit of an overreaction. Well you know how you feel sometimes after a great holiday. How coming back to work is hard." He looked rueful. "I've felt like that sometimes, I think we all have, but Spencer, well he seemed down. He seemed frustrated."

"Had he talked to anyone else, about this wanting to change?"" I wondered out loud.

"I asked him that but that's when he said he didn't have a family. Both his parents were dead. Said in a plane crash. Said he had a sister, but they didn't get on. Said she had done him out of his inheritance. You can imagine how shocked I was when his mum walked into the church today. And then you know it didn't really add up at the time either. He'd never really talked about his family, hardly at all. Even back in Bath. Then out of the blue I met his sister and her husband, Jim I think he's called. Well they were in Rome one weekend. Spencer came to work one day. Said they were in town and he had grudgingly arranged to meet them. Said he didn't get on with his sister. Mumbled something about his inheritance again, but said he'd decided to try, you know to make an effort. Asked me to join them that night. Then when I met them, they seemed perfectly nice. But Spencer was in an odd mood. We only ended up seeing them for fifteen minutes. He made an excuse and we left. We went to another bar and he said he couldn't stand to be in their company anymore."

I suddenly felt cold and very sad. I hadn't picked up any of this via his recent emails. They been jokey, fun. Admittedly mainly about the practicality of meeting up but he'd seemed perfectly fine, not depressed about his job and nothing about his sister (of course) and his inheritance. It was strange too. It was the exact opposite of what Helen had told me the day before. I couldn't figure it out. Something didn't add up. Marco paused for a while playing with the paper under his glass before going on.

"But this year when he came back after the last dive, after the Easter holidays, he was different somehow," he said, looking up.

"Different, what do you mean?" I asked scrutinizing his face.

"It's hard to explain. The first week he seemed like his old self again, you know, happy-go-lucky, the old Spencer. There was a lot of preparation that term for year-end exams. They were coming up and we needed to prepare the students, organise revision sessions, you know. The previous year, Spencer spent the entire term complaining, but this year, rather than moaning about the lack of talent, how the students would all fail or scrape through as he often did, he just made light of it. Said that he was feeling positive about their prospects. That not everyone could be 'professor material' as he put it but said that it didn't matter. But then, again, this positive approach quickly wore off as the the last term progressed. By the end, he was fighting with everyone again. He seemed restless. Had a huge bust up with another professor…and as the term came to a close, he was keeping himself to himself more and more. He didn't want to go out so much and when he did, he was a bit surly, not so talkative. He'd become a bit unpredictable, I guess. But one thing was for sure, he didn't seem to care about his job much anymore. When we did go out, he didn't want to talk archeology either. He just wanted to chat about football, diving or whatever." Marco paused, and fixed my gaze.

"He also seemed to be hanging around with Bruno much more." I studied his face. He suddenly looked ever so slightly bereft. Like he was remembering a friend he'd lost well before the funeral.

"And what about it? I quizzed him. "Wasn't that natural – after all, Bruno is a widower, right?"

"Well, to a point." He went on. "You'd often find the two of them in Bruno's office but when you went in, they'd stop talking all of a sudden and the atmosphere was odd. Like they didn't want you hanging around. At first, I thought I was imagining it but then the other lecturers started commenting on it too, making jokes. In the beginning I thought it was great that they were hanging out so much. Bruno had lost his wife to cancer five years before, he'd been lonely and had lost much of his interest in things, in life. That's why Spencer had invited him to join his usual gang for the summer holiday in the Caribbean the previous year. Bruno hadn't been so interested to begin with but when they came back from the first one it was clear that he'd kind of 're-found' himself. But their sudden friendship, well, it was too much. It wasn't normal. It's a hard to explain but it was almost like, like they were trying to hide something, you know, when you walked into Bruno's office, they looked furtive almost. It was strange."

"And what about Bruno? What about this theory Marco? You were talking about it today. Does it have something to do with him?"

Marco took a deep breath and pushed his glasses further up his nose as if to collect his thoughts. Looking at me earnestly through them he smiled. It was a nice smile. Genuine.

"I know you're going to think I'm completely crazy," he said looking almost embarrassed. "I've talked to some of Spencer's friends about this and they think I'm, how do you say in England, 'barmy?'"

I laughed. Marco had picked up some great colloquialisms, either directly from his mum or the time he spent in the UK. He could see my reaction and was smiling too. I studied his face. There was something warmer about it than had appeared in the cold light of day, or was that the effect of the subdued lighting? Or perhaps the half bottle of wine? Suddenly I couldn't help noticing that Marco wasn't bad looking either. How come I hadn't noticed that before?

"Please go on Marco. I promise I won't think you're barmy." I smiled back blushing slightly. He laughed and, encouraged by the humor of the situation, carried on. For a moment we both seemed to forget that today we'd been at Spencer's funeral and then he was serious again.

"Well, one thing I didn't mention yet was that the week after Spencer came back from his diving holiday this Easter. I met him for dinner in our favorite restaurant in Trastevere. It's a lively place and he was in an excellent mood. He looked good too, tanned for an English, if you know what I mean. Anyway, he told me that on the last few days of the holiday, they'd split up as the group had been in some disagreement about the best place to spend the last couple of days diving. He'd gone off with Bruno, just the two of them to one spot they'd fancied and the other five to a completely different location. Something to do with the fact that the five wanted to dive where the coral was supposed to be good, but Bruno and Spencer were keener to spend time looking for a wreck they'd heard about from some of the locals who were convinced it was a wreck of a ship owned by the pirate Sir Henry Morgan. You've heard of him I guess?" I nodded. He carried on.

"Seems that the other five wanted to make sure the last two days were not a waste and, if they'd gone to this spot, where the wreck might've been, there weren't any reefs nearby and it might've been a complete waste of time, mainly because it's not always possible to drop right down on a wreck like that. The locals can get it wrong and take ages to locate it again, if at all. Anyway, Spencer and Bruno had gone off to find this wreck with a local lobster fisherman called Juan. Seems Juan found the wreck after a couple of hours. Melody, Spencer was just full of this story. Talked about it like it was the most amazing thing. Swore me to secrecy. I mean, told me I couldn't tell anyone about it. Like it was a super big deal. Said that there might be some really valuable 'things' down there on this wreck and that he was dying to get back there and take another look around. He said he'd done a deal with Juan to keep this one to himself so that he and Bruno could go back there this summer. Paid this Juan off I think, I mean to keep him quiet. Said he would convince the group to go back to the same area that very summer. I think actually when it came to it, they had a few arguments about that one. They usually picked a different location each year, but eventually he got his way and they agreed to go back to the same place this summer too. Said that he'd go there on his own if he had to, like split away from the group, but the group didn't want that. Seems they were a pretty tight bunch and didn't want to spoil things with Spencer going off on his own, so they compromised. Anyway, think about this Melody. On holiday this August, the first thing he and Bruno did on arriving in Panama was to get straight out to that wreck. The group didn't think much of it at the time. They said that Spencer and Bruno played it down; that they wanted to go back to explore the same location whereas the group wanted to go somewhere slightly different. But what happened in reality was something different. Seems a tropical storm was coming in that direction and the group decided not to take any risks and stay at the hotel relaxing for the first day or so, until the storm blew over, but Bruno and Spencer took themselves off without telling the group."

"Sure, that's what Spencer's sister Helen told me" I said, "So what about it?" I asked, keen to get to the point.

"Well, and this is where you'll think I'm crazy…" he said looking confident one second, hesitating the next.

"Go on," I encouraged. "I'm all ears"

"Well, I don't think that Spencer died in an accident." He said pausing for effect.

"What do you mean, he didn't die in an accident?" I asked, somewhat bemused.

"I think Bruno killed him." He said, looking up at me from his wine. "I think on the dive that day, Bruno and Spencer found something. Something special and probably worth a lot of money. Something they'd suspected might be there from the Easter trip. Something they had been studying since then and that's why they'd been acting cagy every time I saw them together in Bruno's office. Anyway, they found it and Bruno, well he didn't want to share it with Spencer. He wanted to keep it for himself, to pay off some kind of debt, and he decided to kill Spencer and tell everyone that there'd been an accident."

"You think this Bruno guy murdered Spencer?" I asked, repeating back what he'd said and staring at him across the table. "Marco, that's pretty strong isn't it?

"I know, I know. It sounds crazy but, think about it. It all adds up. When you look at the facts, the way Spencer and Bruno have been behaving, since they came back this Easter, what Spencer said to me about it and now this happens. Think about it. It makes perfect sense! It all adds up! They come back from the Easter dive holiday and Spencer is buzzing. Like he's a different person. Then the two of them become inseparable. Like they are always in Bruno's office, pouring over documents, talking, you know, secretively, hiding stuff when you go in. Then they go back there and within days of arriving are over the same dive area, and before you know it, Spencer's dead...? I also heard that for some reason Bruno might be in some kind of debt. It's just a rumor that was going around the university, but if it's true, that would be a motive too…"

'And what do the police say?' I asked.

"Well the Panamanian police pronounced it death by misadventure. And the Italian police – I haven't spoken to them…" he said sounding defensive.

"If you really believe this theory, don't you think you should? I mean why haven't you spoken to them already?"

"Well, think about it, Melody. What would I say? That I think this old guy, 61, a well-respected university professor of upstanding character has killed one of the junior lecturers? I mean? And like I said, the local police in Panama filed a report of 'death by misadventure.' And after all, what have I got to go on? The first thing they'd ask me is on what grounds I'm making the accusations and actually…I don't have anything. And the debt rumor is just that. A rumor." he said looking almost angry, not with me but with the situation I guessed.

"When I spoke to Spencer's friends, other lecturers, they all think I'm crazy. *'Pazzo'* as we say here in Italy. Then I was thinking today at the funeral about Spencer's mum and Helen. If they heard that I was thinking like this, it would really upset them. But Melody, whichever way I look at this, I'm sure there's something wrong here. Bruno's hiding something. I just know it." His glass was empty and mine was too. He drained the dregs of the bottle into them. The aroma of the last two glasses of the deep, dark, blood red, *Nero d'Avola* filled the air and mingled with the musty smell of the bar.

We were silent for a while. I needed time to think. I had to admit that this was all a bit 'left field.' I didn't know Marco at all, and it was hard to get a sense of what he was saying; If it added up, if there were any legs to it or if he was totally off the scale. He seemed the stable and sensible type but then I'd only just met him that day and spoken to him for a couple of hours. And this Bruno guy; he'd seemed like a nice, old, respectable guy. The truth is my mind was racing.

"So, you see," Marco went on, "I feel like I've got to do something to try to find out the truth. Spencer's friends don't want to know. Like I said, they think I'm 'Pazzo,' But I just have to try to find out." He was fixing me with his gaze. I could almost smell his determination.

"What exactly do you mean?" I said wondering where this was leading.

"Well, Bruno is taking some time off to get over his 'ordeal,' he said. I heard that first thing tomorrow he's going down to Sicily for a long weekend. Seems he's got a sister down there. Anyway, I'm going to use this as an opportunity." He said draining the last of the wine from his glass.

"What do you mean, 'an opportunity?'" I said slowly, wondering where on earth this was leading.

"To do some snooping around," he said, looking slightly uncomfortable at this proposition and shifting on his chair.

"Snooping around? Like where?"

"Well, as a start I have the key to Bruno's office," he said, producing a key from his left jeans pocket. He held it up in the dim, light of the bar. A small, ordinary Yale-type key. For a moment we both studied it. I took a sip of wine.

"You are kidding, aren't you?" I said, putting the glass down. "You know you could get into trouble doing that Marco." I suddenly felt protective and mildly faint at the thought.

"And how did you get the key?" I carried on, beginning to wonder at the same time if I was underestimating this guy.

"Well last week there was a problem with the air conditioning in all our offices, so I went down to the basement to talk to the caretaker about it. While I was down there, I noticed the cabinet where they keep copies of all the keys, you know, to all the offices. So, while he went off to check something, I found the key to Bruno's office. He never noticed it was missing. I got a copy cut that night and the very next day I went back while he was on lunch break and put it back. He didn't know anything about it. It was easy." he said, grinning like he was almost enjoying himself. "It'll be fine," he said as if reading my thoughts, "Don't worry! It's August. Everyone's on break. La Sapienza is deserted right now."

"So, what are you going to do exactly?" I found myself asking.

"I can go into the building one night when no one is around and let myself in to his office, just to look around. No one will even know I was there. That's the easy bit. Like I said, nobody is around, all the lecturers are away on holiday. The place is practically empty. Thing is I'd like to get into his email, but I don't know his password and I don't know if I can trust the IT guy in the office or not. He'd get me into his email, I'm sure…so I'm still trying to work that one out. And then if he's in Sicily he won't be home, so I have to figure a way to get into his apartment…"

"Holy shit Marco, are you for real?" I said putting my now empty wine glass down. Was I hearing things?

"Melody, I think if I'm really going to find out if there was any 'foul play' I need to get into his apartment and onto his personal computer too. Don't you think? I want to investigate this debt rumor and see if there's anything hanging around about what they found on that dive."

"Marco, look that's really insane. You can't do that! That's breaking and entering. You could get into some serious trouble for that. You could end up in jail."

"Look, I'm going to see what I can find in his office. But if I don't come up with anything there, I don't think I've got any choice, do you?"

"Sure you have, Marco. You can just forget this whole thing and face up to it. Spencer died in a diving accident. There was a storm, these things happen. Just last night I was talking to a sailing instructor in the hotel bar. She's over here on holiday from Miami. I somehow got to telling her about Spencer and what happened, and she said that this type of thing happens sometimes."

Suddenly I noticed that the bar wasn't so empty anymore. We'd been so lost in conversation we hadn't noticed the place filling up. Looking around the crowd seemed quite studenty and a little 'grungy'. Mario the barman was busy serving and there was lively chatter all around. The surrounding scene seemed in vivid contrast to the earnest, almost surreal conversation at our table. Someone by the entrance spotted Marco and waved over.

"That's Pietro. He's one of the lab assistants. Helps the students with their analysis, mainly carbon dating, and he used to join us sometimes playing five-a-side on Wednesdays." Marco waved over and turned back to me. "I told him my theory too. Thinks I should give it up."

I could see Pietro looking over, wondering who I was no doubt before turning back to a group of friends and continuing his conversation. I could hear laughter. Some of the group turned to look over at our table. I was sure they were talking about us and I felt mildly uneasy but turned my mind back to the matter at hand. Marco pressed on.

"Melody. I know Spencer. I talked to him after that last diving holiday at Easter. I'm telling you. They found something down there on that dive. Something interesting. Interesting enough, and valuable enough, that it convinced them to go back looking for it again, whatever it was. I think they found it this summer and Bruno killed Spencer to get it for himself. And whether you agree with it or not, I'm going to investigate it. I owe this to Spencer.

Now…what I want to know is…are you interesting in helping me or not?"

For a moment I was taken aback.

"Me, help you? What? How…?"

"Look, I'll be frank. Like I said, everyone thinks I'm crazy with this theory. They've all told me to forget about it. Actually I 'm not talking to anyone else about it anymore. I've spoken to all of Spencer's friends and they've all told me to leave it, so I have to be careful now. I don't want word getting back to Bruno that I'm on to him. So when I met you today, at the reception, I kind of got the vibe from you that you being a journalist and an old friend of Spencer's…well, I thought you might want to 'help out' I mean, Melody, don't you care, don't you want to find out the truth?"

I decided to walk back to the hotel. I needed some air and time to think. It was a good 40 minute walk, but the taxis weren't cheap, and the evening temperature had reached perfection. Reflecting on the evening, one thing was clear, Marco was hell bent on his plan, and the more I mulled it over the more I couldn't get away from it, I was intrigued. You see I'd told him I'd do it. That'd I'd go with him to La Sapienza the following night. This was way too interesting to pass up on. My curiosity had been piqued, and Marco was far too pervasive. Or was that the wine thinking. Whatever the reason, one thing was clear.

Amalfi would just have to wait.

Chapter Nine

The next morning, I woke late after a fitful sleep. In the early hours, as the weak morning light eked through the shutters, I lay awake reflecting on what had possessed me to go along with Marco's plan, a half-baked one at that. All things considered, Bruno was surely just a nice old guy, a mild mannered academic. I cast my mind back to what I'd seen at the funeral, and he didn't look for one minute a murderer. And then what about the police report from Panama recording Spencer's death by misadventure? And another thing; if Helen suspected something, surely, she be onto it, wouldn't she? In a flash, it all seemed clear. Marco and the wine had gotten to my head. They'd colluded and become a persuasive combination.

But persuasive or not, as the light in my room brightened, promising to itself and me another sweltering Roman day, I told myself that I could still back out of Marco's crazy plan. I could catch the 9 a.m. train to Amalfi after all. Thanks to my dad's cash, the hotel was pre-booked and *Villa Cimbrone* was expecting me (I was already one day late). My room with sea view was empty and expectant, a five-course dinner on the Terrace of Infinity reserved for that evening. To make it even more tempting, Termini railway station was just a ten-minute taxi ride away and a car pick-up in Naples the only remaining detail to book. I could check out of my Aventino hotel that very morning and be on my way as planned.

Yet something still stopped me.

I'd arranged to meet Marco at 7 p.m. that night and the day was stretching ahead. I didn't have the energy or will for more sightseeing, so had a late breakfast and started on a newspaper but couldn't settle and switched to a book. Bad choice, it was a murder mystery. Getting my laptop out I attempted some work. I had the next *Melody Talkin'* page to write and a bunch of small features my mum had passed to me from her contacts in the South London locals. I needed the cash and the clock was ticking. She'd told me if I did a good job on these there could be more coming my way, but I still couldn't settle.

Spencer's funeral had left me low in spirits and it was way too hot and humid to go far, so deciding on a stroll I headed down to *'Testaccio,'* a working-class quarter of Rome, a stone's throw from the hotel and a neighbourhood peppered with shops, bars and restaurants.

The bright morning was fast turning gloomy. The confident weather of the day before had been beaten into submission by the arrival of some heavy, amber clouds. They sat low in the sky and felt ominous. Humidity was building up and wandering around *Testaccio,* it felt half empty, subdued, even a little sad. A lot of the shops were closed, my basic Italian helping me understand the handwritten signs which announced that their owners were on holiday and wouldn't be back until September.

After a while I found one of the few places with a bit of life; a main square with a bunch of children kicking a ball around and some old men out with their dogs sitting on benches chatting. It all felt very sleepy. Then I spotted a bar.

The bar *Oasi della Birra* had a handful of wooden benches outside and an impressive collection of beers and wines on the menu, so I sat down, ordered myself a glass of red from a friendly waiter who introduced himself as Maurizio and started on a roll-up. The wine went down well, and I would've ordered a second, but Maurizio came out and told me they were closing. Paying for the wine and feeling a little out of luck, I headed back to the hotel for a nap. Lying on the bed half in and out of a sluggish sleep I could hear the distant rumble of thunder. Before long, it started raining, light drops soon turning into a more determined effort, a crack of thunder announcing itself directly overhead good and proper.

"Africa," explained Gianni later that afternoon as, on my way out, I handed in my key at the reception.

"Africa?" I asked, not understanding.

"Si. The weather. Africa. How do you say 'sabbia' in English? Sand?" He pointed up to the sky.

"Oh, I see." I nodded in understanding. I'd read about this phenomenon. The storm was from North Africa. As these summer storms crossed the desserts, they picked up sand and then, crossing to Europe, the clouds carried the sand with them. Now I understood. That's why the afternoon sky had a brown, yellow glow. The clouds were full of Saharan sand.

The rain was still coming down, large globules were turning into a torrent in the street outside, running down hill and around the bend in the road, and it didn't look like it was going to stop any time soon. Apart from the inconvenience it was almost a relief from the stifling heat and humidity of the morning and, grabbing a hotel umbrella, I made a dash for the taxi that was pulling up outside. As we pulled away, I could see what Gianni had been talking about. All the parked cars were covered in hundreds, thousands of small yellow splashes. The Sahara was arriving in Rome drop by drop.

I'd arranged to meet Marco directly at the university '*La Sapienza'* and pulling up I immediately spotted him, umbrella in hand, taking cover under what looked like the main entrance to a big imposing 1930s building.

"Hi Melody, come this way," he smiled, as I dashed under the entrance for cover. "It's quicker this way. Here. Take my arm. Try not to get wet." We huddled under his umbrella and dashed around the side of the building to a smaller side entrance. Showing his security pass to the guard, once inside we took the opportunity to dry ourselves as best we could.

"My office is on the third floor," he said, putting his glasses back on after wiping them on a tissue and studying me through them. "Bruno's office is down the corridor on the same floor. Shall we go? We can take the stairs."

La Sapienza was large and institutional like. It was getting late and the place was already empty. As we climbed the stairs Marco explained. "There's nobody around here in August. Everyone's on holiday. If we come across anyone in here tonight, I'll be surprised. So, it's perfect for us…"

We were soon on the third floor and along the corridor at his office. Small, dim, with just one window overlooking a small courtyard garden, it had an air of organized chaos. The walls were covered with posters of what looked like museum exhibitions and events. In the corner there was what I imagined to be the life size replica of the head of a Roman. It was carved in dark grey stone, had strong Roman features with blank staring eyes. It gave me the creeps, staring out in the gloom.

"Nero," said Marco, catching my gaze. "My favorite Roman emperor. Please, take a seat," he said, indicating at the only armchair in the office and stepping forward to clear off what looked like piles of student coursework. Old and battered, the chair looked like it had seen better days and a very long time ago at that.

"So, this is your office" I said looking around, stating the obvious. "It's err, very …homely."

"You mean it's a mess?" He smiled, glancing over the desk which was festooned with open books, journals and what looked like student papers too.

"I know, I keep meaning to tidy up but well, tidying is just so boring."

"So, why's he your favourite?" I asked, sitting down and looking back at the bust, trying to get a sense, curious to know more. Marco went over to the bust, studying the face, like an old friend.

"I don't know, his story always just captured my imagination. It has everything. A scheming mother – she was called Agrippina - who married her uncle the emperor Claudius, then persuaded him to name Nero as successor rather than his own son. Then she got too much for him – so he eventually had her killed. Imagine that. Having your own mother murdered! You know at the beginning, he was OK, I mean apparently, he started off quite generous and was reasonable, by the standards of the day. He even lowered taxes and allowed slaves to bring complaints against their masters. But he was also quite a one for self-indulgence, wild parties, you know. Had affairs – like they all did of course. But then after Agrippina was murdered, he really did go off the rails. Not just debauchery. He became tyrannical, killing opponents, he was ruthless. You know, in the end he knew they were going to get him, his enemies I mean, so he killed himself, but, well, he couldn't go through with it on his own so got someone to help him. I mean, what a story…you couldn't make it up. Of course, he's also the emperor who was supposed to be playing a violin while Rome burned to the ground. They estimate that around 75% of it was lost. Rome burned for ten days. Some thought he'd started the fire on purpose. You see he wanted to build a new villa, the Domus Aurea, or Golden House on the spot where the fire started. I studied that for about six months last year. Anyway, that's what he's most famous for, I guess. Playing the violin while Rome was on fire. But I've always been more interested in his psychology. I mean, did he go off the rails after he had his mother murdered? Did that affect him? They were different days, back then of course, but I've always thought so."

He paused for a moment, studying the bust, lost in thought. Then in another instant, he was back in *La Sapienza*, in his office, with me.

"Now, can I get you a coffee, there's a vending machine down the corridor and I want to be sure that there's nobody around before we try Bruno's office. Better not to have to answer questions. I don't drink the coffee out of machines normally, but while I get one, I can look around."

"Sure, I'd love one."

"OK, I'll just be a sec," he said before disappearing round the door. I had to smile. Marco passed as English with this colloquialism and funny turns of phrase. Sitting there I couldn't help wondering if I'd be doing the same in Italian if I ever moved to Rome. I'd always wanted to learn a second language and Italian was an attractive one at that. I was really enjoying hearing it on this unconventional holiday.

He was soon was back with two espresso's in small plastic vending machine cups and a handful of sugar sachets.

"Sorry, no milk," he said, passing me a coffee and some sachets smiling. "And not the best coffee in Italy, but better than nothing I guess."

"No problem. Still better than any of the coffee in the UK." I admitted.

"So, I image you're wishing you were down on the Amalfi coast right now?" He said, sitting behind his desk and for a second looking like the young, intellectual university lecturer he was.

"Well, now you come to mention it, I have to admit, today at the hotel I was kind of thinking about that amazing swimming pool." I managed without much difficulty. "I mean, this weather is just awful…"

"Well, if it makes you feel better, my dad lives down in Naples. I spoke to him today and he said it stormy down there too. Very unseasonal." He said emptying two sugars into his expresso and giving it a stir with a little plastic stirrer. I did the same.

"But actually, I didn't mean the weather, I was thinking more about you hanging out here at 7 o'clock at night, keeping me company on this 'wild goose chase,'" he said smiling.

"Wild goose chase! Where did you learn that saying?" I laughed.

"Oh, you know, having an English mum helps. Then languages have always fascinated me. It was one of the reasons I stayed in the UK to do my PhD. That and the pubs."

"Oh, you like English pubs?" I asked in surprise. "Not the food and the weather then?"

"No definitely not the weather, but you're wrong about the food. I'm a big fan of international cuisine and London is one of the best places for that. And I love English beer. All those local breweries." He said taking a sip of coffee. I took one too. I was scalding hot. He didn't seem to notice.

"So, tell me about the UK, about London," I ventured, blowing on the coffee to cool it.

Marco told me that he grew up in Italy when he was young but when his parents separated, he moved over to the UK with his mum. He was 17 at the time. He'd gone to University in Exeter, had done the Masters in Bath and move to London after that, living just off Clapham Common. He told me that when he first got to the UK, he didn't know anyone, so he'd spent all his weekends in museums. Then when he started to make friends, how he developed a love of the English social life. How he missed the pub culture (not the excessive drinking) but also British music. Before long, the conversation turned to me. He asked me about why I'd ended up as a writer, a journalist. Why I wanted to get into more investigative journalism. The more we talked the more I liked him. He was warm, funny and interested in me. It was refreshing. Then suddenly the conversation came to a pause and I noticed that it was dark outside and, in the office too. We were sitting there, almost in pitch black. Marco was more a silhouette now against a thin light showing through from a glass panel above his door. Leaning over he switched on the small desk lamp on his desk. It was one of those old-fashioned types with a green shade and brass stand, you know, those types that journalists used 100 years ago.

"I got this from and antique shop near Camden market," he said, explaining, clearly seeing my admiring glance through the dark.

Though the lamp had a green shade, it cast a yellowy light down onto the desk but not much elsewhere. Hugely impractical, but beautiful. I liked that in a man. Someone who could chose an object for its beauty rather than just its practicability.

Suddenly we heard a bang, a clang in the corridor outside. I jumped and looked at Marco.

"What's that?"

For a while I'd forgotten why we were there, waiting in his office for the building to close down, to go to sleep for the night.

"It sounded like a door slamming. I'll take a look." Marco remained unfazed, and quietly got up and peeked around the door into the corridor.

"Cleaners," he said, still peering out through the crack. "They should be gone soon. I think it will be all clear then. I'll just make as if I'm getting another coffee and have a look around. See if any of the other lecturers are still here. It's Monday, late and August, so I really doubt there be anyone here, but I'd rather check. Some of the PhD students are fanatics too. They don't have a life out of this place." With that he disappeared around the door and it gently closed shut.

I suddenly felt a creeping unease. Sitting in the dark, punctuated only by the green desk lamp and the muffled sound of Roman traffic from the street below was unsettling. Marco was gone for what seemed like a very long time. I started to think he was never coming back, then suddenly he appeared, from the gloom of the corridor.

"Looks like everyone's gone. The cleaner has finished and is back downstairs getting ready to go and it doesn't look like anyone else is here at all. Seems we've got the entire building to ourselves."

It was true, you could've probably heard the proverbial pin drop. Going over to his desk he opened the top door and produced a flashlight.

"OK, shall we see what we can find?" he said with a smile. "Oh, and here you go." He said passing the flashlight to me. "I always keep one here, we have power cuts sometimes. And I brought another," he said, taking another small one out of his pocket and showing me.

"Marco. Bruno…he's…definitely left Rome, right?" I asked, feeling suddenly unsure.

"Sure. Don't worry. He's in Sicily. He told me at the funeral that he was leaving today on an early morning train." He'll be in Taormina or halfway there by now. And look, he'd never be here at this time of night in term time, let alone August. Don't worry. Really."

Marco led the way down the long corridor on our right. Despite the dark, there were enough windows to create a grid pattern of light on the left, with an occasional beam of orange streetlight seeping through on the right. Then around a corner and it suddenly became almost black.

"That's Bruno's office," Marco whispered, his eyes no doubt slowly trying to adjust like mine. "There, that one on the right."

Bruno's office was tucked away right at the end of the corridor in the darkest spot, away from any light. No windows, no streetlights, it was as black as a bag. Taking the key, for a second he struggled to find the keyhole but eventually, after some fumbling, the key slipped in and a second later we were in his office.

"Better if you use your torch rather than putting on the light. You never know. I mean if the security guard downstairs does the rounds. I've never been here at night before, so I've no idea if they do or don't."

I didn't like the sound of that. What if the security guard passed by and caught us in here with torches? How the hell would we explain that! But rather than complain I closed the door. We were there now. Might as well get on with it.

"Hey, shall we lock the door from this side?" I asked.

"Good idea," said Marco, turning the key in the lock.

"We should still be careful, see those windows up there onto the corridor. Anyone passing by would see the light. Anyway, let's try to be quick."

He was right. Above the door was a panel of glass. I really hoped the security guard we'd seen downstairs was the lazy type. Thankfully, he looked it.

"So, Sherlock, what are we looking for?" I asked, wondering if Marco had acquainted himself with Sir Arthur Conan Doyle while in London. Ignoring or missing the reference, Marco switched on his torch and moved over to Bruno's desk. The office was bigger than Marco's, spacious almost. A large desk, on the left with two filing cabinets on the right, a sofa by a large window, also looking out onto the same courtyard garden, a coffee table and a wall-to-ceiling bookshelf, jam full of books and journals.

"I don't know, I guess anything which looks 'suspicious.' You know, about scuba diving, Panama, anything which might give us a clue to what they found down there on that dive…use your investigative journalistic skills," he said, looking up and smiling despite the tense situation.

"Ok," I said, flashing the torch over the sofa, coffee table and bookshelf. "I'll start with those documents over there."

At first sight Bruno's office wasn't much tidier than Marco's but on closer inspection the place seemed to have order to it. Scanning the coffee table, for a moment I wasn't sure what I was looking for. Once again, a feeling of 'you idiot' welled up inside. What was I doing here apart from an unhealthily sense of curiosity, and...then there was Marco… Pushing the words, 'curiosity and cat' to the back of my mind, and trying to ignore the slightly uncomfortable sensation that I may actually there more because of Marco than anything else I started by grabbing a handful of documents from the coffee table. A quick scan and they seemed like various printouts of emails, student papers, an invitation to speak at Edinburgh University next term and a bunch of bills including what looked like some electricity bills from an address in Rome.

"What have you got there?" asked Marco, not looking up as he worked his way through the draws on the left side of Bruno's desk. "Anything interesting?"

"Not much," I told him scanning the documents again to be sure. "These look old and they all seem to be correspondence with some lecturers in the UK, but there are some in Italian here too so I think you should take a look to be sure. The rest look like magazines, subscriptions, promotions that kind of thing.

"Nothing here either," said Marco, closing the last desk draw on the left and starting on the right cabinet. "Just a load of stationery and office supplies in these drawers."

Picking up the next bunch of documents I quickly flicked through those too – more magazines, journals a few pieces of what looked like Italian charity direct mail, one from UNICEF, another from Amnesty. Then I spotted something – a phone bill, quite long, two–three sides, and flipping it over, I could see some international calls too.

"Hey Marco, what about phone bills? That could be interesting right?"

"Absolutely!" said Marco, glancing up for the first time. There's a photocopy machine down the hall, put them to one side and I'll do a copy before we leave."

Moving on from the coffee table I started on the shelves, but nothing there either. Full to the brim of history and archeology books, journals and papers. As far as I could see, nothing of interest to us.

"You're very quiet over there" I said glancing over. In the limited torch light, I could see that Marco had a frown of concentration on his face. "Found anything?"

"No nothing at all. He said, running his hand over his head and looking up. I expected more…something, I don't know, documents, something related to Panama…but I can't see anything. Even in this right-hand draw there's just another bunch of journals, papers and student thesis. Nothing at all related to his holiday, scuba or Panama." He slumped back on the chair.

"Well, maybe this guy keeps personal and work life separate," I said. "I know a lot of people who do. I mean, after all, why would he keep any documents, or anything related to his holidays, here?" I said by way of explanation.

"Maybe you're right," he agreed. "But I thought there might be something in here. I saw him and Spencer pouring over things loads of times between Easter and the recent holiday. I don't know what they were, but when I came in once, Bruno looked very shifty, and he quickly covered it up. But looking in here tonight, I don't think we're going to find anything here of interest after all - so it's a good job I found these."

Marco held something up. He'd put his torch down on the desk and in the darkness, I could see something hanging from his hand.

"What do you have there?" I asked squinting, trying to make out the form of the small dark thing he was holding.

"Well, if I'm not wrong, the keys to Bruno di Franceschi's apartment," he responded, grinning.

Chapter Ten

"*So*, you're being serious?"

We were sitting at the dining room table in Marco's living room and I was focused on the bunch of keys which Marco had dropped down between two glasses of Lambrusco.

"I mean, you really want to go into his apartment?" I asked picking up the glass nearest to me, taking a sip and shifting my gaze to study his face. The wine was light, fresh, ever so slightly sparkling. In contrast, and for the first time since we'd met, Marco looked tired, heavy and a little worn around the edges. I tried to imagine what he was thinking, how he was feeling. After all, Spencer, his best friend, was dead, and no doubt he was still grappling with this new reality. For a moment I felt a rush of sympathy, of understanding. I was tempted to lean across the table and touch his arm, to feel closer to him in this tragic situation, but something stopped me and in an instant the feeling had passed and there it was again, a little niggle in the back of my mind. Marco. I didn't really know him at all, not yet.

"But really, can you be sure that these are actually the keys to his apartment?" I persisted. "I mean, they could be anybody's keys. And even if they're his, they could be keys to something else, a garage or…I don't know…just because you found them in his desk drawer, doesn't mean they're his apartment keys."

Marco got up and went into the kitchen, to the fridge. His apartment was compact and the small kitchenette and living room open plan. From the table where I was sitting, I could see him in the semi-darkness, his face and glasses illuminated by the fridge light as he scanned the shelves.

"Bruno went away last summer for three weeks and he asked a colleague, Anna, to water his plants, you know, pass by his place a couple of times a week while he was gone," he said, taking out packets as he talked.

"He's got a large balcony full of plants. I was there once for a faculty drink. It's very nice, very green. Says they're his pride and joy and I guess in the summer they need quite a bit of water," he continued, bringing the packets and brown paper bags over to the table.

"Anyway, I remember, he passed these keys to Anna during lunch in the canteen. She lives near him and he was happy she could do him the favour." Marco started laying the packets down on the table, taking out the contents, unwrapping them. The smell of an Italian delicatessen filled the air as he opened the bags to reveal various salami, cheeses and cold meats. Smelling the tangy aromas, I realized I was ravenous. No wonder. I hadn't eaten all day and it was now well past eleven.

"You see, I remember these keys very well. See that *Leaning Tower of Pizza* key ring?" he went on, pointing at the keys. "I remember thinking how tacky it was."

He was right. The key chain had one of those cheap looking touristy key charms. It was a leaning tower of Pizza.

"In fact, I commented on it," Marco continued, setting down a couple of plates and producing a basket of bread from the sideboard on the right. "I said it was stylish, as a joke. Bruno laughed and said that his niece had given it to him. Normally he would've thrown it away, but he didn't have the heart, seeing as it was gift. Help yourself." He indicated at the food. "Sorry it's a bit basic…we could've grabbed a pizza I guess..."

"No, this is great, thanks." I said helping myself. The salami and hams tasted rich and full. The cheese was creamy and strong.

"OK, so the keys are Bruno's and they're for his apartment. But you really think it's a good idea to break in?" I asked through a mouthful of bread and salami while Marco topped up the wine in my glass.

"Well, I wouldn't call it breaking in" he said putting the bottle down, taking a sip from his own and studying me through his specs.

"After all, strictly speaking it's more like 'letting myself in.'"

"Oh, come on Marco. It's going into his flat illegally. I mean you... you, could be arrested. And how on earth would you explain it to Bruno? You could lose your job."

"Well, I'll just have to make sure I'm not spotted. Probably better to do it in the early hours, when there's no one around."

"But then if you're spotted it'll look really suspicious at that time. Maybe better in broad daylight, like mid-afternoon?" I ventured. "Looks a lot less suspicious, no?"

Marco gave it some thought. "No, I think it's better at night. It's just too risky during the day. Bruno mentioned once that there are a lot of retirees in his block and I think they're all pretty friendly too. I could easily be spotted during the day and any one of them could have Bruno's number, give him a call down in Sicily if they saw something that didn't add up. Night-time is better. As long as I'm quiet and there's nobody around, hopefully his neighbors will be in bed, but I think your right. Perhaps its better if go in at say 10 or 11 p.m. That way if it's dark, I'm less easily spotted, but at the same time if they hear something, it's kind of a normal time, you know for there to be some activity or noise."

"And what would you be looking for?" I asked, thinking more aloud.

"Same as in his office I guess," he said, looking thoughtful, putting down his wine to grab some more ham.

"Just something that might give us a clue. Bank statements, tickets, emails, anything on treasure hunting. Talking of which, let's take a look at that photocopied phone bill."

He jumped up, went to his bag and pulled out the photocopy. For a second, I got a flush of excitement. Perhaps it would give us even a small inkling of if something was going on, if Bruno was implicated, or then maybe it would turn nothing at all....

Marco pulled his chair round and sat next to me at the table. It was the closest we'd been physically and, pouring over the document together, it was cosy, almost intimate. And he smelt nice – still fresh from the rain, but in a manly kind of way. Focusing on the task at hand I tried to turn my attention from Marco to the bill.

"Here, look, international calls," he said, indicating to the second page. "He's made quite a few calls here. I wonder where some of these are for. Do you know any of these international codes?"

"No idea. Do you have a computer?" I suggested, feeling a little embarrassed at my lack of international knowhow. "We could look on the internet?"

"Good idea."

Marco soon had his laptop out and started googling international dialling codes.

"Tell me the codes you have there." He said from behind the laptop taking down a decent gulp of wine. I ran down the list with my finger calling out the international codes as they appeared. Nothing surprising, Switzerland, France, China, and then…

"507," I called out. It was the last code on the list.

"Sorry, did you say 507?" Marco asked, quickly looking up from the laptop.

"Yes, why?"

"That's Panama" he said. "What was the date on those call?"

"Look, here." I said indicating with my finger. "There are a few calls, about three, let me count. Yes, four actually. And the date…well… let's see…last week. He made these calls last week!"

We looked at each other.

"Why would Bruno be calling Panama last week?" I asked, almost to myself. "I suppose there could be lots of reasons...could be anything. Calling Panama – it isn't exactly a crime..."

"'You're right but I think it's strange," said Marco, closing the laptop. "I mean, why would he need to call Panama? And four times? And look at the length of some of these calls. He was right. Some of the calls were twenty, thirty minutes long."

"A girlfriend?" I asked, with half a laugh.

"I don't think so," said Marco more seriously "But you never know. I do know he's been desperately lonely since his wife died of cancer, about five years back, I think. After all, he's only 61... he could've made a lady friend over there I guess."

"Like I said, could be anything though," I insisted "Err, I don't know, he left something in a hotel, booking another holiday?"

"Yes, I know," he said, thinking, taking a sip of wine. "OK, what next?"

"I guess we could call some of these numbers, then maybe we'll get an idea of who he was calling?" I suggested, conscious that I was making this up as we went along.

'Good idea. We can do it via my Skype account" he said, grabbing some more cheese and bread. "You're making this up as I go a long, aren't you…" he smiled over.

"That's for sure," I grinned back.

Opening the laptop again, he quickly pulled up his skype account and he was soon typing in the first number. In a second or two the number was connecting, then a ring tone, then a voice. "Buenos días, *Hotel Miramare*. How can I help you?"

Marco hung up.

"Well that's the first," he said, noting down the details of the call. "A hotel. We can look it up on the web later. Let's try some of the others." The next call was a bank called Banco General. The one after that was another hotel called Al Natural. The next a woman answered in what sounded like Chinese. It sounded a bit like she said a restaurant name, there was noise in the background too. Marco tried to ask some questions, but she hung up. It was a bit odd, but we pressed on. Then we tried the non-Panama numbers, but they seemed innocuous enough. Hotels and the like. A conference centre too. Marco remembered that Bruno had been on a circuit of archaeological conferences that month, so nothing particularly odd. Just the number in China remained a bit of an unknown, with no answer. Marco closed the laptop and studied my face.

"He could be planning another holiday?" I ventured. "But why the bank? Isn't that a bit odd? I mean unless you live in Panama, why would you be in contact with a bank there?"

"Who knows," said Marco, draining his glass. "Investments, property, transferring some money to pay for something, could be any number of things. It's hardly a crime, but I do think it's odd though. Bruno has never mentioned he's got something going on in Panama - outside of the holidays with the guys of course. We could ask them by the way, I mean if they have another holiday planned, but… well, what with Spencer I really doubt it, and to be honest I don't feel like asking them right now, it's not the time...Anyway, getting back to the point, I really must take a look in his apartment now. Who knows what I'll find?"

"Mind if I smoke, on your balcony?" I indicated to the small balcony I'd spotted earlier off the side of the lounge. It was a little humid in Marco's place, I needed air to think and I desperately wanted a cigarette.

"Sure, go ahead, there's an ashtray out there. A couple of my friends smoke," he explained. "I'll just clear up these things."

Out on the balcony everything felt damp but at least it was cool and fresh. There were two chairs, a little marble top table and some cacti in pots hanging from the balcony rail. Some of the cacti were submerged in water, the effect of the earlier downpour. I got rid of the worst over the side of the balcony rail and after drying my fingers on my top, started on my roll-up, trying not to get it wet. The sound of a tram trundling past, wheels against tracks, drifted up from the road below. An ambulance siren punctuated the low-level city hum as it hurried by, insistent and repetitive, moving north south, east west, I had no idea. I'd completely lost my bearings and had no sense of where I was in relation to the hotel, *Trastevere* and *Isola Tiberina* - the bits of the city I'd come to recognise these last few days. I'd just finished the roll-up when Marco appeared with our wine glasses."

"Everything OK?" he asked putting my glass down on the table with an inquisitive look as I tried to light my cigarette. I had a cheap plastic lighter and it was low on fuel, the sparks not igniting into anything close to a flame.

"Here, have this," he said, taking another lighter from a metal box on the table. Somehow it was dry and, when he lit it, the flame sprung up, catching the tobacco at the end of the cigarette and igniting it into a hot red point in the dark night's air.

"What are you thinking? You know, about going into his apartment? Wild goose chase? Tell me," he quizzed, smiling, putting the lighter back in the box and studying my face suddenly more serious. I took a second drag.

"And look, you know, I don't expect you to come along with me. I've decided. I'm going to take a look in there, while he's down in Sicily – it's my perfect chance - but I don't want you to think you have to come with too."

I took a slip of wine. For some reason I felt perfectly calm, serene perhaps for the first time in the last few days. The rain had started again, just a light, fluffy drizzle almost hanging in the air now, but the sky was still heavy with clouds and it was hard to tell if the earlier storm was passing by or on its way back. Taking another drag of my roll-up, I studied Marco. I liked his face. It was a good, kind face with soft, dark, thoughtful eyes. Although they were hidden a little behind his glasses, glasses that caught the evening light, I could still just about see them in the dark. And for the second time that day I noticed… he wasn't unattractive, in a geeky, studious kind of way.

My mind was made up. It had been made up from the start.

"When are we going in?" I asked.

Chapter Eleven

As luck would have it, Bruno lived in San Saba, a quiet, leafy, residential neighbourhood, just a twenty-minute walk from my hotel in Aventino. The storm had passed, and the sky was clear. As I left the hotel, a smattering of stars was even visible through the amber glow of the city light pollution, but the weather had been changeable these last days, so I had a small, fold-up umbrella with me just in case.

Walking down from Aventino and once at the bottom, I crossed over the main road, *Via Mamorata*, and took a left. Soon I was passing the Egyptian pyramid, famous in this part of the city - illuminated against the night's sky - a sharp triangle of ancient creamy-white stone. It seemed lonely and misplaced behind a surrounding fence - wrought iron bars, a prisoner of a modern-day city. On a different occasion I would've stopped to study it more closely, googled it, pulled up some information on my phone, taken a photo. It was in fact a curiosity; why the Romans had brought it back from Egypt and rebuilt it here perfectly stone by stone. But the pyramid would have to share her secrets some other time, I had more pressing current day matters on my mind and I didn't have the time for a nocturnal sightseeing detour.

Arriving at the *Piramide* Metro station, and following the google map indications on my phone, I veered left and headed up the steady incline that formed the San Saba hill in the direction of our agreed meeting point. Although it was only 11 p.m. the streets felt deserted, abandoned. Most of the buildings were in darkness, many had their external shutters down and looked locked up, empty or both. A dog barking somewhere in the distance was the only sound as I arrived at the small square where we'd arranged to meet. Scanning around for Marco, a flash of headlights from a car parked on the far side told me that he was already there and waiting.

"It's quiet around here," I said getting into the passenger side of his Fiat 500. I'd never been in one of these tiny Italian cars and it was cute, but even in the dark I could see that this 500 had seen better days. A ragged dent across the bonnet, the cream paint peeling around it, suggested an accident sometime in the recent past. Inside the leather seats were tatty too. The stuffing poking out between the seams in some of the most well-worn parts cried out for a refit.

"Well it's a very quiet, respectable neighbourhood," Marco replied, glancing around from behind the wheel. "You need a lot of money to buy a place around here these days. It's because it's so central, leafy and quiet. And it's probably even quieter right now with half of Rome on holiday."

"So, Bruno's OK for money then?" I ventured, trying to build up a picture of this man, the man I'd only seen once at the funeral but was getting to hear more about day by day.

"Well not necessarily," Marco said, turning his gaze back to me, perhaps reflecting on the rumour that had gone around the university of Bruno being in some kind of debt.

It was hard to pick out the details inside the car, parked there in the dark, shadowy street and with just the orange street lights for any illumination, but in spite of his casual denim jacket and unshaved face, I could still see he looked tense, his expression tight.

"He told me he'd inherited the flat from his parents when they died. That would've been years ago, like even back in the seventies," Marco explained

"He certainly wouldn't've been able to afford to buy it otherwise, not on a salary from La Sapienza. Believe me. None of us are earning enough to buy places round here, especially not these days. Some of these larger houses and flats are worth millions now, but his parents probably bought it before the war when this part of Rome wasn't expensive. Things were different back then..."

"Wow," I said, glancing around again. "I had no idea Rome was so pricey."

"Like London, no?" he said studying my face, his eyes searching, thoughtful for a second.

"Anyway, you good to go? Second thoughts?"

"No second thoughts," I told him. "Did you remember the flashlights?"

"Sure," he nodded, reaching over to the back seat and passing one to me. "Here you are. I put new batteries in to be sure. It's probably better we use them when we first go in, especially until we make sure the shutters are down. People in the block may know Bruno's away and they might get suspicious if the lights go on. Let's go then. It's just over there. Follow me."

Crossing the *piazza,* we entered a dark, narrow, tree-lined street and started to walk down it. A light wind was agitating the trees making their leafy shadows dance both on the road and the terracotta walls which ran shoulder high down either side. Clouds were still tracking across the sky. Glancing around it looked like there was no one in sight, but it was hard to be sure, with all the dark nooks and crannies, the trees standing in line down the road, partially blocking the view. Considering we were about to enter someone's flat illegally, it was a little unnerving.

About halfway down, Marco tapped me on the arm and indicated that we'd arrived at Bruno's block. It was set back from the street, looked 1950s or sixties by my best guess and each apartment had a generous wrap-around balcony on the front and sides.

"Bruno's place is on the first floor. See, that one, there." Marco explained pointing up to a large looking apartment on the right. It looked like a nice place. The balcony was overflowing, full of plants; vegetation of all types, some small shrubs, some climbing vines. A large bougainvillea in full bloom was a key feature trailing down in generous swathes. It was beautiful. I could see why it was his pride and joy.

"Listen, once inside the building better use the stairs not the lift. They can be a bit noisy in these sixties buildings. From what I remember in the entrance there are two flights, we need to take the one on the right."

Marco pulled out the keys from the top pocket in his jacket and we both looked at them and then each other.

"OK. Let's go," he grimaced.

Checking out the road to be sure one last time that no one was in sight, we headed over to the external street gate. It took a couple of seconds for Marco to find the right key, but he'd soon figured it out and we were in. Then, up the short pathway to the main entrance of the building. Luckily, this time he found the right key first try, and super quick, without a sound, we were inside the lobby. Glancing around, Marco beckoned me to follow him, and pointed to the flight of stairs on the right. In no time we were heading up, Marco taking two steps at a time, and in front of Bruno's door. I kept expecting to hear voices, a neighbour on their way in or out, catching us in the corridor, keys in hand outside Bruno's door. How would we explain that? My heart started thumping just at the thought.

Without a word, Marco had a third key in the top lock of Bruno's door and was turning it slowly, trying to make as little noise as he could although in the silence of the building, every turn sounded like a very loud clunk. Then he found the last key, got it in the bottom lock, turned it three times and was opening the door. Without a sound we were through the entrance and he gently closed the door behind us with a barely perceptible click. We were inside.

"Phew," I whispered. "That was a bit stressful."

"I know, worst bit over. Now we're in we can relax a bit. Nobody will disturb us in here if we don't make any noise," he said, glancing around.

"Looks like they might be away next door at number three. I noticed outside that all their shutters are down."

It was very dark in the apartment entrance, and switching on his torch, he flashed the beam around.

"OK, look, I've been here once before. A year ago we had a faculty drinks here one night," he whispered. "I think his study's through there. Guess that's the best place to start."

Scanning around, I took in the apartment as best I could in the dark and the limited light from my torch. It felt strange and wrong to be there, but I tried to push the uncomfortable sensation to the back of my mind and headed into the lounge. Looking around, and from what I could see, the furniture looked very seventies, worn, and old. Rugs lined the floor, it was hard to tell the colours in the dark, but then I wasn't there to study his interior design tastes.

"This way." Marco indicated with his torch, flashing the beam through the darkness of the lounge to pinpoint a door off on the right.

The study was small with a patio door onto the balcony at the far end. The shutter was up and a pale, orange glow from the streetlamp filtered through from outside giving off just enough illumination to make out a sizable wooden desk and two chairs in one corner, an old style winged armchair in another, book shelves and an old record player on the right. Vinyl records were piled up on the floor and stacked on a small unit against the wall nearby. Bruno clearly hadn't made it to CDs let alone iTunes yet.

"Delibes, Lakmé. He must like opera," I said, picking up one of the records from the top of one pile and studying the cover with my torch. I hadn't seen vinyl in years. Feeling the weight and size of it in my hand, looking at the old DECCA cover it felt like something from a museum.

"Let's put the shutters down, then we can put on the light and see much better. Better not to take any risks," whispered Marco, keeping focused on the task at hand.

Once the shutters were down, he switched on the 70s angle poise lamp on the desk and sat down scanning the top of the desk.

"That's better, now we can see what we're doing without these," he said, switching off his torch. I did the same.

"Ok, now what?" I asked, putting the record back down and looking around for inspiration.

"Let's start by looking in the drawers or anywhere there are documents. How about you start over there, I'll look in these drawers here. I wonder if I can get into his computer…"

Now the light was on I could see that the study was a bit of a mess. Not only but it smelt a little musty and stale. There were papers and documents everywhere, a few cups with coffee dried at the bottom here and there, even a couple of dirty plates balanced on the top of a stack of magazines. Not only but a strong smell of cigars seemed to have permeated the general disorganisation and clutter. Clearly Bruno was a smoker. Moving an ashtray full of cigar stubs to one side, I started sifting through the first pile of papers, print outs, brochures. From what I could make out in my limited Italian, they all looked inconsequential to me. Meanwhile Marco started looking through the desk draws and was booting up the old desk top computer. It felt like we were back in La Sapienza all over again.

"Aha! I wonder what's in here," he said, pulling out a notebook and skimming the pages.

"Interesting…let's see…I wonder if...woah, look at this. These looks like passwords, don't you think?" He said flashing it at me.

"Fantastic! Thanks Bruno. You've done what you should never do. Note down your all your passwords so that someone like me can find them!"

"You're kidding?" I said, coming over.

"No, look at this! This has to be a string of passwords, doesn't it? I'm going to try logging into Gmail, Hotmail, see if I can get into his email...with a bit of trial and error and some luck…"

He was soon typing away on the keyboard, trying various combinations of email providers, usernames and passwords from the book. It took him just five minutes, then:

"Bingo! Look, this combination works, he's got a Hotmail account!"

Hardly believing our luck, I pulled up a chair and Marco started scrolling down the inbox. The uneasy sensation washed over me again but worse. Not only being in Bruno's place like this, but looking into his personal email account too, but I pushed aside my personal sensibilities and thought of Spencer. I wanted to know what happened to him. I wanted to be convinced that Bruno wasn't involved, and now Marco had planted his theory in my head, this was certainly one way, perhaps the only way, of doing it.

Then, I spotted the KLM booking.

"Look, what's that? A KLM booking?" I said, indicating at the screen. Marco clicked on the email and the contents popped open. A reservation confirmation for a flight to Panama City scheduled to leave in a month's time. The ticket was one-way.

"Nothing worth a life sentence in prison for," I said, already conscious that we had to keep everything we found in perspective and not let our imaginations run ahead.

"But that's odd though. A one-way ticket? And it's the start of term then," said Marco, immediately countering my train of thought, scratching the stubble on his chin. "Why would he be planning to go away then? We aren't supposed to take holidays in term time, especially not the first few weeks. That's the most hectic week of the year too. It's odd…"

Marco noted down the details in a small black notepad which he'd pulled out of his denim jacket pocket, and we pressed on. He was clicking around on various emails, some about work, some about social arrangements then he glanced up. "Look here, a booking for seven nights for that hotel. Remember the one? *Hotel Miramare*? It was on his international call list. And the dates match with the arrival of the flight in Panama." Scrolling down, he added, "I don't see any other hotel bookings though, so I wonder what he's going to be doing after that…" Then flicking even further down the emails, suddenly:

"What's this email here?" He said, the light of the computer reflecting on his glasses, the concentration in his eyes visible for a second as the pages flipped from one to the next.

"This is an odd email address, no? Atlas世界收藏家 @gmail.com?"

Clicking on the email it read:

Confirmation noted. Drop off in Panama confirmed at agreed meeting point on agreed day. Payment will be made in cash. No paper trail following this email. Purchase phone and local SIM card on arrival in Panama. Contact number will be sent by text in the next 5 days to your current number. No further emails will be sent following this. Delete this email once read (including hard drive).

Atlas 世界收藏家

"Woooah," Marco said, leaning back in the chair. "Now tell me that's not odd. There you go! Something's going on. I knew it!"

I read the email again, at least twice, while Marco copied it down in his notebook. "Err, yeah, I have to say that does look suspicious." I conceded, a sense of excitement and foreboding welling up.

"And what's that? Is it Chinese?"

I was starting to feel that weird sensation in my stomach again. The one I was getting a lot these last few days when something didn't seem quite right. A combination of panic, nerves and adrenalin condensed into a knot that made my stomach turn.

"It sounds, well, very like subversive. Kind of like there's something illegal or underground going on." I said it as much to myself as to Marco.

"I told you!" Marco said, glancing up from his notebook and studying my face. Even in this light I could see that he'd gone pale, the realisation that he might really be onto something not the comfort, the ending, he'd been looking for perhaps, after all.

"They found something down there on that dive. I'm convinced of it. Bruno's now arranging to sell it. I'd put money on it. And it looks like there's some Chinese connection going on. Hey, remember, one of the numbers in Panama sounded like a Chinese restaurant, maybe that's no coincidence if this really is Chinese. And then there was that number in China, the one we never got a response from when we called. Maybe we should try it again. Once we've finished with this email, let's copy and paste this Chinese into google translate and see what this bit here says," he said, indicating at the screen.

"Anyway, there's something going on here - and like I said, I've just got that feeling, whatever it is, whatever they found, Spencer got in Bruno's way...and that's why he ended up dead…"

I had to admit it, I could see where Marco was coming from now. For the first time I began wondering if he was really onto something, if Bruno really had murdered Spencer.

"Hey, why not forward this email to yourself?" I suggested. "Then we can look at it later. As long as you remember to delete the email from the send folder, Bruno will never know, then you've got a copy in your inbox. Who knows how that could be useful somehow? Evidence even?"

"Great idea!" Marco nodded and, without another moment, it was done.

Marco continued searching the rest of Bruno's inbox, while I went back to the papers piled up on the floor and shelves.

"And look at this," Marco said, waving me over again some minutes later.

"He's been checking out property in Panama! Look at all these emails from real estate agents, they've been sending him listings – all since he came back this Summer – look at the dates – and all the properties listed are for over $1m. And luxury yachts too. Now where would he suddenly be getting the kind of money to even consider buying something like that? And you know that ticket to Panama was in business class. Did you notice that? I've known Bruno for years, and he's just not a big spender. I mean, look at this place, it hasn't been updated since the seventies. He's always looking to save a euro here and there, I know him."

"Another inheritance?" I suggested weakly. But Marco was right. Glancing around the place, it looked old and long in need of an upgrade. The furnishings were tired, old fashioned and worn out. His computer and stereo were from a different era too. But the listings from Panama showed flashy new $1 million plus properties with private plunge pools and ocean views. The Yachts were in the million-dollar range too. Something didn't add up.

"Ok, anything in those papers?" asked Marco.

"Nothing," I noted back. "Just looks like an overspill of work stuff from the office. Hang on, what's this?" I said, scanning a letter and bringing it over to Marco. It looked like a letter from the bank, with United Bank of Italy (UBI) printed in letterhead at the top.

Marco scanned the letter and looked up at me from the desk, ashen faced.

"It's a demand from his bank. Says that they're expecting his monthly instalment of five thousand euros on his three hundred-thousand-euro loan. Looks like he's behind on his repayment too. So, it is true. Bruno is massively in debt. This was from just last month." We were silent for a good while. Thinking. Adding things up in our heads. Why was he checking out million-dollar properties in Panama while massively in debt in Italy?

"OK, let me look in the send folder here in Hotmail," Marco said, collecting himself and getting back to the task at hand, "that might give us some more clues if we're lucky and…."

It was then that the sound came from the entrance. It sounded like a key in the lock in the front door. My stomach lurched. For a second, I really thought I might faint.

It *was* a key in the front door.

"Marco!"

"What the…?" Marco was aghast. "*Cazzo*! Shit!" He barely managed in a whisper. "It must be Bruno. We've got to get out of here, now!"

Marco flicked off the desk lamp and we froze. With the shutters down it was pitch black in there now. I couldn't see a thing.

"But where, how?!" I whispered, unable to see even Marco, almost in a blind panic.

I could hear Bruno. He was already inside the flat, in the entrance hall. A small, thin finger of light suddenly appeared under the study door. It sounded like he was turning the key in entrance door from the inside, locking the door, then the sound of a heavy bag dropped dead on the floor. Within seconds he'd moved into the living room. The sound of keys clattered on a glass top coffee table. It gave us a start and highlighted how the internal walls were paper thin and how he was just on the other side of them. Then for a second I though he was about to walk in, I could almost see his shadow in the sliver of light under the door, but instead his footsteps headed in the opposite direction, into the kitchen on the far side of the lounge. A tap running, the clatter of plates - it was our chance to get out, but how?

"Over here!" Marco whispered close to my ear. "Onto the balcony!"

I could hear that Marco was already over at the balcony door and had started slowly and quietly winding up the shutter inch by inch. It was painfully slow - he couldn't afford to make any sound. When it was waist high – just high enough up to duck under - he opened the balcony door a wedge, we slipped through and he gently pushed it closed behind us. I breathed a sigh of relief. At least we were outside – better than being trapped in the study - but we had to get off there and fast.

Marco wasn't wasting any time. He was frantically scanning around, looking over the balcony railing, down to the street below.

"Melody, over here," he whispered, beckoning me over to the corner, behind what looked like a small olive tree in a large terracotta pot.

"I think we just got lucky." He continued under his breath. "Look. It's not a long way down if we can jump and land on that wall, right there…" he pointed down. "Do you think you can do it? I'll go first and be there to catch you."

It looked like a pretty big drop, but he was right. It was doable. Just. And, after all, there weren't any other options – we certainly couldn't risk trying to exit the flat by the front door.

I sized up the height of the drop and the width of the wall. The wall was broad – wide enough to land on - if we got it right. I nodded and gave the thumbs up. A light went on in the bedroom behind us on the left. Bruno was moving around, unpacking perhaps. I detected the waft of cigar smoke too. He could come out ono the terrace at any moment and from any of the patio doors, directly from the bedroom the study, or lounge. Not only that, but it was perfectly natural that after a weekend away he'd step out to check on his plants. We had to get over the side and we had to do it now.

Marco climbed over the railing, shimmied, half jumped, and made it down onto the wall. He wobbled a bit but caught his balance. Steadying himself, he turned and looked up to me. He suddenly seemed a very long way down. Climbing over the balcony rail, somehow, I got stuck, one leg still over the rail, balcony side. It was awkward and I wasn't very nimble but twisting around I managed to get my second leg over, pushed myself off, and landed on the wall next to Marco.

"OK?" he asked, grabbing me tightly, more from relief than necessity.

"OK," I managed back, shaken but relived to out of the flat. Marco jumped down to the pavement and turned back to help me down. Then we were off, down the road, running back to the car.

"For fucks sake Marco. I thought you said he was in Sicily!" I exclaimed when were safely back in the 500 and driving away, still breathless from the run and the blind panic of it all.

"That's what he said!!! Fuck *'Cazzo'* that was crazy!" He was driving the 500 a little too fast, the adrenalin still no doubt at play. I wasn't going to tell him to slow down though. I wanted to get away from there fast and I wasn't about to worry about going twenty over the limit.

"Sorry Melody, really. I'm so sorry. He was supposed to be away. I don't know what happened! He must've decided to come back early. That was too close for comfort. Shit."

"I thought we were done for," I exclaimed, my hands still shaking. "Shit, I've never been so scared in my life."

We drove on a while in silence, reflecting on what had been much too close a call. I hadn't asked where we were heading, but I didn't really care. I was just relieved to be out of there and putting some decent distance between us and Bruno's place. As we pulled up to a major intersection it was clear however that Marco was thinking, something was troubling him. He had a concentrated look on his face, one that I was beginning to recognise. After a while he turned to me.

"He might go into his office at La Sapienza, sometime soon, even tomorrow. Who knows? I'm thinking that perhaps we should pass by his office now and put the keys back in his desk. I think it'd be better to be on the safe side just in case and it'll only take a few minutes. You can wait in the car. You know, I just don't want to take the risk that he goes in there early, looks for the key and they're gone..."

"Agreed," I said, "No more risks."

We drove to La Sapienza in silence, the shock of Bruno's return still sitting on us. Marco parked down a side street by the main building and I waited in the car. The streets were deserted and dark, the security guard nowhere in sight, the only soul in the vicinity a little feral black cat. I watched it skirt the entrance and scurry to the opposite side of the street. With a cursory glance back at me, it was soon through some railings into a park and gone.

Time was dragging and I needed to calm down, so I found my tin with tobacco and papers from the bottom of my bag and started to make a roll-up. Only then, taking in the smoke, did I start to wind down, feel more relaxed, although watching the minutes on the dashboard clock tick away didn't help - Marco was only gone thirteen but if felt more like thirty.

"Done, no problem," he said to my relief, dropping back into the driving seat and turning to me. "Listen, do you want to come back to mine? We've had a shock. I know I need a drink – if you'd like – and we can discuss what we found and what next?"

"Yes, that would be good," I admitted, taking in a final drag of my cigarette, throwing the butt out of the window and winding it up.

"I could use a drink."

As soon as we got to Marco's place, after pulling off my jacket, I dropped down his sofa. I felt exhausted and my ankle was starting to hurt. Clearly, I'd twisted it, most likely jumping onto the wall. I hadn't noticed at the time, in the sheer panic of the moment, but it was killing me now. Kicking off my trainers I gave it a rub.

"You OK?" he shouted over from the kitchen.

"It'll be fine, just a sprain I think," I said as he came back with an open bottle of white and two glasses.

"That was a bit too much for one evening," I said as he poured out a generous glass and passed it to me.

"I know," he said, pouring one for himself, shaking his head.

"When I heard his key in the lock, I just couldn't believe it," he admitted, almost laughing, although we both knew it wasn't funny.

"Me neither," I agreed, the absurdity and panic of the situation hitting me, all over again. "Oh boy…."

"I'm sorry Melody, I mean for dragging you into all this, but, well, thanks for coming. That would've been so much harder on my own. I think I underestimated this whole thing. But look, in the end, despite what happened, it was a good night, no?" He half smiled, clearly feeling more relaxed now.

"I mean all those emails! All that extra information…the flight reservation, hotel booking, those property listings, the letter from the bank and what about that Atlas email…. If only we'd had time to look at the emails he'd sent too." He reflected, a focused, determined look returning to his face.

"I know, it's a real shame. I would've loved to see if he'd responded and how," I admitted, taking another sip of wine.

"But hey, we still got a lot of interesting stuff. I mean I think you could be right. It's freaking me out a bit to be honest. I mean, that this guy might've had something to do with Spencer's death. We've got to follow this up now. And that Atlas email. That was the clincher for me. Hey, let's take another look it. You know, the one you sent to yourself," I said, putting down my wine. "I'd love to give it another once over, or the just version of it you copied down in your notebook. I'd really like to read that again…wh… what's the matter?"

Marco had jumped up, a look of panic, on his face. "Shit!"

"What? What on earth's the matter?" I said standing up too, the look on his face, unnerving me all over again.

He was banging his jeans pockets, looking around the flat, frantic. "Where's my jacket?" he mumbled, rushing to the entrance where it was hanging, searching in the pockets there too.

"Oh no…Oh no…"

"What's wrong? Tell me!"

He came back over into the lounge, hands on top of his head.

"You're not going to believe it!"

"What Marco? What's the matter?!"

"What an idiot I am. Oh shit!" He looked at me, panic now tearing at his face.

"For fucks sakes Marco, what?"

"I think I left my notebook on the table in Bruno's study."

Chapter Twelve

For a moment we just stood looking at each other. Silent.

"You're kidding, right?" I asked.

"No, I'm not," he said, sitting back down on the sofa with his hands back on the top of his head, the colour draining from his face. He took off his glasses and, flinging them down on the sofa, rubbed his eyes. Looking up, he went on.

"It was there on the desk in the study, by the computer, I think. I was copying down details; you know of the emails. That's when he arrived. When he sees it, he'll know someone's been there, in his flat. That someone's on to him. I think we left the torches there too… Shit, fuck, 'cazzo.'"

"Was there anything in it, the notebook I mean, connecting it to you?" My mind was racing, I was trying to think straight and not panic, although I was feeling nauseous and mildly faint.

"Let me think…"

"Yes, please think Marco. What was in the notebook? If he can link it to you…"

"No, I don't think so. Wait a minute. Well…"

"Well what?" I was really was starting to panic. I was worried, not so much for me, but for him. If the notebook could be linked to Marco who knows what could happen next. In a flash I'd already imagined him losing his job, being interviewed by the police, jail… and if Bruno really was who Marco thought he was…a murderer…even worse. Bruno could be leafing through it now, planning his next move…It didn't bear thinking about…

Marco was concentrating, trying to remember the notebook, the contents.

"Let me see, I have a few notebooks, in this one, well, there were some notes on Roman history from the 200 AD period. Just a couple of pages at the front. Let me think… yes, I think that's right. But unless Bruno's a handwriting expert, he wouldn't be able to link it to me. It could be anyone's. I hadn't put anything personal in there. It was a new one. I put it in my jacket on the way out tonight, just last minute really, you know, it occurred to me I might want to write something down."

"But he'll think that it belongs to someone from *La Sapienza*, when he sees the historical notes, no?" I ventured. "And if he asks around, people might say you've been talking about him..."

"Yes, that's possible, but first he's a member of quite a few archaeological circles here in and outside Rome, so it doesn't totally link it to *La Sapienza*, not 100%. Then I don't think any of my friends would ever talk to him, I mean tell him about me and what I've been saying. He's got a good reputation but after all, he's the boss and not 'one of them' if you know what I mean. They might've thought that my theory was crazy, but they're not friends with him either. I don't think they'd say anything. The main point is that nothing links the notebook directly to me. But one thing's for sure. As soon as he sees it, and the torches, he'll know someone, people, were in his place and that most likely they're on to him. I mean if it were just the torches, he might think it was burglars, but not when he sees the notebook. Damn though. How could I make such a stupid mistake! You know, it was just in the heat of the moment, I was, was so freaked out, you know, that he was coming into the apartment. I kind of lost it for a moment..."

I studied his face and sat back down next to him on the sofa.

"Lost it? I thought you were great." I smiled reassuringly, rubbing his arm.

"After all you got us out of there, and well, from what you're saying, thankfully he'll never know it's yours. The notebook won't give you away. Thank god!" I was starting to relax, feel relived, a bit. "And another thing, maybe in an odd kind of way it's good he knows someone's on to him. When you go back to *La Sapienza* you can watch him, see if he's jumpy, no?"

"I guess you've got a point," he said mulling it over, turning to me, thinking.

"We could try and turn it to our advantage…You know Melody, I'm so glad you agreed to help me with this" He grimaced, the relief that the notebook wasn't the end of the world clearly visible. I smiled back – and I felt little butterflies...

"So, shall we take a look at that email again?" I ventured, trying to put Marco's smile out of my mind, turning back to the task at hand. It was hard though. I couldn't help noticing that, without his glasses, his eyes were very dark and kind, and quite sexy…

"You know, the one you sent to yourself?"

…and what a nice profile he had, how strong his cheek bones were, and that this unshaved look really suited him...

"I mean it really is…"

Suddenly Marco was kissing me. Warm kisses that tasted of wine and salt. Then he was pulling me closer to him, softly, but his arms felt surprisingly strong and firm. Soon I was leaning back into the soft depths of the sofa and he was above me, insistent, his hands slowly pulling at my t-shirt, kissing my neck, my shoulders. Then he was kissing my mouth again, small soft gentle kisses, his hand pressing into the small of my back, a strong, urgent embrace. Hot passion was starting to envelop me, taking me over as his kisses got deeper. I could taste and feel his desire.

"Melody," he murmured between the kisses. "I, I think you're wonderful. '*Mio dio,'* you're, you're beautiful too. Really, beautiful. Will you, will you please, stay the night?"

"I, I don't know Marco," I said, pulling back, hesitant looking into his eyes.

"I'm not sure… I…"

"Just stay here, sleep here in my bed, nothing more if you don't want it …I promise… I know this has been a crazy night, I just want to spend the rest of it with you Melody...and like I said, if you don't want anything more, that's fine, we can just sleep, but don't go… not tonight..." Then he was kissing me again, his hands feeling surer of themselves, reaching up my back under my t-shirt, exploring, pressing me to him. His mouth moved to my neck, his tongue soft but firm making a trail down to my chest then back up to my mouth

"Ok, I said, between the kisses. His mouth back on mine, his eyes dark and full of longing,"

"I'll stay, I'll sleep here but, well that's all… OK?"

"OK." He pulled back, his eyes smiling before planting another kiss on my lips, "Very OK."

The next day I woke with the light streaming into the bedroom and the sound of Marco, pottering in the kitchen. Until then I hadn't seen Marco's place in the daytime and taking it in from his bed at eight in the morning was, let's say, an unexpected way to do it.

The light grey walls, and dark wooden bed had a manly, bachelor feel about them, the only decoration a large oil painting on the opposite wall. I studied it in the sunlight, from the comfort of the big old bed. It looked like the forum and a 19th century work, the kind of thing you'd pick up in an antique fare. It spoke of taste and an interest in art. I liked that in a man. But lying in the bed the sounds of Marco in the kitchen brought a sudden tightness to my chest that started to grow. It was Spencer… He was never far away.

"Good morning." I ventured from the bedroom door. He glanced up from the stove where a pot of coffee, hissing, sounded like it was just coming to boil.

"Good morning," he smiled back, a little awkwardly.

For a moment I couldn't work out quite what he was wearing.

"I've been out for a morning run," he said, as if reading my mind. "I go most days. Helps me stay in shape and I like the time to think."

Now I got it. He was wearing a running kit - shorts, an old t-shirt, trainers. He looked sweaty, flushed and sporty. He looked nice. He turned off the gas, got two cups down from hooks where they were hanging above the sink and started pouring the steaming coffee into the first.

"Coffee?"

"Yes, thanks, I'll err, just use your bathroom first if that's OK?"

"Of course," he glanced over again, with another self-conscious smile. "You know where it is, right? First door on the left."

In his tiny bathroom, I took a quick shower, dressed and made the best of things with the limited contents in my bag; A lipstick and powder didn't go far, but it was better than nothing. Pulling on the same jeans and t-shirt from the night before didn't feel great either. They looked grubby and crumpled and with the heat and humidity already starting to build I needed something lighter. Sweat was already started to bead on the back of my neck and the cooling effect of the cold shower would soon be wearing off. Looking at my reflection in the mirror, I tried to ask myself what had happened the night before. Marco definitely had something; he was a cute, good looking in a geeky kind of way, thoughtful, intelligent - he seemed like a good man – but I just couldn't shake the feeling, that in spite of everything, much as I wanted him to be, he just wasn't Spencer...

When I'd finished, I found him sitting in the living room.

"Everything OK?" he asked, perhaps a little tightly, passing me a coffee. "Milk?"

"Yes, thanks," I said, taking the cup, putting in a dash of milk from the carton on the table and sitting down. Studying him more closely I couldn't miss that he looked tense, nursing his expresso in its tiny cup at the other side of the small dining room table. I don't know what I was expecting but after the passion of the night before it wasn't quite this. There again, I wasn't feeling quite myself either…I was disorientated, confused. I wasn't sure what to think let alone what to feel.

"Melody look …I've got something to do his morning – something came up," he said, shifting on his chair, looking uncomfortable.

"But I can meet you later, is that OK?" he said, leaning across the table then, taking my hand in his, kissing it. Holding it gently, fixing my gaze, I couldn't help feeling that he looked a little lost, a little sad. Not a surface, superficial kind of sadness, but a deeper one. Something was up.

"What's wrong, Marco?"

"Nothing, nothing at all. Something's just come up, that's all and I've got to dash now," he said, smiling gently.

"But can we meet up later?" he asked, squeezing my hand again, smiling through whatever was behind his demeanour.

"OK, Sure" I said uncertainly. "Is it something to do with Bruno? With Spencer?" I asked, studying his face.

"No, nothing to do with that." He almost laughed, looking for an instance more relaxed.

"Look, I'm sorry, really. But we can talk later. OK? We can meet at my local bar. Would, say two o'clock be OK for you? Will you at least let me call you a taxi? Sorry I can't give you a lift…I have to grab a quick shower and get going…"

Back at my hotel I turned on the aircon, lay on the bed and stared at the ceiling. I was trying to figure out what I was feeling but my head was spinning, the wine of the night before finally catching up with the lack of sleep.

Pulling myself off the bed to go to the loo, I checked my phone and saw a missed call. Jake.

"How's things Mel's?" He sounded cheery down the phone. "Enjoying Italy? You're in Amalfi now, right?"

"Not yet. It's a bit of a long story…" I managed between yawns.

"Oh, really? Actually, I was just calling to check-in, see how things are going, you know, with the feature, but mainly I wanted to make sure that you're going to send the September *Melody Talkin'* page soon. Final draft's due next week..."

I wasn't in the mood for this call let alone Jake checking up on me. I needed some sleep. But it seemed the chance I needed to bring him up to date, so I told him about Spencer, the funeral, about meeting Marco and entering Bruno's flat and I told him what we'd found. He was quiet down the phone. I could hear the silence all the way from Soho.

"Wow Mels, that's… that's terrible. Sorry to hear," came his voice after a good while. "I know you were, well, you were fond of this guy. Terrible. And quite a story, I mean what this guy Marco is claiming, and then, you guys going into this man's, what's he called? This man's place like that. That was a bit risky you know…"

"Bruno, he's called Bruno. I know. I know, but look, what do you think, do you think I can still make it work? The article I mean?" I said, pushing aside the concern in Jake's voice, opening the mini bar, looking for something cold to drink.

"Look Mels, it's up to you. Sounds like it's turned into something quite different. But I think you can get something out of it – I mean wow, what a story, if this guy really is implicated. Of course, it'll depend a lot on what happens next and how you spin it. I'd suggest you get online and start doing some research into the area too. You know, international laws on treasure, underground illegal trades it the stuff. But I must be honest Mels. I've done my bit fighting your corner. Mac's expecting a draft feature or two from you by end of summer if you want any chance of the contract come January. He's talking about a total relaunch too, so everyone's contracts are going to be up in the air. If you submit a different story to the one you proposed, that's your call...and it might be fine… if it's good. You know what I'm sayin', right?"

"Right, I get it. Don't worry. You can't pull any more strings."

"Shit, look at the time. Really sorry Mels. Gotta dash. There's a board meeting starting in five minutes. Look, I'm, I'm sorry about Spencer. Really…Speak soon? Keep me posted. And remember, like I said, your *Melody Talkin'* deadline is coming up next week. Don't let me down…" And with that he hung up.

I sat on the end of the bed staring at my phone. I'd completely forgotten about September's *Melody Talkin*' deadline. My relaxing holiday in Amalfi was not going to be so relaxing after all, and the way things were going, I wasn't even sure I was even going to make it down to Amalfi either. I needed to see Marco and I needed to figure out what next.

Later that day as planned we met in Propaganda, a stylish cocktail bar on a corner back near Marco's place in *Celio*. The Colosseum was in plain sight at the end of the road but somehow the bar was surprisingly empty when I arrived. Not a tourist in sight.

Marco was on a high stool at the bar and already finishing off an Aperol Spritz.

"Try one of these? It's a bit early for *aperitivi* but hey who cares," he said, looking a little dejected, waiving to the bar man who he clearly knew well when I nodded a yes.

"*Due in piu,*" (Two more) he shouted over, pointing to the drink.

"*Aperol Spritz*. One of my faves. You're getting more English by the day," I said with a weak smile. Grabbing a stool, I sat down and took in his face.

"Err, sorry? What do you mean?" he asked, draining his drink through the red and white striped straw.

"Maybe not the *Aperol Spritz*, but the mid-afternoon drinking." I explained.

"Oh right. Yes. Look, I'm sorry for what happened this morning," he said, a little stiffly, putting down his empty glass and ignoring my attempt at a joke. "I mean having to dash off like that..."

"What's going on Marco?" I asked.

Marco, looked uncomfortable, fiddling with the paper napkin under his glass. It was like he couldn't really look me directly in the eye.

"Last night was, well, wonderful, I think… I think you're amazing, believe me. But, look, I don't know how to say this but, I'm not sure…well, I'm just not sure if last night was a good thing, a good idea." He said, sitting forward in his chair, finally looking at me square on and taking my hand.

"Go on," I said.

"This is going to sound awful, but I have to be honest with you…but… well…actually, I didn't mention it before but, look, I've, I've got a girlfriend and well, thing is we haven't been getting on recently, we nearly split up, but we planned just a couple of weeks back to try and make another go of it. You see, we've been together for five years. Anyway, thing is I'm still not sure where it's going. Last night, I think the emotion of the whole evening got to me and, the wine and you're attractive…

"Oh, I see," I said, my face flashing red, a burning starting behind my eyes. I was stunned. He had a girlfriend and had cheated on her with me? Not only was this rejection, but it was coming not even 24 hours after the event. It was a slap in the face and a hard one. Instinctively I pulled my hand away. He winced.

"You see, it's just, just that, well, my life's a bit complicated right now." He continued, seeing my reaction, fixing me through his glasses. He looked pained, confused.

"It's the situation – with my girlfriend, and not only that, well she's got some heavy family stuff going on right now that I'm a bit involved with. Don't get me wrong, you're wonderful, just wonderful – I'd, I'd love things, us, to get together..."

He'd love us to get together but his life was complicated? Heavy family stuff? I felt anger rising in me, bubbling under the surface of my skin, visceral, real and fast approaching boiling point. Perhaps Marco was a player and I just hadn't picked it up? Another typical man who was happy to have a one-night stand and move on. And cheat on his girlfriend in the process. I had every right to be livid and

I was. I had every right to walk out of there, and I was about to but then, in a flash as quickly as it had come…the anger was gone. In an instant it had fizzled out and I just felt flat. There was only one person to blame. Spencer. Sitting there, all I could think about was him. About making love to him and how much I missed him today, and every day of my life. It was what I already knew but it resurfaced again, there and then, the same feeling I'd had in Marco's bed that very morning. I tightness, a longing. But not for Marco. And in a flash, it was suddenly clear. I wasn't ready for any relationship – with anyone, including Marco.

"So, you see, the reason why I had to go this morning, well it's my girlfriend, and…"

"Marco, you know, its fine. It is what it is." I said interrupting, holding my hand up to make him stop. "You know, I think you're great too. Last night was… lovely. But look, I have to be honest with you too. I should be livid – I mean that you just told me you cheated on your girlfriend to spend the night with me. The fact you never even mentioned you had a girlfriend, but …well I'm not – livid I mean. I realise, I'm not angry at all. It's a bit of a relief. You see, I think I'm still not over Spencer. Strange as that sounds, I mean we were only together a year more or less, and it was four years ago now, and, well, now that he's dead…I know it sounds crazy, but I'm still just processing it all and I just don't think I've got the emotional space right now anyway, I mean for a relationship with someone else, so look, no need to explain. I'm not ready, and you have a girlfriend. Let's agree to just chalk it up and move on. OK?" Marco looked surprised, and for a moment a strange expression of sadness crossed over his face – I thought he was going to be relieved, but he didn't seem relieved at all.

He was about to speak again but I went on.

"Marco, can we just leave the whole thing behind us?"

"OK," he grimaced back. "I didn't realise that you're still getting over Spencer. I thought there was something between us, like you felt something too. And I feel like I should at least explain running out on you this morning…"

"No need to explain yourself to me Marco." I insisted. "Like I said, you have a girlfriend, and I'm not over Spencer. I think it's pretty simple really. Look, we're OK just as friends, aren't we?" I said trying to smile.

"OK" he said, looking resigned and for a second a little retched.

"OK, good," I said, resisting the temptation to take his hand back and squeeze it. Our spritz had arrived and I drank in the alcohol, grateful for the cool, aromatic aromas, the bitter taste hitting the back of my throat. After a few seconds had passed, putting down the glass I pressed on.

"So," I said, trying to change the tone, change the subject.

"Thoughts, on Bruno? Now we've had time to sleep on it?" I blushed, immediately.

"Sorry, I errr…well I know we haven't had much sleep but…." He smiled. The situation immediately more relaxed. I laughed, too. I had to.

"After last night, what we found, I have to admit you were right. There's definitely something really odd going on," I said, biting into a small pasty that the bar man had just pass over as a complementary nibble.

"But next steps? What are you thinking?" I said with a mouth full of puff pastry and anchovy.

"You said about going to the police, but do you think that's a good idea? I mean, how will we explain getting access into Bruno's computer?"

"Ah, well, that's no problem," Marco said, also making a start on one of the nibbles, another sign that things were normalizing between us, appetites back at play.

"I have a good friend here in the police – Luca. We go way back to school days. I was best man at his wedding. At least he can give us some advice – off the record like. I phoned him up earlier this morning. He's going off on holiday to Sardinia tomorrow, but our luck's in. He's in the office today and he said if we go over there this afternoon, he can spare us half an hour. I don't know if he'll be able to help much but it's better than nothing and a start. What do you say? Are you up for it?"

"What do you think?" I said giving him a grin.

"Let's get the bill."

The police station was on the other side of Rome in a part of the city called *Prati* and just a few blocks from the Vatican museum. In the car on the way over Marco acted as impromptu tour guide, pointing out notable monuments, statues and fountains. The afternoon was in full flow, and while he chatted about the city and told me about his favorite zones, bars and restaurants, I couldn't help noticing how frantic and frustrated the traffic was. Coaches with tourists clogged the narrow arteries of the city, like a cholesterol overload. At the same time locals tried to navigate a city not built for the quantity of vehicles modern day life wanted to force through it. But with Marco's know-how, punchy driving style and some creative short cuts, we eventually emerged near our final destination on the river near the impressive *Castel Sant'Angelo.*

"One of my favourite monuments in the city, a fortress and the home to many popes and Hadrian's mausoleum of course," he explained, catching my gaze. "You really should go visit sometime. The views from the top are breathtaking. And see this bridge?" he indicated as we pulled up at the traffic lights on the *Lungo Tevere*, the fast moving, cobbled, frenetic traffic artery running each side of the river. "There's a great legend about it and a ghost story too. The ghost is called Beatrice Cenci. Cenci lived in the late renaissance. They say she was treated terribly by her farther so one day she plotted and murdered him. She was beheaded for it right there on the bridge. They say every September, for one evening, her ghost crosses the bridge. Some say in a carriage, some that they've seen her walking with her head under her arm. I've haven't seen it, yet." He grinned. "But I've always thought it would be fun to hang out sometimes here late at night and try."

Luca's office was on the third floor in a large building that looked like it had seen better days. A labyrinth of functional but shabby corridors and small offices, Luca's was no exception to the others I glimpsed on the way up and was dingy and cramped. Waving us in the old beat up office furniture looked like a set of bad eighties cast offs, his desk top computer a model I hadn't seen in years. A grimy desk fan was turning the same hot, limpid air around with no discernible effect.

After some exuberant back slapping with Marco, and a more formal shake of my hand, Luca pointed and the two chairs in front of his desk and gestured for us to take a seat. I liked the look of Luca. He had a switched on but thoughtful gaze and a gentle kindness about him that I wasn't expecting from a policeman. A photo on his desk showed a full-on family life; a wife and two smiling toddlers, a girl and a boy beaming up from what looked like a happy beach holiday somewhere windswept and sunny.

Luca didn't speak any English, so Marco started explaining in Italian while Luca listened carefully to the story, focused, a small frown between the eyes, swiveling ever so lightly in his chair in concentration. I heard the names Spencer and Bruno. Then *La Sapienza*, Panama, San Saba and a whole lot more I couldn't follow at all. Luca listened carefully concentrating, sitting back in his chair and appeared to be carefully mulling over what Marco was saying. From time to time he put up his hand, paused Marco, asked a question, then Marco went on.

When Marco had finished, there was a longer pause, then he leaned forward. He seemed to be giving Marco advice. Marco was shaking his head. He looked down and resigned. He was nodding, then shaking his head. Another second there was a more heated exchange then without another word, the exchange was over, Marco was standing up, they were smiling, and laughing, shaking hands, hugging and Marco beckoned to me. I said goodbye and we were soon back outside on the pavement in the blistering heat of the late afternoon sun.

"Well?' I asked. 'What exactly did he say? I couldn't follow any of it to be honest."

"It's not good." He said, with a frown "Come on let's walk. I'll fill you in."

We headed back to the car which we'd left a couple of blocks back. The afternoon was ending, but it was still baking hot, not helped by the combination of cement, tarmac and stone which was radiating the heat between street, cars and the big building or *'pallazzi'* of the zone. I needed a cigarette and a cold drink, but Marco was on a roll.

"He says that first, we can't use anything we've got from Bruno's place as we got it breaking in." Marco said with a frown. "In fact, we could get into trouble for that if it ever comes out. The police would need to get a search warrant, but the thing is he says we don't have enough to justify a search warrant. Moreover, if the police in Panama say that Spencer's death was accidental, and the family have a certificate as such, how can he now propose a search warrant? On what basis? Best he can do is have a chat with Bruno, to see if anything comes out of the conversation, like if something doesn't add up with his statement in Panama. He said he can get a copy of that from the authorities but that will take time. But Melody, let's face it. What good will that do?" he said, stopping suddenly in his tracks turning to me. "Essentially nothing. Not only this, but he's up to his eyes in cases right now. He probably won't even get to have that chat with Bruno until next month. Today is his last day in the office until early September – you know how Italians love their Summer Holidays – well he's off to Sardinia with his family tomorrow." He said picking up the pace towards the car. "He's been going for years. It's all booked and paid for. Understandably he has no intention of letting anything get in the way of that. Especially on what I've just told him – given, well, he said we've got nothing really – legally I mean."

"But what about the Atlas email?" I asked. "Doesn't he think that's worth anything?"

"Like us, he says it's really suspicious, but he can't really do anything about it."

We'd arrived at Marco's 500 and it was clear. The trail was going nowhere. With the police that is. It was about as beat up as the Fiat and there didn't look like there was a whole lot we could do about it either.

We drove back to Aventino in silence. I felt exhausted, like we'd driven the 500 off a cliff with us in it. I was hot and beat, and I needed to sleep in a dark airconditioned room and take stock. I'd been on a bit of a roll since the night of the funeral, swept up in the possibility that Marco was onto something, and it was all starting to catch up on me. Then there was *Zenith* and my conversation with Jake that morning. I needed to get my projects back on track and I needed to do, my *Melody Talkin'* page fast. Not only that, but I still had a bunch of small features for my mum hanging over me not to mention the Facebook feature to figure out. I had no idea what new direction to take with that now and hadn't even had time to give it a good think through. All this was swirling in my head as we pulled up at my hotel in Aventino and Marco killed the engine. I was starting to feel overwhelmed.

"What next?" he asked, turning to me, fixing my gaze.

I thought I was hearing things. "What next? Nothing I guess Marco. I mean, what do you propose? You heard Luca. Even though we found those emails, there's nothing we can do. And we nearly got caught red handed by Bruno in his place, too. That wasn't much fun. I won't forget that in a hurry. I for one don't fancy getting banged up in an Italian jail in the near future. So please no more suggestions about 'breaking in.'"

"But do you at least agree there's something fishy going on?" he asked, fixing me in the eyes, not letting go.

"You want my honest opinion? Yes, I think there is. But who knows? Maybe there was a freak accident and at the same time they'd found something valuable that he's now trying to sell on the black market. I don't know much about these things, but I guess a trade in black market pirate treasure might exist. But it doesn't mean he killed Spencer, does it?"

"Well Spencer's my friend and I'd like to find out one way or the other. And from our conversation today, when you said that you're still in love with him, I thought you might feel the same too," he said hotly. His jaw was set.

"Look at the facts Melody. He's got a ticket to Panama in a month. He's opened a bank account in Panama, and he's got some odd shit going on with an anonymous person with a secret rendezvous and the guy is talking about paying in cash. Then not to mention all those real estate listings for million-dollar properties and yachts too. Come on. If that isn't fishy, I don't know what is."

I knew Marco was right, but I just didn't want to deal with it anymore. The conversation with Jake kept repeating in my mind. I need to get a good September *Melody Talkin'* page done. I had to get some decent features to Mac. I needed my contract at *Zenith.* I didn't want to be out of a job, and I needed to pay my bills.

"Look Marco, I get it but, I just can't do this anymore. You said your life's complicated right now. Well mine is too. It was a great adventure, but I'm out. I wish you all the best but, you're on your own."

"What, wait what are you saying?"

"Sorry, but I've also got my own personal shit going on right now too. I need to get some work done or I'll be out of a job. And maybe you need to get your situation sorted too. I mean leave this Bruno obsession behind you and focus on your relationship instead. No?"

"But what about Spencer? Don't you care what happened to him?"

"Marco, I told you today. You know that I still have a huge place for Spencer in my heart. I mean, I know it's stupid and a long shot but coming over here to meet him, deep down I realize now that I was hoping we might get back together, you know? There. I've admitted it now. And if not, at the very least, to understand why he dumped me all those years back. And now I'll never know. I'll never know if I meant anything to him or not and why he dumped me. And of course, if something bad happened to him I'd like to know. But, finding out Spencer's dead, well it's knocked me for six. So now I think I've just got to put closure on Spencer and well, this wild goose chase just isn't helping, OK? So, I'm sorry but that's me. Ciao Marco."

And with that I got out of the car, walked into the hotel and didn't look back.

Chapter Thirteen

A dazzling sun, the sea, a pool. The colors blue and white with a splash of lemon zest. 37 degrees and siestas at noon. Cicadas relentlessly grate in the canopy above. The view; a sheer granite rock face before a tumble of olive and lemon groves below and then the sea: quite distant, we are so high up here, but still I have the sensation that you can reach out and touch it, saltwater on your fingertips. The Mediterranean always takes my breath away, and even more so from here where you can see its full majesty morning, noon and night.

A pile of books, a pool-side lounger with a fluffy yellow towel folded carefully on the end. The hours melt into days, into nights and back into days all over again. A leisurely breakfast, a dip in turquoise water, lunch, an afternoon nap, a gin tonic, and dinner at a small table at the very end to the terrace. Always an elegant, fresh yellow rose, my company for dinner. Which day? Monday, Tuesday, Saturday?

Bliss.

Thanks Dad. The money was well received, the final bill, of no concern, for once.

A bell boy called Stefano wearing an old-style hotel uniform including hat met me in the small, tranquil central piazza in Ravello with a hotel trolley in one hand, and a white be-gloved handshake ready in the other. Soon he was trundling my luggage out of the piazza and along a narrow stone footpath, winding through tangled yet cultivated vineyards, past a convent and church and a small hamlet before we arrived at an imposing high, ancient looking stone wall and the heavy wooden gates which formed the entrance to *Villa Cimbrone*. The Mediterranean glistened and was mesmerising in the distance, the cicadas loud and not going for a siesta any time soon.

Situated right at the end of the peninsular with spectacular, sheer views down the Amalfi coast, the Villa was nestled in blissful gardens of fragrant honeysuckle and Instagram bright bougainvillea. The splash of a controlled, no doubt elegant, dive hinted at a pool yet to be seen and was they only sound from the grounds as I entered the cool reception to check in. Everything oozed style and poise.

I'd always been a budget traveler, a backpacking type. Flea pits in Asia, some pretty cheap hostels on a recent trip to Morocco, and jaunts around the med. I think I'd reached rock bottom in Turkey sleeping on a park bench one night due to dwindling funds at the end of a trip. For a year or two, Dad's 'guilt money' as mum would call it, had dried up while he'd been saving for his wedding to Cheryl, his second wife. But these past few years he was back to his older habits, at least two or three thousand Canadian dollars arriving in my bank account twice each year. And it made a difference. I might regret spending the money on a fancy hotel when my meagre savings account was drained, again. But this time I didn't care. It was true though, I understood why mum worried and I wasn't planning on telling her that for once I was splashing out. She worried as she never had very much money for herself, and certainly couldn't give any to me to help me out between contracts. And despite doing just OK, she never forgotten her working-class roots and the rent, the mortgage, the bills whatever they were had to be paid. That had been a sticking point with Dad. He came from a wealthy family. But when times had been hard, when she'd just had me and was at home washing out cloth nappies, without a penny to rub together and with dad's career not taking off, they'd never helped out, even though they could. Not a penny. I know that got to her at times.

"That's your dad's side of the family." She'd reminded me of this many times, whenever she could when some news surfaced from somewhere, who knew where, on the Meeks family. I can see her now, frowning at the kitchen table in her modest flat in

Balham. Her G&T in one hand her cigarette in the other. She'd pause for effect, taking a drag, and frown some more.

"Well off and bloody tight."

But *Villa Cimbrone*, perfect as it was, had come at a price those first few days. I couldn't completely relax with Jake breathing down my neck all the way from London, so I'd sacrificed time on the pool loungers and, back at the writing desk in my room, done a first draft of my September *Melody Talkin'* page. Relief washed over as I pressed the send button and the electronic 'whoosh' indicated it was on its way. Jake would be happy, relieved to see it appear in his inbox. And I was happy with it too. Being away from London, having a change of scene, had done me good. I felt refreshed, revitalized. I knew it was my best *Melody Talkin'* page in a while. And not only that, but a first draft of the Facebook feature was now also confidently sitting on my laptop. On the first night at the villa I'd taken a G&T to the Terrace of Infinity. The terrace was situated at the far end of the hotel grounds, down a long leafy, semi overgrown gravel path. It was open to the public by day but after dark the grounds were closed, and in the evenings, I'd found that I mainly had it to myself. Sitting there, gazing down at the sheer drop below, looking at the twinkling lights along the coast, I told myself I wasn't leaving until I'd figured out the spin, the angle of the story. I lot rested on this. Mac was not an easy man to please. I had to get it right. An hour later and the G&T drained, I'd settle on an approach as close to the original idea as I could. The take was about how we should use Facebook and social media to connect more, to *really* be in touch rather than just using it to snoop and show off. That life was short. Why wait and potentially regret it. I had plenty of examples to use, then of course the Spencer story. The summary concluded with what I thought was an emotional 'life is short' message, with Spencer front and center. Spencer as someone who lived life to the full but how we never know just when our number was up. And because of this how we needed to connect more, especially given the disparate lives we are all living. I thought it worked, just. But was it edgy enough? Mac would be the one who would ultimately decide. But days later, the article still on my desktop, I still hadn't sent it. Something just kept niggling me about it. That there was a bigger story to tell, a story about murder, treasure, an underground trade in historic artifacts, a story as yet unfinished...something much more exciting, more investigative, more the new *Zenith,* and more to the point, that I was settling, again, not pushing the boundaries. Always the same Melody, playing it safe. Like Rome hadn't happened, no snooping in Bruno's office, no going into his flat, no Atlas email, no Marco.

And the niggle followed me to my bed. I couldn't sleep - and the Villa wasn't helping. I was used to the constant background noise a city generates but in *Villa Cimbrone*, there was no noise at all. Nothing. The nights were silent. It was like a soft dark, velvet glove was pressing down on that isolated hotel at the end of the peninsula, muffling all the sound around it. The quiet was so pervasive, so total, it almost felt like the fingers in the glove had slipped in my ears and were softly putting a pressure on my ear drums.

And then there was Spencer - floating in and out of my dreams. Four years later, but still the lasting memory of the scent of his sweat mixed with his cologne. The way his eyelids flickered in his sleep. And the stories he'd tell. The details would often change depending on how many pints he'd had and who he was telling - but that hadn't mattered at the time. He had a way of telling a story, drawing you in. The evenings in The Maypole, a group of us; seven or eight, and Spencer, holding court, telling a story. How he'd tricked a teacher at school, how he'd snuck into the local casino underage. You name it, Spencer had a story for it. Now he was gone, and the stories too. And that's where it started, to keep me awake at night, the niggle in the pit of my stomach, turning into a larger knot. Minor details in a story down the pub, that was one thing. But why did he lie about his parents? Pretend he didn't have a sister? Tell Marco that his parents died in a plane crash and me in a car accident? Would I ever make sense of it?

One day, after a night tossing and turning, my agitation finally getting the better of me I tried calling Spencer's sister. After all, she'd given me her number. I figured we could speak on the phone. Perhaps arrange to meet up if she was still in Rome, or even when I was back in the UK. But she didn't pick up. Was that strange too or just normal for someone in mourning? I'd never been there, never experienced loss like hers myself and I didn't know her, but it didn't make me feel any better, just made the knot in my stomach grow.

Then there was Marco.

I'd set my phone to silence but kept finding his missed calls on my phone. Then a voice mail too followed by messages that I didn't open. I knew he was calling about Spencer, but I just didn't want to listen anymore.

He'd called again during the night. My phone vibrating on the bed. I watched for a while then turned away. But instead of feeling better, not speaking to Marco was making me feel worse.

Eventually I crumbled, and called my mum, told her as much as I could bear. When I finished, I could hear her frustration down the phone.

"Why on earth don't you want to speak to this Marco? You're not being logical, Melody," she pointed out, a fact I already knew.

"I know, it's just that, well, it's complicated," I tried to explain.

"Complicated? Oh… I see." I could almost see her nodding down the phone. Taking a swig at her gin and tonic.

"So, you slept with him, and you quite like him?"

"Mum!!! Look, yes, no. It's not that simple. I think I'm still hooked on Spencer and, well Marco, I found out he's got a girlfriend. And he cheated on her to spend the night with me. Even worse…"

"Melody, I know. You keep telling me it's complicated. But actually, it's really quite simple." she said gently. "I know how much Spencer meant to you but, well, Spencer's dead. You need to try and move on. I know it's hard, but you have to try and draw a line under it. Look, just give this Marco a call back. Maybe he's got something to say, something you might want to hear. What have you got to lose at this stage? At least hear him out."

The next day over lunch, feeling annoyed that my mum was right after all and with half a bottle of Chardonnay for support, I gave Marco a call.

"Melody, finally!" he replied sounding relieved, anxious.

"Bad time?" I asked, a little cheekily, trying to sound disinterested, nonchalant at the same time.

"*Cazzo*. Shit! I've been trying to get in touch with you for days! Why didn't you get back to me? Was it my message!?"

"Which message? I've had a problem with my phone," I lied.

"The one I left in your pigeonhole in the reception, you know in *Aventino*. They said they'd give it to you in the morning. That one?"

"Oh no, I didn't get it," I responded, perplexed, trying to get the attention of the waiter. I was sitting at my usual table right at the end of the terrace. The view was stunning and the only thing to make it more perfect was a desert – preferably something with chocolate on it.

"Oh, I see," he replied, sounding surprised, a little put out, or confused, I couldn't quite tell.

"That's annoying. It was important, I wanted you to understand."

"Understand what?" I asked.

"Oh, err, Melody. Look, I can't have that conversation on the phone. It was something I wrote, I wanted you to read… forget it, now's not the time perhaps. But listen. I wasn't just calling about that. There's something else. I've been trying to get in touch with you about Bruno."

"Bruno? What about him?"

"Bruno, yes. I have some updates for you. Well I found out something important. He's leaving for Panama."

"Yes, I know that," I said, smiling at the waiter. He was good looking, and we'd been flirting a little. It was all innocent really, and I'd noticed there was no ring on his wedding finger, so he wasn't totally off limits. "*Gelato,* (ice cream) *Si*, Strawberry and chocolate. *Grazie*."

"No, you don't understand, he's leaving tomorrow." Marco pressed on.

I sat up in my chair.

"Tomorrow? What? Really?"

"Well he came into work two days ago, apparently. I wasn't there so I just heard about it. I went in to get some things sorted out with the admin office. Anyway, turns out he just resigned. Like that. He's supposed to give three months' notice, but he refused. Says he's got a sick relative in Sicily and is moving back there immediately. You can imagine how surprised and pissed off the Admin office is. Leaves them with no senior lecturer and the start of term just weeks away. It's a breach of contract. I don't know what they'll do about that. But anyway, that's not the point. After that I was on the way to my office to get something and I went over to his office, he wasn't around and I tried the door, it was unlocked. So, I went in and took a look in his desk drawer."

"Are you crazy!?" I asked putting my glass down, feeling faint. "If he'd come back, apart from anything else, he would've put two and two together and placed you in his apartment too."

"I know." I could almost hear him smiling down the phone. "Anyway, he didn't come back and for a good five minutes I had a snoop around, and I found a new print out for a ticket to Panama leaving tomorrow. Melody, it said one-way. Like he's not coming back."

"Well, that's a turn up isn't it?" I said trying to think on the spot. "But it still doesn't mean he killed Spencer."

"Melody, listen. Then I called back the hotel Miramar in Panama. Remember the one we found on the telephone bill? Well I said that I've got a friend arriving on Saturday and I have a message for him. When I told them the name, they didn't contradict it. They said, sure we can pass on your message. At that point I hung up, but don't you see. This and the ticket. He's not going to Sicily at all, he's going to Panama, for sure. And it looks like he's not coming back. My guess is that he found my notebook, the flashlight. He knows someone is onto him. He's moving on and he's not wasting any time."

I had to admit my mind was racing. Marco was right. It was true. It all made sense. Marco was still on the end of the phone, silent. My ice cream arrived, and the waiter winked, a cheeky smile on his face. But I wasn't interested in double chocolate chip or boosting my confidence with cute waiters anymore.

"Melody, you still there? Melody? Look I thought I could go back to Luca, tell him this latest development, see what he says. He's on holiday right now but I'm sure he won't mind if I give him a call. Really, I don't know what else to do. That's why I wanted to speak to you."

"Sure," I replied, "Let me know what he says. Give me a buzz later."

I hung up and looked at the ice cream. It was already startling to melt, the red strawberry sauce on top was congealing in the dish, like blood and I didn't really feel like eating any of it anymore. I'd lost my appetite.

Later that day, I hadn't heard back from Marco and I went for a pre-dinner stroll around Ravello. The sun was going down and Ravello village was enchanting with its winding cobble lanes, a smattering of bars and restaurants, churches, convents and heavenly views but I couldn't shake the sensation that, I was after all said and done, alone. Couples and groups were everywhere, and I seemed to be the only one out by myself. Arriving back at the Terrace of Infinity where I knew I could sit without feeling self-conscious, I chose a bench with the most uninterrupted view and started on a roll-up to pass the time before dinner. Normally I didn't mind solo travel at all but tonight it had really bothered me, and I was rattled.

Between school and university, I'd taken a gap year and gone traveling with a friend. We'd backpacked around Asia most of the time, but our plans didn't always line up, so we'd spent some weeks apart before meeting up again 'at base camp' as we'd jokingly called it. Base camp being Chunking Mansions in Hong Kong, a notorious high-rise block in Kowloon stuffed to the brim with tiny shops, hotels, restaurants and hotels: all dives, all cheap, all low end. Chunking had served as base camp on and off for a good six months and, thinking back to that trip, seven years ago, it seemed like another life. We'd been adventurous, or so it had felt at the time. Then university had been a blast too. We all thought we were already so grown up, but on reflection we'd just been playing at life in the secluded confines of the colleges. And I'd loved my English Lit course at Cambridge. I knew I'd made the right choice from day one. The journalism thing came much later – probably my third year at Cambridge. It was Spencer who suggested it, put it in my mind, just two months before the end of my last term.

We were in the Maypole and he'd just bought us a second round of drinks. I'd arrived back from my smoking spot out at the back in the carpark, no doubt smelling of cigarettes, not that Spencer cared. He planted one on my mouth, his tongue hot, wet and firm, telling me that he was ready for some action later that night. But I pushed him playfully away and he grinned back, knowing it was just a game, that I wanted him there and then too, just the same.

"Ok, look, help me out," I said with a smile, taking a sip of my pint and getting back to the conversation we were supposed to be having,

"So, like I said, I'm toying with publishing or something in magazines, but none of them are easy to get into right now..."

"But your mum could help with journalism, no? Why don't you consider that? You know, newspapers," he said, leaning back on the bench, pulling open the packet of salt and vinegar crisps and taking out a handful. "I know you said last week that you feel funny following in her footsteps, her shadow, but I don't get that. If you want to do it, why not? Strikes me from everything you do and say, that's really where your heart is. Why fight it because of her?"

"Funny you should say, I've been thinking of journalism myself a bit more recently too. I guess being honest these last years I was blanking it out because I wanted to rebel and do my own thing." I shrugged. "But, well you know I think you're right. More I keep thinking, more I keep coming back to it. Despite her. If I'm honest, these last months I feel more and more that it's what I want to do. But, if I did do it, I'd do it standing on my own two feet. I'd never ask my mum for help," I said, a little annoyed at his suggestion. "If I'm going to do something, I want to get somewhere on my own merit, not because of her."

"Oh, come on," he said, taking a sip of his pint. "It's dog eat dog out there. Why wouldn't you? In any case, it's not like she ended up having a totally glittering career in the end anyway, is it? She can probably only help you so far, I mean, where is she working now? The Local Yokel Times of Nowhere. Some shitty local rag, right? But anyway, the point is you should use all the contacts you have. You'd be stupid not to. Everyone else will. And I think you'd make a great journalist. That piece you did for The College Times on the tension between students and locals was great. Not to mention all those you did last year. You'd be better than her. That's for sure."

As he was off in the men's room and I was getting in another drink in the bar later that night, I thought about what he'd said. It stung a bit, about my mum being at a crappy local. It seemed condescending, harsh, and even a bit cruel. Why was he like that sometimes? He'd never met my mum. He didn't understand how she'd struggled, even though I'd tried to explain. But I did know he was right. Why not give the journalism thing a go! If he thought I'd make a good journalist, maybe he had a point. And as I was mulling it over at the bar waiting to get served it ignited something in me, standing there I felt excited about life after Cambridge for the first time. I thought about how I'd always been interested in current affairs, an avid reader of the Sunday supplements, and how I could combine that interest with writing. Yes, journalism. Maybe it was somehow in my blood after all. I knew deep down that I'd probably been suppressing it for years. And another thing, I realised standing there, that maybe I'd passed the phase of wanting something different to my mum. Of pushing it away like I probably had done in a teenage rebellious phase when I was younger. But If I did go for journalism, I'd do it on my own merit. I didn't need anyone's help. I'd make my own way, take my own path. It would be a different path to mum's and not only that, I'd make my mum proud too. I'd make up for the career that she never had…because of me.

Putting the finishing touches to my roll-up, I lit it and breathed in the sweet, strong tobacco before expelling the smoke into the still warm early evening air. I couldn't help wondering what Marco was up to. Out with his friends? Perhaps even in the Propaganda bar near the Colosseum, or with his girlfriend? There it was again, a soft something flipping, fluttering inside my stomach at the thought of him. Then Spencer came back into focus, only this time the photo of him from the funeral. I suddenly felt mildly queasy, not helped perhaps by the earlier rich lunch, the Chardonnay and one too many *Aperol Spritz* aperitivi. Nevertheless, I took another drag, studying my nails. The clear gloss looked chipped and in need of a refresh. It was years since I'd had a professional manicure. My toes were the same. The polish old and flaking. I wondered what Marco really thought of me. The Italian women were so well turned out, so feminine, polished, with long flowing hair, strolling around Ravello in their high heals and matching clutch bags. And there I was: short red hair, little leather backpack and flats. I'd never been a matching clutch and shoes type of girl and I knew I wasn't every man's cup of tea with my tomboy style, boyish looks and figure. My mind flashed to the look on Marco's face at the stove, seeing me at his bedroom door. He'd looked so awkward the morning after, so uncomfortable.

Pushing this from my mind, I stood up and went to the rail, to take a better look at the view. The sun had gone down and the sky was on route to a deep indigo blue but even so, I could still perfectly see the spine-tingling drop. Looking down made my had spin. It was steep, sheer, and deadly.

I carefully put out my cigarette and threw the butt over the edge and watched as the little cream spot disappeared out of sight.

Taking in the view, somehow and without warning, all at once, everything came into sharp focus. I knew what I had to do. Deep down I'd known the second Marco had called.

I made for the hotel. Dinner could wait. I had some things I needed to do online and there wasn't much time.

"So, I've decided. I've bought a ticket on the next flight out after Bruno. I'm leaving tomorrow morning. Will you come too?" I was back on the hotel terrace, nursing an *Amaro* night cap and feeling the calmest I'd felt for a while.

"What? Are you joking?" Marco's voice came down the phone.

"I'm sure if we follow him, out there, we'll find out what's going on. I mean, we know that Bruno looks up to his neck in something seriously dodgy, maybe even something illegal. At worst… well, I know what you think about that. So, Marco. You started this thing. Won't you come too?"

"Panama? Me? Now? You're serious, aren't you?"

"I've never been more serious in my life," I said, resolutely taking a sip of Amaro, gazing up at the stars and tracing the big dipper across the horizon.

"I can't do that!" Marco exclaimed. "I mean, are you crazy? Like, just jump on a flight and go to Panama, tomorrow?"

"Yes, why not?" I insisted.

"And what will we do when we get there?" he asked, showing he was maybe one step ahead of me, more practical.

"I don't know yet. We'll figure it out as we go along. Put a plan together, on the plane. And look, I'd like to think that we've forgotten what happened the other night, right? I mean between me and you. I think we've put that behind us. This is purely as friends. OK?" I paused, let it sink in.

Silence.

"Well, I'm going, I've decided. And like I said, you started this thing, and you know, I could do with the help to be honest. You said it yourself. Don't you want to get to the bottom of this? I've been down here in Amalfi trying to put this to the back of my mind, move on, but you were right. I can't and I owe it to Spencer. We owe it to him. You said yourself, even if Bruno didn't kill Spencer there's definitely something fishy going on. Apart from the fact that this guy might've murdered your friend. And now the fact that he's brought his flight forward, now he knows someone's on to him – it's obvious - he's getting out of here. Probably never coming back.

"So, you're going there for Spencer?" he asked, still uncertain. Something bothering him I couldn't pinpoint.

"Yes, of course. Come on Marco, you started this. Come with me, what have you got to lose? Help me finish it. Together."

"I don't know…its' all a bit, out of the blue. And, Panama? Really. Have you been before? Know anyone there?"

"No" I laughed. "I don't know anyone there. I don't know the first thing about it. I don't even speak any Spanish. But I did check online and on a practical matter, we don't even need visas, just a flight, that's it. Look, the flight is leaving at 10:30 tomorrow morning from Rome Fiumicino and I'm going to be on it."

Later that night I was packing my bag when my phone pinged. A message from Marco.

"Going to book the flight now. Meet you at the gate. You're either crazy, dangerous or both."

"Are you sure?" I texted back.

"No, I'm not. I'm bloody confused. What am I doing! ☺ " came back the message.

I laughed. There were no worries on that one I thought to myself. I was already confused enough for both of us.

INTERLUDE

The Caribbean Ocean
Somewhere off the coast of Panama
1665 ca.

Wicks marked the spot, and the men started shoving their spades into the hard, sodden earth. The captain wanted a hole eight feet deep and eight feet wide, and the compact mud and tangle of roots made the digging hard and slow. As the night progressed, the trees around the clearing became agitated, as if they knew that something was afoot. Wicks glanced up and went over to Morgan.

"Once back on the boat with all the torches out, Marquez won't see us, but we'll have to leave within the hour to still have the cover of dark."

"Aye," Morgan said, studying Wicks' face in the orange lamp light. Wicks' stubble had been turning grey these last years and the rum was starting to make his jowls puffy, give him broken veins and bags under the eyes. It was a reminder that they weren't getting any younger, the frequent missions starting to finally take their toll. They'd been on many together and a flash of remorse washed over Morgan for an instant when he thought about what he was planning to do, then it was gone, his mind back on the task at hand.

"We're lucky it's not a full moon and there's cloud about," Morgan said, "but looks like a storm's on its way...we'd better make haste. The breach in The Satisfaction's hull won't stand too rough a tide."

Wicks knew the captain was right. He'd seen the breach up close and he could see that it wouldn't resist high seas. Not only, but by the way the trees were moving above, a storm was arriving, and he already guessed the voyage to Port Royal might not be a smooth one. Taking a lantern from the clearing floor, Wicks walked to the hole, to see the progress made. Looking down he could see that the two men at the bottom were sweaty and grimy with mud. They glared up, the hard work, heat and dirt turning to resentment. Wicks sized up the space. It was not quite eight by eight, but it would have to do. The time it would take to dig another few feet wasn't worth risking The Satisfaction for.

Wicks nodded to the captain. "It's deep enough. Put the chest in lads," he shouted to the group of buccaneers on the left who had taken the digging turn before last and were swigging rum from one of the remaining flasks.

The men heaved up the chest. It seemed heavier than before, exhaustion had made sure of that, then carefully, they lowered it to the bottom of the pit on coarse hemp ropes.

Then the shooting began.

Morgan took the first aim with his left musket. Two shots and two men on the left of the clearing fell hitting the sodden earth with a thud. Spice was next, taken by Wicks with a bullet between the eyes. Spragge was the fourth.

Then Bates. He was shot in the back as he took a dash to the edge of the clearing. The captain finished off another buccaneer with his second pistol and left the last two men for Wicks. They were down in the hole with the chest and didn't stand a chance. Within seconds, pistols smoking, all eight buccaneers were dead.

It was then that an eerie sound descended on the clearing – Howler monkeys - high in the jungle canopy. Their primordial screams carried over the night's air as if demons had been let loose on the island, but Morgan didn't flinch. He knew the noises of the jungle well and didn't fear them.

Moving quickly, Wicks dragged Bates, Spragge, Spice, and the bodies of the other men to the hole and rolled them in. They fell with a thud on the top of the chest. Perhaps the men hadn't wondered well about why the hole had been so big for an average sized trunk, but if they'd been alive to see the scene it would've all fallen into place now.

Then Morgan turned to the Banyan Tree.

The girl was still there, behind an enormous, tangle of moss and roots. She was barely visible, but with closer scrutiny her eyes reflected in the light of the lamps. She moved into the clearing and looked down into the pit.

"May the spirit of the forest take their souls," she said, making a semi cross over her chest. She turned to the captain. "Morgan, mi darling, what makes you bring mi to witness an awful 'ting as this, me being the woman ya love?"

The captain raised his pistol. "I'm sorry, Lotta, but you know, I just can't trust you with all that's in that chest." Her yellow eyes flashed with realization, and even though the oil lanterns were almost out, the flames low, they still cast a dying brown light on the clearing, and for a second she seemed to glow in it.

"Morgan, no, my love I..."

A flash of white, the force of pistol fire, her body crumpled on the clearing floor.

To an untrained eye, for a second, Morgan seemed to catch his breath.

"Better than you having to cut her throat," came Wicks' voice from behind, from the encroaching dark on the other side of the pit.

Pistol still smoking Morgan put it on the floor, picked up the waif-like body, almost gently, and rolled it into the pit along with the other men.

Wicks and Morgan worked quickly then. Morgan wanted the earth to be well packed, the pit completely hidden. He was taking no chances. The chest was worth too much to him to finish the job badly. The island was remote, the clearing well hidden, but in these parts you could never tell. Someone could land, find the clearing and if not well concealed, the chest. And then there was The Satisfaction crew. They could plot a return, seek out the chest, find the clearing. Not only, but he didn't know when he might be back. It would all depend on his final cut of booty from this trip not to mention the state of his plantation and finances. Before heading out he'd heard a blight had taken out a neighboring sugar cane plantation. All had been lost. He'd been gone for weeks and didn't know what he'd find back in Jamaica. A return trip could be months, even years later. So, he wanted no trace...he needed to be the only living sole to know the chest was there, and he trusted no one.

The trees above were swaying harder now, the storm percolating above like a brew of black coffee raising to the boil, so they finished the job in haste with no time for a separate grave for the men. It would be unpleasant digging up the chest whenever he got back, unearthing not just his prized booty but the decomposing bodies too, but he'd seen worse and he knew he could stomach it.

Within minutes they were heading back to the cove, Wicks in the lead, back on the trail they had already cut, making as best they could with the last two failing lamps. Then taking a rowboat, pushing it down from the beach, into the sea.

Pulling hard on the oars, they labored back to the ship, a looming black silhouette on the horizon.

"With the sails up The Satisfaction'll *make good speed with this wind behind her," Morgan said, almost shouting to be heard above the crashing waves which were breaking on the reef, even stronger now with the wind behind them.*

"Let's just hope she'll hold until Port Royal - and with just a handful of men on board to sail her – t'won't be easy."

"It's been done before," Wicks returned with determination and a grimace, indicating that pulling the rowboat along in the swell was no easy feat.

Morgan knew he was right. They'd make it back, even if limping. He'd make sure of it, though he was conscious that a little light was starting to seep out low on the horizon on the right, a sign that dawn was soon breaking and that with Marquez on their trail they had to get moving fast.

It took them a good amount of time with just the two of them on the oars, fighting the wind and waves, which were stirring more and more with the approaching storm, but soon they surpassed the reef and were getting closer to the ship.

"At least the treasure is safe," said Wicks. "Safe as a... what the...."

It came as a surprise to Wicks. He'd been by Morgan's side for the last five years. He'd trusted Morgan and Morgan had trusted him. Until now. But greed does strange things to men. Desperate men. And although the captain never seemed desperate, he was. He was tired of forever sailing the ocean for plunder. He craved a quieter life with his wife Mary on his sugar plantation in Jamaica. And he intended to do it in style. He wasn't going to share or risk his future, even with Wicks. So, Wicks just had to go. He was sorry, but if truth be told, just for the seconds it took to push Wicks body over the side into the sea. The days were ruthless and the men ruthless with them and Morgan was no different to the rest.

Slowly, and some who didn't know him well might say with a little heaviness, the captain climbed up the rope ladder on The Satisfaction *and landed himself on deck. The remaining crew gathered to his side. He could see in the creeping morning light from the east that they were ragtag bunch of a crew at that; a dreg compared to that which he'd set sail with weeks ago. Most had wounds, they were tired and worn thin to the bone. They gathered around, faces hard, dirty, and questioning.*

"Natives," he said aloud so they all could hear. "We were ambushed. All are gone. It's a miracle to god that I survived."

The men were silent and still, taking in the news, weighing the captain's words in the humid, salty morning air, the sound of the reef and the creaking rigging of the boat the only noise for a good while.

"All?" shouted Mr. Roberts, the ships doctor from the back of the group. "All dead? That's strikes me as mighty strange." He pushed forward and faced the captain. "And Wicks?"

"Wicks too," said the captain, turning to Mr. Roberts and fixing back his eye with grim determination.

"Like I said, natives. We got to shore, made it into the jungle, and mayhem ensued. I made it back to the cove, lost sight of the men in the jungle. But I heard and saw enough. I managed to get the boat down the beach, out into the sea in the cove and waited there a good while to see if any men would make it back to the beach. Aye, I waited at least an hour by my reckoning, but nothing. I heard plenty of screams though. The devil only knows what fate had in store for them. But 'tis for certain they're all dead, god rest their souls."

"How can you be sure they're all dead? We should go back, see if any survived!" shouted one buccaneer at the back.

"Impossible," said the captain, turning to face the man. "We've just one rowboat left, and Marquez is on our tail. It's almost dawn and we have a hole in the hull the size of a barrel with a storm coming up. I say we set sail. Does anyone say otherwise? If so, speak now. Let's hear it!"

A mumbling went around the men. It travelled from one side of the ship to the other. Mr. Roberts took another step closer, fixing Morgan again, studying his face. The men went silent. A moment passed. Then he nodded to Morgan and the men and moved over to the captain's side and addressed the crew, it seemed as second in command.

"The captain's right. I'm with him. It's too dangerous to go back now. We should press on, but only if he can promise us right here and now that we'll get the share of the silver due to the men who've been lost. That seems only fair. What do you say, captain? What do you say to me and the men?"

"I give you my word," said the captain addressing the group. "With so few of us now there be more silver and plunder for those left here tonight. I guarantee you that."

At that a subdued mumbling went around the crew.

"And that chest?" said Mr. Roberts, turning back to the captain. "What of that? You never did explain to the crew what was in that chest and where it is now."

"That's not for this crew," said Morgan, also turning to facing Mr. Roberts straight on.

"We all agreed to that from the outset. Just one item, to be kept out of the spoils. Everyone here tonight signed up to that, and I'm not about to change it now. The chest is mine, always was, and it's of no concern to the men, or to you, Mr. Roberts. But like I say, the rest of the booty to be shared equally. So men, do you all agree?"

The crew glanced around and after some muttering said aye. Morgan then addressed the crew. "Let's make haste! Brace the main sail – and look lively about it. We're sailing for Port Royal this morning and an extra half bag of silver for each of you from my personal spoils if we get there in five nights instead of six!"

There was a loud cheer and the ship was once again a hive of activity. In minutes, the sail was up, billowing, full to the brim of wind and the boat was ploughing through the ocean. The reef was soon behind, the course set and Morgan back in his cabin.

The captain was a drinker, but in moderation by the standards of the day. He took a decanter out of a padlocked cupboard and poured himself a measured glass of quality rum in his favorite cut crystal glass. The candlelight twinkled on the crisscross patterns precisely cut into its breadth as Morgan took a sip. It had been a bittersweet night. The captain was known for the fair treatment of his men and nobody would imagine the slaughter he had perpetrated on the island. On arriving back in Port Royal, he knew there'd be hordes of men ready to join his crew again. Not a bad thing, He wouldn't want to leave the chest there too long. He needed the contents now. But he knew that this time the crew would talk, speculate, that his story didn't quite add up. As he took another sip of rum, he ruminated that he needed to formulate more detail. He needed to sound convincing if pressed about it. This type of tale would be told, recounted, and passed around the drinking holes of Port Royal for years to come. But on this he wasn't greatly concerned. He'd done it once before and he'd do it again and in a blink. And he knew that if Port Royal appeared on the horizon within the week, he'd be fine. The only niggle was Mr. Roberts. He sensed Roberts was suspicious, that he knew something was afoot. He mulled it over, finishing the rum and then, just to be sure, got up and he turned the key in the lock on the door of his small but comfortable cabin.

Once done, he took a seat in front of a large worm-infested wooden table he used for his maps. These were the best maps to be had, commissioned from the honorable Mr. Smith-Brown, official map maker of Port Royal. He studied them again using an eyeglass made for the job. He wanted to be certain he hadn't made any mistakes. No, he was sure. The island was not shown.

It was completely missing from the detail of the inlets and islands which peppered Bocas del Toro. A nice and useful mistake if ever there was one. He could be certain that, officially at least, only he, his crew, and handful of buccaneers who had crossed these waters knew that the island was there. The chest and its contents should be safe, buried deep and concealed in the clearing. Pouring himself a second glass of rum, he mused over the alternative. If only he could've gotten it safely back to Port Royal on The Satisfaction *on this voyage. He could've immediately paid for the construction of his new sugar plantation house and more. But much as he wanted the gold now, his retirement projects already pressing on him heavily, he knew that he would have to be patient. He would have to return one day to claim it. He just couldn't've taken the risk with the Spanish on his tail. Just the thought of Marquez getting his hands on this precious hoard. No, he'd prefer to bide his time, take his chances and leave it on that god forsaken island than risk it to the Spanish.*

He took out the parchment so carefully folded into his pocket on the island where he had marked the exact location of the chest and set about reducing it in size with a sharp, silver fruit knife. Eventually it was small enough to be folded into a tiny square of paper. He took tweezers and placed it into a large gold locket and then brought over his finest red wax candle to seal the locket with hot molten wax. Turning it in his hand while it cooled, he admired the trinket intensely and with great pleasure before taking a small metal box from a draw and placing it inside. Sealing this with wax too, he placed the metal casket inside the ship's safe. Turning the key in his hand, he strung it on a chain and put it over his head.

"Someone'll have to kill me before they get their hands on my loot," he said to himself with a satisfied grimace before poring himself another large glass of dark, molasses rum.

Chalk Farm, London,

Now

If you asked me today, if you said, “Melody, what made you get on that plane, travel halfway across the world to Panama? What changed your mind? What prompted you to go?” I’d take out my tobacco tin and papers, roll a cigarette, light it, take in the smoke and reflect. If I could, I’d pour myself a glass of Amaro, take a sip and think some more. Then I’d likely say that time is a strange manipulator. It often blurs the sentiments of a moment. Feelings and decisions which were once clear somehow don’t seem quite so obvious, even days, weeks or months later.

But this is different.

I can remember the precise moment with clarity.

Sitting on the Terrace of Infinity in Ravello, looking down onto the Mediterranean stretching far off to the horizon, I spotted a little white sailboat.

The sun had just gone down, and the little boat bobbed into view from behind a peninsular on my right. I watched it cross the horizon on its way back to port. It was starting to get dark, but I could still just make out that it was an old wooden boat, with a white hull and sails and, against the ocean I could see the outline, small but clear, of four men, silhouettes against the sea. The wind was soft, but a sound travelled up from the boat to where I was sitting – the hint of talking, laughing, some music. A little onboard boat party was taking place amongst friends.

Listening to that sound my mind went back to the photo on the wall in Spencer's apartment. Spencer on a boat in the Caribbean with his friends, loving life, and how his life had been cut short, how he was no more. Just the thought of that almost sucked the spirit out of me and, in that instant, I knew. I needed closure. I needed to know: Accident or murder.

Perhaps if the little boat had taken a different course that day, the rest of my life would've been different. Not a taxi to the airport, a plane and a transatlantic trip to Panama. Instead, more lazy days by the pool and a flight back to London. Then Chalk Farm, tidying up the Facebook feature and submitting it to Jake. Meeting Emma for a drink after an evening stroll on Primrose Hill. The *Zenith* office, holding my breath, fingers crossed, studying Jake's face in the hope that Mac liked the feature. Perhaps some more Tinder dating…

Of course, that never happened, and the course of events were very different…

It's autumn now. Winter is on its way.

I'm back at my cozy kitchen table and, as I continue to type this story, the condensation is building up inside on the window. It's getting colder now too. I just turned on the radiator.

I reach for a blanket and wrap it over my legs, reminding myself to start saving for that double glazing I promised myself. (I say the same thing every November and never do.)

The bright, sunny Terrace of Infinity is so worlds apart from the cold, dreary scene outside and the cozy one inside for that matter.

And so is the Melody of then compared to the Melody of now.

Some might say that the Melody of then was naïve. I think perhaps that's true. After all, sitting on the Terrace of Infinity, watching that little boat bobbing across the horizon, I don't think I really understood that everyone has their secrets. Nor did I understand the true nature of nightmares. I sometimes wonder if the bad dreams will ever let go once they've entered your sleep, entered your days, like unpleasant house guests overstaying their welcome, following you around wherever you go.

But most important of all I've realized that there might even be something far worse than murder.

Betrayal.

Chapter Fourteen

The flight was eleven hours via Madrid. Somewhere over the Atlantic, after the food and drinks trolley had passed around, and we'd settled in for the long haul. I shared my idea with Marco. It was simple enough - check into the same hotel as Bruno, try and tail him, see what he was up to, where he was going, who he was meeting. We'd have to stay out of sight, while at the same time be careful not to lose him. Of course, I'd never done anything like this before and had no idea how easy or hard it would be. But the night before, after packing my bag in Ravello, I'd gone online, checked out the details of the Hotel Miramar and a quick scan indicated it was big, impersonal, and corporate - which was good news. We could probably stay out of sight, incognito, in a hotel like that. We'd have to be careful though. We knew if he saw Marco, it would be game over and although he'd met me just the once at the funeral, the problem was my distinctive, short red hair. I tended to stand out from the crowd and there was every chance he'd recognize me. To compensate I'd already picked up a big floppy sun hat and new sunglasses during the transfer in Madrid. A corny disguise, but chances were that Bruno would never recognize me in it, even if I was right in front to him.

"We'll need to rent a car, to tail him from the Miramar," Marco pointed out, draining the last from his mini screw top of red into a plastic cup and taking a swig. "I'm happy to drive and I've got my license with me so that shouldn't be a problem," he added, as if reading my mind.

"Great, I was going to ask you about that," I said, thankful he was willing to take on the driving, which had never been my strong suit.

The plane landed, just after 5pm local time. We knew Bruno was on the earlier KLM flight and should've landed already by a couple of hours. Passport and customs seemed to take forever; our bags were the last off the carousel. Eventually we emerged from the terminal into the early Panamanian evening.

I'd read on the internet that it was 'winter' in Panama – and the forecast looked about right. Winter in Panama meant rainy and hot, the combination of which enveloped us like a hot wet towel in a sauna as soon as we stepped out of the terminal building.

"It's a bit chilly," Marco said sarcastically, grinning and taking off his glasses to wipe off the condensation while I fumbled with an umbrella. It was now 6:30 p.m., still 35 degrees and bucketing down.

We were soon in a taxi and speeding along a darkening highway, the wipers working overtime, the lights of Panama City, blurry through the rain on the horizon. It was surreal and such a far cry from the streets of London or Rome. Banks of modern high rises twinkled in the distance, looming like monolithic giants rising from the surrounding flat green belt. And then we arrived, from a semi-lit, concrete underpass, thrust into the city: a jumble of shining towers, malls, apartment blocks and hotels. Sweeping down from a flyover, within seconds we were cruising around the central bay.

"Look, Hotel Miramar," said Marco, pointing ahead as we approached and just before we swerved to turn left and enter the hotel forecourt. Full of palms, banana trees, and a host of tropical vegetation, I couldn't help thinking that it looked like something out of a stage set for Jurassic Park.

The Miramar was big and flashy, but from a decade or so back. The lobby was shiny and polished to within an inch of its life. It was colored and cut-glass crystal overload. Not my cup of tea but then we weren't there to admire the interior decoration. At least it looked clean, had all the amenities and, most importantly of all, was where Bruno should be staying.

Within minutes we'd checked in, I'd taken a shower and was on my way down in the lift to meet Marco in the hotel bar. It was a strange feeling knowing Bruno was in the same hotel, somewhere. Perhaps he was taking a shower, watching TV in his room. Perhaps the lift would stop on floor 2 and he'd get in, perhaps he was already sitting at the bar enjoying a drink. Fact was it was impossible to relax knowing I could come face to face with him at any time. Worse still were the questions in my mind, questions I couldn't shake: 'What in god's name was I doing there?' 'Half-baked plan or best thing I'd ever done in my life?' being the two most front and center.

Pushing aside this mounting unease, and with a constant eye out for Bruno, I soon found the hotel bar on the ground floor. It was at the back of the hotel and overlooked a marina which was crowded with boats gently bobbing in what looked like a low tide. It had stopped raining but there were still the flashes and flares of an electrical storm in the sky.

The bar was perfect; dark and discreet with plenty of booths, where we could meet while remaining tucked out of sight. I selected a booth at the back, ordered a Mojito from a very smiley waiter called Luis and waited for Marco.

"Hi, how's things?" Marco said strolling up, dropping down into the seat opposite. "Did you freshen up? I feel so jet lagged – like awake and dead all at the same time."

"You're not ready for 'Operation Treasure Seeker?'" I smiled. Marco grinned back and waved over the waiter.

"Actually, if you really want to know, I'm wondering what the hell I'm doing in Panama. But what the heck. I'm here now, right? What's that?" He said pointing to my drink which happened to be one of the largest Mojitos I'd ever seen.

"If it's a Mojito I might just join you. Looks good." Luis came over. He ordered and then turned back to me.

"OK, listen," I said, trying to put out of my mind how Marco was looking quite handsome in the soft, mellow light of the bar. Why did I find men in glasses so attractive? Or was this one just growing on me…

"I just took a quick look around the place. It's perfect I think," I said, pausing as the waiter returned with another smile, another huge Mojito and two heavily iced glasses of water.

"What do you mean?" he asked taking a sip of the Mojito once the waiter had moved on.

"First I think we should double check – I mean check that he's actually staying here. We don't want to screw up on that and find out in two days he never checked in, had a change of plan. So, I'll see if I can find out from Reception. Like, I don't know, maybe say something about my friend Bruno is staying here, I want to meet him for breakfast, did he check in yet? Then assuming I get the confirmation, how about this. Like we discussed on the plane, we come down to breakfast super early. We can take a corner table I spotted just before. It's tucked out of the way but has a great view all the way to the reception and entrance. That way we can see when Bruno comes down and leaves. Before that though we need to try and rent a car. My guess is that Bruno will use taxis to get around or else he'll hire a car too – so we need to have one ready to follow him around. I heard someone on reception telling a client that's what most people do here – get taxi's or a car. Apparently, they're easy to pick up and just a few dollars a ride – the taxis that is. That or Uber. But he's sure to do something like that. I don't see him using public transport. If we've got a car, we can follow him anywhere he goes by taxi, Uber or even if he's driving himself. If we're careful that he doesn't clock us of course. I just hope Bruno doesn't leave so early – like before breakfast. We can't camp down here after all. Oh, and by the way, the AVIS office only opens at 8:30. If he does leave earlier, we'll just have to try and wing it."

Marco nodded in agreement. "And what did you mean about this place being perfect?"

"Oh, sorry, yes, - just that it's big, and there are plenty of quiet corners and hopefully it'll help us not come face to face with him. The only real issue is the lift. I guess we can try and find out what floor he's on and try and avoid it. Like even take the stairs if necessary."

"Have you done this before?" he grinned, taking another sip of the Mojito. "Like were you a detective in another life?" I blushed and felt a little proud of myself. The plan for day one was set.

Back in my room later that night, my head was spinning. Two huge mojitos, being up for 24 hours, jet lag and too much excitement about being in Panama was all adding up. Part of me was excited, sure I'd done the right thing embarking on this 'adventure.' But the other half of me was still wondering what the hell I was doing on this hair brained romp in Central America - and persuading Marco along too. I started to feel responsible. I mean, Bruno the mild-mannered senior lecturer, dealing illegally in historical artifacts? Even murder? Now I was here, thousands of miles away from home, I was beginning to wonder if Marco and I had dreamt the whole thing up too and if so, it was my fault for dragging Marco to the other side of the world. Still, I reminded myself - I'd seen the Atlas email with my own eyes and now Bruno was back here. That was a fact you couldn't get away from. Had he murdered Spencer? Whether it was murder or not, what if Bruno was into something deeply illegal? I didn't fancy having to deal with the Panamanian police, who didn't have the best reputation in the world. Not to mention if Bruno was linked with criminals now. From the little I'd seen of Panama City – just from the drive in, this city had a mix of slums and super rich. No doubt there were drugs gangs and all kinds of stuff going on here, you could bet it. They didn't call the high rises here the 'cocaine towers' for nothing. Bruno could be dealing with a Panamanian Mafia, who knows what. And if Bruno was involved in selling whatever he'd found in the criminal underworld I for one wasn't planning on taking any chances coming face to face with them.

And then there was Marco…he'd looked quite cute after two mojitos…

I set my alarm for 5:45 a.m. and then laid awake for most of the night, thoughts of Spencer, Marco, Bruno, and what the hell I was doing in Panama doing a salsa in my head…

Chapter Fifteen

We'd arranged to meet in the hotel restaurant for breakfast at 6 a.m. I'd just drifted off to sleep when the damn alarm went off. With just a few minutes to jump out of bed, shower, get dressed, and get an adequate coating of mascara and lip gloss in the right places, I headed down the stairs.

When I got to the restaurant Marco was already there, looking as fresh as a daisy. "How did you sleep?" I quizzed, amazed that he'd beaten me down and already had scrambled eggs in front of him.

"As they say, like a baby," he smiled taking a sip from a jumbo-sized cappuccino. Were all the drinks made for giants over here?

"What you woke up every hour crying?' I smiled back.

"Something like," he said, grinning. "Hey, want one of these? Not quite Italian cappuccino but not so bad…" He beckoned over the waitress before I could speak, he already knew the answer.

"*Dos mas,*" he said pointing at the cappuccino. "*Gracias.*"

"I got down here just as they were opening up, but no sign of him yet," he said, turning to me. "Did you check on reception?"

"Sure, I came down to speak with the receptionist before I went to bed last night. I didn't want her to know which room the enquiry was coming from, just in case they mentioned it to him. This young receptionist, very nice, called Doris, said yes, he checked in earlier that night. She even gave me his room number, he's in 1534. That's 11 floors above us. Asked if I had a message for him. Of course, I said no. I mean, really, she could get into trouble you know. They're not supposed to do that, I mean give out guest room numbers, information. Glad she did though!"

"Great, that's good to know," said Marco. "I mean that he's actually here and I suggest that as we're just on the fourth floor, we take the stairs. I for one don't want to blow this by coming face to face with him in the lift."

The two cappuccinos arrived, and after taking a glug, while the coast was clear, I grabbed a few bits and pieces from the breakfast buffet, keeping one eye through to the lobby and reception while I was at it. No sign of Bruno. Unlike us he was probably having a lie in. Then the waiting game started. It seemed like hours. It was hours. No sign of Bruno. I was already getting bored and it was only the first morning.

When 8:30 came around, Marco jumped up. "Keep an eye out. I'm off to AVIS to get that car we need hired. I'll just be over there," he said, indicating at the AVIS office to the left of the entrance.

"Hey, let's check our phones are working," I said, pulling out mine. "I want to be sure I can text you if I need to." Once done, Marco headed off and I sat and read my iPad while keeping an eye on the lobby. By habit, I always checked the newsfeeds, read The Times cover to cover, whenever I could, and my Hotmail inbox got a once over too. Nothing was happening back home on the work front. The European summer holidays continued, with most offices running on empty, half the staff no doubt on Mediterranean breaks by now. I skimmed The Times and checked Twitter again.

And suddenly, there he was. Bruno.

I didn't spot him immediately. He looked different in a linen shirt, knee length shorts, and a Panama hat, but it was him for sure. Tall, gaunt, and slightly stooped, with a soft looking brown leather satchel under his left arm. There he was at the reception, chatting with the concierge, and then he was heading in my direction. Turning away as he came into the restaurant, out of the corner of my eyes I could see him finding a table, putting down his room key and satchel, and then we was over to the buffet and ordering coffee. Thankfully, he didn't give my end of the restaurant a second glance. Just to be sure though, I put on my hat and, finding my phone, texted Marco.

"He's here having breakfast! How's it going? How long till we get the car sorted?"

"Almost done," he came back right away. "Meet me in the AVIS office. Come now."

I grabbed my things, stuffed them into my backpack and, with a '*Gracias*' to the waitress, headed out.

Marco was taking the rental keys just as I arrived at AVIS. "Good timing," I said, glancing back to the hotel reception. "I think he'll be out soon – depends on how long he takes over breakfast. I don't think he'll go back to his room. Had a satchel with him. My guess is that he'll be heading straight out."

"Good," said Marco. "Let's find the car and find a spot to park where we can see him leaving the hotel. I did a quick look around last night before going to bed and think I found just the spot, just hope someone else hasn't parked in it."

"Great!" I said, "I'm impressed!"

"This way." Marco took the lead and we headed down two floors in the lift to a large, underground parking facility.

"She said that it's a white Hyundai, parked in bay number 23," Marco said, glancing around. "Over there!"

Once in the car, it took him a couple of minutes to figure out the dashboard, to get the gears into automatic, then we were pulling out, heading up the ramp into the bright sunlight of a fresh, Panamanian morning. There wasn't cloud in the sky.

"Shit. The parking spot I had in mind's gone!" said Marco, frowning.

"What now?"

"Damn. Let me think," he said, turning around to get a good look at the options. "We'll have to park outside the hotel entrance, I think we can, just on the left. Let's see. It might work. I think from there we might just have a view of the taxis and cars that exit the hotel. We need to be able to see if Bruno's inside. We're assuming he's going to get a taxi, but he might take an Uber or even hire an AVIS too. We need to keep our eyes peeled on everything coming out of the hotel just to be sure. Then we can try and tail him from there."

"OK Starskey," I said.

"What?" He glanced over, looking puzzled.

"Starskey and Hutch? The TV show from the seventies?" I said. Marco looked blank. "Never mind." Clearly Marco's British upbringing didn't stretch as far as bad seventies cop shows.

"He's wearing a Panama hat," I told him. "If he keeps it on, it should be easy to spot him."

Marco swung out and down the short hotel drive onto the road outside. Pulling up to park at the spot he'd suggested we had and OK view of the taxis and cars as they stopped to pull out into the oncoming traffic. We were there just fifteen minutes, then…

"There he is!" I jumped up in my seat. "I just got a silhouette of him, I'm sure it's him, in the back of that yellow taxi coming out now."

Right enough it was him in the back. The taxi pulled up giving us a five second view. Panama hat off now and concentrated on a mobile phone, I got a good side profile of him, before the taxi edged out into the morning rush hour flow. In a second Marco had also put his foot on the gas and pulled out and pushed his way into a spot directly behind. I was impressed with his maneuvering, but we'd only just got started and it wasn't easy keeping up. It was a little after 9 a.m. and the morning traffic was intense and, while it was moving at a steady pace, there were cars constantly changing lanes, moving in and out, barging here and there. It was a different style of driving to Rome and Marco would have to get used to it and fast if we had any chance of keeping up. Bruno's taxi continued along Avenida Balboa, a three-lane highway, which swept along the bay, then pulled into the left-hand lane before taking a left turn into a busy main street. Marco managed to stay right behind by almost skipping a red. Then, after another two minutes, the taxi slowed down before pulling up outside a block of modern office buildings in what looked like a bustling financial district. We pulled up a little way back on the opposite side of the road and watched as Bruno got out, satchel still in hand, and strolled into a modern glass and silver high rise. Over the entrance it said Banco General.

"I'll go in," I said to Marco, "Try and see what he's doing,"

"OK. Be careful," said Marco, passing me my hat and sunglasses from the back seat.

I slipped out of the car, and dodging oncoming traffic, crossed the road, stuck on the hat, and headed in.

Inside it was air conditioned and extremely cool. The entrance opened into a large lobby area. People were buzzing around everywhere. The working day was clearly underway. On the right a row of cashier windows and a long line of customers waiting to be served filled the space. On the left a series of desks and seated bank employees having one on one conversations, consultations with clients was in full flow. For a second, I panicked, thought I'd lost sight of him but then I spotted him at the far side, in front of a row of management offices shaking hands with a young bank employee. Then after what looked like a polite chat, the clerk was leading him towards a door. Above it was written '*Cajas de seguridad.*' Then he disappeared inside. I took a seat on one of a cluster of sofas by the entrance and tried to look occupied on my phone while keeping an eye on the door at the back. Around fifteen minutes later, Bruno reappeared with the same young clerk. They shook hands and he strolled out. After waiting a couple of second I followed him out and saw that the taxi was still waiting for him, and he was getting in. And something struck me. Was it the satchel? Did it look slightly fuller? He was carrying it across his shoulder now. As quickly as I could without getting run over, I dashed across the road and jumped in next to Marco, and within seconds we were pulling out a few cars behind and tailing him again.

"*Cajas de seguridad*?" said Marco, glancing over as he was driving. "You know what that means, right?" My Spanish was bad, I had no idea. "Safe deposit boxes!" said Marco. "Safe deposit boxes! I can't believe it. I bet he's gone in there to collect something! If he did, whatever it is - it's relatively small and he's got it in that satchel he's carrying."

This was starting to add up. Marco had been right all along. Bruno had something in that bag. Something worth enough to keep it in a security deposit box at the bank. Something he had with him now and was taking who knows where for god knows what. I'd seen this kind of thing in films. I couldn't believe it was happening for real, here in Panama and with Marco on I on the scent.

"I mean, I've heard about safe deposit boxes but, well, I've never ever seen one or known anyone who uses them. I can't believe it." I said looking hard at Marco as he concentrated on the traffic. I was electrified.

We continued following the taxi, no idea where we were heading or how long it would take. We didn't know the city, so we might have been going to the best part of town or to the worst, most dangerous part. It was a disconcerting thought. Marco was concentrating on not losing the taxi while trying to navigate the chaotic lanes of traffic. It wasn't easy. To make it harder, all the taxis were yellow and a lot of them were beat up and rough around the edges; Bruno's was no different.

Despite all the confusion and our overall navigational challenges, we soon realized that we were heading in a loop back in the opposite direction.

"There's the hotel Miramar," I pointed out as we went sailing by on the right side this time.

"Hey, let me put on roaming. Will cost me a bomb but at least we can try and get a sense of the city and where we might be heading via Google Maps."

"Great idea," said Marco as he concentrated on getting past the next set of lights so not to be left too far behind and risk losing him for good.

As quickly as I could, I got onto Google Maps and a blue dot pinpointed where we were and where we seemed to be heading. And glancing around it looked like we were approaching a different part of town. My Google Maps told me this was called 'Casco Viejo.'

The layout and buildings here were completely different to the bustling financial district in the modern part of the city. Clearly the old part, it looked like a mini Havana. Some buildings looked newly renovated, others were building sites under construction, and the rest were derelict, dilapidated, some mere shells, the facades revealing a tangle of weeds, trees and garbage at the center where once the core of the building used to be. It was a strange mix. The roads were narrowing down, cobbled and one way. The traffic slowed down to a crawl. It wasn't that there was so much traffic, just that the roads weren't really built for it at all. Locals hung around on street corners, salsa blasted out from what looked like squats and cheap local joints to eat or drink. I wasn't sure how safe this place was and was starting to feel nervous. Then suddenly a few blocks in it started to look more upmarket, and we spotted tourists – they were here and there, some taking snaps of what looked like the central square, of the churches and were generally wandering around.

Bruno was a couple of cars ahead by now, but we hadn't lost him yet. It was easier to tail him here in just one line of slow-moving cars.

Then his taxi swung left, cruised around a square and parked. Bruno got out and light-footed it into what looked like a large, newly renovated, colonial style building. There was no sign outside, but Marco, glancing down pointed at my screen and tapped on an icon. A photo and advert popped up.

"The American Trade Hotel. I bet that's it. Very nice. Looks classy and a bit high end. I'm relieved, I have to say. Some of those places we passed back there looked really dodgy. I'm grateful we didn't have to get out and try and follow him into one of those."

"I'll go in again," I said, making to jump out, conscious that it would be easy to lose sight of him somewhere like this.

I was soon in the lobby, and just in time. Bruno was disappearing into the lift and in seconds to the doors slid shut. Pulling out my phone, I sent Marco a text. "He's gone up in the lift. My guess is to a room. Waiting in lobby." Then I had an idea. "When he comes back down, let's split up." I typed in. "You follow him in the car. I'll wait here, see if anyone comes down, someone with the satchel perhaps. Who knows? But worth a try?"

"OK, Roger," Marco responded. I smiled. OK he'd seen some of those crappy TV cop shows after all.

There was nothing to do except wait in the lobby. This 'detective work' could be dull, I decided right then. But at least it gave me time to take in the surroundings. The American Trade Hotel was large, cavernous, cream and colonial in style. Heavy designed patterned mocha tiles paved the floors. Huge parlor palms and large ceiling fans circulated the heavily air-conditioned air. It was mid-morning and I could see local businessmen already meeting colleagues, perhaps planning to do deals over an early lunch.

I'd being sitting in an armchair with a good view of the lifts when just fifteen minutes later Bruno emerged. This time I noticed immediately. The satchel was gone.

"Wooah,"' I said almost out loud to myself. Marco had been right. He'd handed something over and whatever it was it had been in that bag. But where's the cash? The email talked about cash. Maybe he was collecting it later? Phone at the ready, I buzzed Marco. "He's on his way out. Stay in touch. See you back at the hotel."

I kept my eyes on the lift. It was busy with guests coming in and out. A young couple, laughing and joking, and older couples, they looked like American retirees. Then suddenly out came two men in suits. And one was carrying the satchel. I glanced down at my phone as they glanced around. One definitely clocked me in the corner chair. I was glad for the hat and cursed that I hadn't had my sunglasses on too, but it was too late for that now. Watching out of the corner of my eye, and trying not to make it obvious, I followed them as they went over to reception. It looked like they were checking out, settling a bill, passing over a credit card and signing the slip. While they were doing that and trying not to make it obvious, I angled my phone to get a couple of photos. They looked Asian, maybe Chinese. Both had buzz cuts, smart suits, and sunglasses. One was slim and medium height, the other not very tall and stocky. Then they were strolling out, with the satchel under the arm of the short one on the right. Careful not to follow too closely behind, given these guys had clocked me once already, I strolled down what I guessed was '*Avenida Central,*' Then up ahead, I saw them stopping, before getting into a large black four-by-four. I hung back, stepping onto the shade of a shop doorway, and pretended to check my phone as the four-by-four slowly cruised by. I couldn't see a thing inside: All the windows were mirrored.

I met Marco back at the hotel.

"Well he went out of Casco and back onto *Avenida Balboa*,"' he said, flopping on the armchair in my room on the fourth floor, the view of the entire bay of Panama City behind him. It was almost midday, the sun was bright, and I was still melting so I turned the aircon up two notches.

"We sailed past the *Miramar* again and right back to Banco General. I followed him in and this time he waited in the lobby and an older guy came out. They shook hands, talked for a while, then he took him over to the cashier's line. I had to hang back a bit. I didn't want him to see me but anyway it didn't matter, it was easy to see what was going on. He pulled an envelope out of his shirt pocket and then handed over a cheque. He signed various papers, I guess to pay it in. Then he walked out and was into the taxi back to the hotel. It's odd as I was expecting a cash deposit, but that's what happened. Perhaps cash just wasn't doable in the end for some reason."

I quickly brought him up to date on the two guys from the hotel and showed him the photos on my phone. The quality wasn't bad. You could seem them well if you used the zoom function. I'd also managed to get a blurry shot of the license place of the black four-by-four. What we'd do with the photos was another matter. For a moment we were silent, mulling it over. The silence said it all. We didn't really know what next. Marco said that Bruno had gone straight up to his room.

"I hung around in the lobby for a good while. Then Bruno appeared again, this time in his robe, with a book under his arm. I followed him out to the pool where he got a lounger and fell asleep."

I glanced down from my window. Even now I could see him stretched out in the sun. I couldn't be sure, but from up there he looked fast asleep. Whether he was or wasn't, it didn't look like he was going anywhere fast, possibly for the rest of the day.

After some down-time we met in the hotel bar that night. It was 7 p.m. and the city was coming alive around us. The high rises on the bay were twinkling again; a combination of glass, steel and concrete, and a harvest moon had just come into view. For a second it almost felt like a romantic vacation, not on some amateur detective romp with someone I barely knew.

"What next?" asked Marco, studying the large cocktail on the table in front of me, something with Vodka and some liquor I'd never heard of.

"Apparently it's called Electric Lemonade." I grinned to Marco as he eyed it up with trepidation and ordered a beer. "They had it on promotion and somehow that nice bar man Luis convinced me to try it. Want a sip?"

"Errr, no thanks," he said, smiling back, "Looks awful if you don't mind me saying. Any food or liquid that's blue shouldn't be allowed." I laughed. I liked his sense of humor, his candid approach to life. I liked him.

"Well," I said taking a sip of the cocktail as Marco nibbled on some nuts while he waited for his beer to arrive.

"I guess we'll just have to play it by ear, wing it, see what happens next. I mean anything could happen tomorrow. Who knows? I do hope that's not it though. I mean, is Bruno just going to hang out at the pool now? That would be boring and wouldn't get us very far. Today was pretty interesting, though, don't you think? I mean, it all adds up to him selling something on the black market. He definitely had something in a safe deposit box, sold it today to those two guys, whoever they are, and went back to the bank with a cheque."

"I agree," he said, taking a sip of what looked like the coldest beer this side of Siberia which smiley waiter Luis had just placed in front of him.

"But what next?"

"That's the trick, isn't it?" I said, pushing the Electric Lemonade aside.

"I mean, what hard evidence have we got and what more real evidence can we get for that matter?" I went on. "I don't think anything we've found would stand up if we took it to the police." For a moment I felt down, despondent. "I mean, maybe I hadn't thought this through very well, but as it looks now, Bruno may have cashed in the money from whatever he and Spencer found. He might be home and dry. Meantime we've got nothing to prove it and I don't know how we'd get it."

"And I'm still convinced something bad happened to Spencer," Marci said, , "something, you know, wrong, but how will we ever find out for sure, let alone prove it?" he added, scratching his head, taking off his glasses to clean them on a paper napkin. "If it were just the two of them on the boat, it's practically impossible to prove anything. Sorry, Melody, I think I've encouraged you into this whole thing from the beginning, without much, if anything to go on. I've always gone on my gut instinct. It's got me into all kinds of trouble on archaeological digs too, but this time maybe I've gone too far…"

We were silent for a few moments.

"Look Marco, let's not give up after day one," I said. "Think about what happened. He's definitely into something here. Only time will tell. Let's stick at it for a few more days and see where this goes. Who knows, right?"

"Right," he said looking a bit more cheerful again.

"You're, you're not pissed off then?" he asked, looking sheepish for the very first time. "I mean, really this whole thing was my idea in the first place."

"Absolutely not." I said, fixing his gaze. "In any case, I was the one that said let's come to Panama. That was my idea. And you know, there's nowhere else I'd rather be than here, right now. Somethings going on, and look, we're going to get to the bottom of it. One way of the other. For Spencer…"

He grinned back and for a moment we were silent, enjoying the salsa music, and I couldn't help noticing those brown, intelligent, studious, kind eyes again.

Chapter Sixteen

The next day, the same routine. Alarm at 5:45 a.m. Down to the breakfast room. Watching and waiting. Minutes and hours. No sign of Bruno. 11:30 a.m. and we were getting restless.

Something was up.

"Let me go over and see what I can figure out at reception. His room number is 1544, right?"

"Right. I think that's what you said when you checked yesterday," nodded Marco.

I went over the reception and said I'd like to use the phone to call my friend. They passed over the phone and I dialed his number. No response.

"Sorry," I called over to the receptionist. "I'm trying to get in touch with my friend. Bruno in room 1544, but he doesn't seem to be picking up."

"Oh, sure, that's right." The receptionist smiled back. "He took the early flight to Bocas del Toro this morning."

"He left? Checked out?" I said, trying to moderate my voice, so as not to sound too surprised."

"Yes, he got the early flight – it leaves Albrook Airport at 6:10 a.m. every morning."

"Shit. Well, what are we going to do?" asked Marco. I was back in the breakfast room. We were getting looks from the staff, they were trying to lay the tables for lunch. We were getting in the way.

"Well, it's clear, no? I think we've got to get on a flight and follow him. Let's go up to my room and book a flight to this place, Bocas, wherever that might be. The sooner the better too otherwise we'll totally lose the trail."

Up in my room, we opened my laptop and checked on flights to Bocas. The next was leaving that day at 5:40 p.m. and would get us to Bocas at 6:30 p.m. After booking two seats we started on some Bocas research. Some searches later all became clearer. Bocas del Toro was on the Caribbean side of Panama, just fifty minutes in a plane. A small town known as a bit of a hippy jumping off point to many of the beeches and islands of the locality, it had a reputation for surf, hippies and nature lovers. Most of the accommodation looked basic, single- or two-story wooden cabana types of thing.

Then I spotted it, Al Natural.

"That was the resort we'd found the number for on Bruno's telephone bill" I said, searching Marco's face for recognition.

In fact, we'd looked at the Al Natural website back in Rome, but it had said it was on Bastimentos Island. I hadn't connected it to Bocas. Until now.

"My money's on that's where he's gone. I'll put a $100 and an Electric Lemonade on it." I said, look up from the screen at Marco.

"We need to book a room there," said Marco.

"But wait, how big is this Al Natural place?"" I asked almost to myself, scanning through the Al Natural website on my laptop again to take another a look.

"Actually, look, it's small," I said, responding to my own question. "Tiny in fact – take a

Look." I knew I was right. Just ten cabañas, stretching in single file along the beach. The website said the room rate includes three meals a day all taken in the central cabin. There was a photo of a big wooden table. He got it immediately.

"OK. We can't stay there. We'd be face to face with Bruno in two minutes of arriving." Searching various sites, I checked out other options. They were limited. The island was small and practically uninhabited, in the middle of nowhere, out in the wilds. Then I came across it.

"Hotel Limbo. This might do," I said, cursing down the page.

A similar looking place down the beach from Al Natural. Google Maps told us it was a 15- or 20-minute walk away. Perfect. Close enough to keep an eye on Bruno, while not too close to be spotted. We still had some time to spare before the taxi pick up for the airport, so I booked us two rooms and arranged a boat pick up in Bocas. It would be dark by then, but the Limbo manager assured us that wasn't a problem. Provided the weather was calm, they did evening pick-ups all the time. Sorted.

"I hope you're right about this," said Marco on the way to the airport. I mean if Bruno's gone somewhere else, the trail is screwed.

So did I.

The flight was fifty minutes, the plane small, old and rickety. It juddered and rattled down the runway, propellers buzzing like an angry wasp. Within seconds we were soaring high, getting a view of the city, Casco Viejo and the bay. I even managed to pick out Hotel Miramar. Then we were circling around and got a birds-eye of the canal; a bendy strip like a brown ribbon winding from inland, widening and disgorging itself into the ocean under the bridge of the Americas. The green canopy below was spellbinding too, the trees like fresh supermarket broccoli, the blue of the ocean in sharp contrast and mesmerizing. Panama it appeared was a pretty special place after all.

Bocas Town was a mix of colorful but shabby, one- and two-story wooden houses, some more substantial while many had just corrugated iron roofs for keeping the heavy rains at bay. Taking a lift to the port in a beat-up people carrier, we got a glimpse of clusters of shops, mini markets, restaurants, hotels, and hostels. It felt half asleep but somehow still had attitude: like it didn't care about anything very much at all.

The driver dropped us at the Limbo Hotel peer with a grunt along with a bunch of young scruffy backpackers. They drifted off in search of a beer or somewhere to stay while we waited for our pickup to Bastimentos Island.

"Interesting place," said Marco, glancing around. "Is it me, or… I don't know, does it have a, like, an odd vibe?"

I knew what he meant. Bocas town was an odd mix of Panama and deep Caribbean, like Jamaica or Trinidad. Kids cycled by with dreads, and strong wafts of weed and the obligatory 'No Woman No

Cry' drifted across from a nearby bar. The locals were out and about, hanging loose on street corners, drinking the local Balboa beer. It's not like they were giving us unfriendly looks, but they weren't exactly friendly either.

"I'm sure the place has a different vibe in the daytime," I said, trying to shrug it off, but I knew what he meant. I didn't feel easy.

We sat on a wooden bench on the peer and waited for our ride. Thankfully, we didn't have to wait long. Gradually the sound of an outboard motor started to eke out of the dark, then a long tail boat emerged out of the blackness with Limbo written on the side. Our ride had arrived.

Prisilio was a local but from further up the coast. He introduced himself and helped us down into the boat and put our bags under some plastic sheeting at the front.

"Can get, wet," he explained, indicating to the bags and the sky, Marco nodded in agreement. Then we were off.

Talking above the sound of the outboard motor, Prisilio told us he came from a tribe called Kuna Indians. He explained that his tribe had their own nationality, own nation even, called Kuna Yala. In fact, you could see he was different to the Panamanians back in the City, or even most of Bocas for that matter. Short, strong, very stocky, he looked almost Peruvian, but with dark weather beaten, deeply wrinkled skin. He told us that he worked at Limbo in the afternoons and at night was a fisherman.

"Your English is good," I ventured, shouting over the motor. "Where did you learn it?"

Prisilio grinned.

"Went to school in Panama. Studied cooking. Gave it up. Wanted a different, easy life. Came here to help family. City was OK. Worked making pizza. But it wasn't good, for me. Miss the sea." He said, without emotion. It was just a fact to him I could see. Like DNA.

As we glided out of the lagoon which protected Bocas town from rougher seas, Prisilio push down on the throttle and before long we entered a slightly choppier open sea. Little inlets and islets were silhouetted against a starless sky suggesting that Prisilio had been right - rain may be on the way. Then after about thirty minutes, we got first sight of Bastimentos Island. Dark and flat against the ocean, just a few pinpoints of light here and there indicating limited habitations. No bars, restaurants, shops, or nightclubs here. Just a scattering of single-story wooden cabins.

Prisilio slowed down the outboard motor and we drifted towards a small narrow wooden jetty.

"Hola, Hola!"

The manger had come out to the jetty to greet us, waving a flashlight. We pulled alongside gently and Prisilio cut the engine. Silence. Just the sound of the ocean lapping the pier, the reef out in the distance and the noise of a nocturnal jungle reaching down from behind a narrow strip of beach.

"Hola, Mr. and Mrs. Meeks. Welcome to Limbo."

Marco glanced over at me. I smiled.

"Actually, we're just friends, hence the booking. You do have it, right? I did book two rooms…" I said clambering up onto the peer with some help and noting the correct room booking right away in an attempt to spare Marco the embarrassment.

"Oh yes, you're right," said the manager, studying a booking form again with his flashlight, grinning and shaking both our hands. "My apologies, we have another couple arriving shortly and I was confused. This way. Please be careful. I don't want you to fall off the side of the pier. That happened last year to an American guest. His wife thought it was funny. He didn't!"

Limbo was perched directly on the beach, a cluster of small independent one-story cabins made of wood and palms fronds. Very rustic, certainly basic, and extremely natural. A single bare bulb hung in my small but comfortable cabin, casting a dim light. With no glass in the windows, no TVs or mini bar, the effect was comfortable camping. A fan above the bed slowly moved the air, a mosquito net hung over the bed and was no doubt a godsend given the close proximity of the forest and the insect life it no doubt housed.

"You're just in time for dinner!" said the manager, who by now had introduced himself as Jose.

"Just over there, see that bungalow on the water? Your table is reserved for nine. See you shortly!" And with that he was off, the flashlight showing his progress back to the main hotel residence, a receding pinpoint into the night.

The restaurant was on a small jetty reaching out from the beach and just a meter above the sea. About eight or nine small tables were dotted around, all simply presented with crisp white tablecloths, candles, and one single red hibiscus flower as decoration. Other couples were already seated, some soft Café del Mar type of music added to the mood.

Taking a table, I sat down opposite Marco, and we ordered drinks. The waitress introduced herself as Sally from Holland, who explained she was on a gap year for some freedom, fun and adventure, before heading off to study economics in the Hague. For twelve months of tropical paradise, I couldn't say I blamed her.

She soon brought us the house specialty fresh passion fruit daiquiris to get us started. (They were insanely strong, large, delicious, and inevitably lethal) and a bottle of chilled white wine to have with our meal.

"Well, this is nice," I ventured, trying to ignore the romancing couples all around us. "I almost feel like we're on holiday, rather than a treasure hunt!"

Marco smiled, in recognition of the slightly awkward scenario. "Yes, I know what you mean," he said, taking a sip of his cocktail. "It does feel a bit like that doesn't it, I mean in this err, location, the romantic setting and all. Can't wait to see what it all looks like in day light. The beach looks amazing. I just put my feet in the sea before and the water's so warm. It's like a bath."

We were silent for some minutes, taking it all in, the surroundings, the soft breeze, the music…

"Melody, you know…you know what happened in Rome that night," he said, shifting in his seat, looking awkward, leaning forward "Well, I wanted to tell you…"

"Marco, please," I said, butting in. "I understand, about your girlfriend and look we agreed to be, well to be friends, right?"

For a moment he fixed me, was about to go on, then, "Spencer?" he said, "Are you… still…?"

"Here's your first course," Sally said, interrupting, arriving at our table with two bowls of what looked like soup. "Local seafood gazpacho with a garnish of locally sourced lobster. Enjoy!" she beamed down, before heading off to serve another table. The moment with Marco and whatever he was trying to ask me lost for the time being.

We sat and ate the next course in semi awkward silence. But the wine was flowing and with more of it in my direction, we were chatting normally again, and if I'm honest, I was probably even doing a bit of flirting. Then before I knew it, we'd had the last course and I'd finished most of the bottle myself.

"Let's make a move." Marco said, getting up to help me up too, perhaps sensing that I was more than a little tipsy.

"We've an early start again, and I'm dead tired, I don't know about you. Hey, be careful there. We don't want you to go over the side, do we?"

One arm around my waist to help steady my way, we made it back to the cabins. He was half holding me up. I was giddy, giggly and at the same time I was beyond tired. The powerful cocktail and the wine were making my head spin, but in spite of my slightly dizzy self I couldn't help noticing again how attractive he was and what beautiful arms he had. Memories of Rome and the night we spent together came flooding back and, arriving at my cabin, a wave of longing came over me. Before I knew what had come over me I was kissing him. My mouth pressed against his. Through my drunken haze he still tasted divine – a mixture of passion fruit, wine, and chocolate. Then he was pulling me to him. His mouth was firm on mine, his tongue exploring my mouth, it felt full of desire. My head was spinning all the more, and this time it wasn't just the fault of the drinks. For a second, we stumbled backwards, into the cabin and towards the bed, cascading down onto it with a thud, the mosquito net straining from where it was hanging as we fell half on it becoming a tangle with us on the bed. He was above me now, looking down, searching for my face in the dark. I thought I wanted him. Didn't I want him? Then, out of the blue, the switch, and Spencer flashed up in my mind. It took me by surprise, but in that split second being with Marco felt all wrong and I was trying to get up, was gently but firmly pushing him away, almost holding him at arm's length. He was confused then, with a flash of realization, I could see a wave of disappointment, mortification wave over him…

"Sorry Marco, I… I can't do this, I can't … I, well you know…oh, I don't know, I thought I wanted to, but I keep seeing Spencer, I don't know, I'm so confused…"

"What?" he exclaimed "Is it my fault? Did I do something wrong?" He was standing up now, his shirt disheveled, his glasses on the bed by my side.

"No, it's not you, it's me! I started this and, well, I was a bit drunk and I shouldn't have. It's my fault. Please forgive me for leading you on. It's so bad of me especially after what happened in Rome, and you have a girlfriend. I'm so sorry. Please, forgive me. Please leave Marco. I think it's for the best. Please go."

"But I want to stay here with you Melody. I need to tell you how I feel."

"No Marco. Please, this is a mess, again. Please just go. Really, I'm sorry I don't know what came over me. Like I said, it must be all the wine, the soft lights, and music. Please, let's forget it, that this ever happened. It's my fault this time…" I was babbling, confused and with that I grabbed his glasses from the bed, stuffed them into his hands and pushed him out of the cabin. I closed the door and was alone. Again.

I stood there for some time, behind the door. He was standing on the other side, it must have been a good minute, no doubt deciding what to do. I half expected, hoped he would knock, but then I heard him making his way down the cabin steps, and across the beach. What had I just done? I wanted him one second, not the next. He had every right to hate me. Damn, I'd made such a fool of myself, getting drunk, flinging myself at him, then seconds later pushing him away. I came across as desperate and confused. What was I thinking? He'd made it perfectly clear in Rome. He wasn't interested, he was back with his girlfriend. How awful of me to tempt him like that. It was exactly what I hated; girls going after other girls' men. Not only that, but I'd told him I wasn't over Spencer, so what must he think of me? I was annoyed with myself; that I'd allowed this to happen.

After collapsing on the bed, I lay awake for some hours, under the mosquito net listing to the jungle. I could feel it reaching down to my cabin, dense and dark, right behind my bed, stretching off into the center of the island. For the first time in a long while I felt very alone. After all, there I was on an island in the middle the Caribbean Sea, with nothing much between me and the ocean and with a dark black tangle of jungle behind me. All around was the sound of insects and calls from what sounded like birds made the forest seem like it was pulsating, like it was a living breathing entity in its own right. In this situation, I was even more conscious that Marco was just a few meters away back in his own cabin. Was he sleeping deeply, or like me, lying awake, tossing and turning in the dead of the night too?

Flicking a bug off the outside of the mosquito net I turned off the light, rolled over and tried to get some sleep and before drifting off my mind back on Spencer, I made a mental note to avoid any more cocktails and wine on this trip.

The next day was bright and the sky was clear. The clouds from the evening before had lifted although the mood at the breakfast table had not.

"So, so sorry," I muttered over coffee and toast. "I was drunk, I don't know what came over me… I…"

"Let's just leave it Melody, shall we?" he said, fixing my eyes, in a sad but resolute way. "Look, clearly you're not over Spencer. And well, when you're ready, we should talk, but until then, yes, better we just leave it, no?"

After breakfast we found the perfect spot to start our surveillance along the beach, and armed with a pair of binoculars, sun cream, and enough water to sink a ship, dug ourselves in for the day.

We soon spotted Bruno on a hammock just after lunch. Shorts, Panama hat and a book. And that's where he stayed all day, the rest of that day and the next two days after that too.

"I think he's on holiday," I finally said, on day three, stating what seemed to be the obvious.

"There's nothing going on here. The most dramatic thing that's going to happen is he'll run out of books!" I was trying to make a joke. Then on reflection it wasn't that funny at all. It was downright disappointing., "Jesus, we really are wasting our time out here…"

"At least I'm getting a tan in the process." Said Marco with a lame smile.

Things had been a little tense and awkward with Marco these last few days, but today we were almost back to how we'd been before. Almost. Every time I saw him my stomach lurched a little. I kicked myself about what had happened on the first night on the island every single day. I told myself it was the booze: A passion fruit cocktail the size of a small vase and too much wine. But as time went on, if truth be told, I was already dreading the end of this adventure. Getting back on a flight to London, back to *Zenith* and back to my *Melody Talkin'* page…without Marco...

Zenith…Zenith. It was always at the back of my mind. Jake had been happy with the last edition of *Melody Talkin'*, and he wanted more like it. I still hadn't finished the Facebook feature and had decided that after our time on Bastimentos, with nothing to show for it, I'd tweak my original Facebook story and I'd send it. It probably wouldn't light up the world, but who knows, it might just be enough to give me a chance of the contract. And as for our Panamanian adventure, enough was enough. I'd said as much to Marco that night at dinner and he hadn't argued otherwise. Just nodded, a resigned kind of nod and said in the morning he'd ask Jose if he could use their computer to book our flights back to Panama City.

Then, just as we were about to give up, go home, purely by chance, we got lucky. We bumped into Prisilio on the beach. He must have spotted Marco and I watching Bruno through the Binoculars. Admittedly, we'd been doing it a lot and had probably started to get a bit too 'casual' about it.

"Why watching that man?' He asked, pointing up the beach, and sizing us up from behind his wrap-around Ray-Bans. As it happened he'd brought is canoe out of the sea for repairs right behind us on the beach and was also working on his fishing net, mending the holes with a blue twine. I could see it was clearly second nature to him. He didn't even need to look at what he was doing. Instead he kept his curious gaze on us as his fingers knotted the thread.

"He's up to something, right? You police?"

Marco laughed, then looked puzzled. "No, we're not police, but what do you mean, 'up to something?'" It was a fair question. Bruno didn't look up to very much at all these days, spending most of them in a hammock with a book and cocktail on the go.

Prisilio paused, sizing us up some more, then went on. "My nephew has a boat. Has been fishing for few years. He tell me, this guy, that one you watching, he pay him to take to island – over there," he said, indicating to the horizon. "Take him four nights now. Goes, at say one, comes back around four. Same every night. Say when he comes back he covered in, how do you say, mud? Bring back things - in bags. Say he goes into jungle, and the next he sees him three hours later, he covered in dirt with bags. My nephew – doesn't like it. Say spirits on that island. They not like either."

Marco and I looked at each other. I couldn't believe it.

"What island?" I piped up, my pulse picking up.

"Big *Zapatilla,*" he said, indicating to the horizon again. "There are two islands, but he go to second one." I took the binoculars from Marco and focused them to sea. There were two Islands nestled on the horizon, small, low dense and windswept. Prisilio went on to tell us that they were national parks, totally uninhabited, except for one cabin where the ranger often sleeps, but that was only when the turtles were laying their eggs and that wouldn't be for another four months.

Marco and I looked at each other. We'd been about to give up, pack our bags and go home. It hadn't occurred to us that Bruno would be out and about at night. But he was. Something was going on and we knew right then that we had to get to the bottom of it. Jake, *Zenith,* and London would have to wait.

Chapter Seventeen

We met Prisilio that night on the beach. It was 12:30. We kept our flashlights off and Prisilio did the same. He'd driven a hard bargain on the fee at $200 for the night. He told us that it looked like a bad tropical storm was coming our way and he'd never normally go out, so the fee was double. We couldn't argue with that.

From the cover of dark and a low-lying palm up the beach, we watched as a small boat pulled away from the Al Natural jetty. We didn't know for sure it was Bruno. All we could see was the pinpoint of a flashlight moving against the dark, inky backdrop of the ocean, but based on what Prisilio had told us it was a pretty good bet.

The trick was to then leave enough time so that we could follow him out to the island but not so close that he'd hear our boat's motor, so we waited a good thirty minutes, and then set off.

The water was calm, the clouds covering the moon made nighttime details tricky to pick out, then suddenly we passed the foaming waters of the reef on our left, and we were out more into the open ocean, onto a rougher sea. The boat was low and narrow and took on a rhythmic bounce as it topped the swelling waves before heading off the next. It was only then that I noticed there were no life jackets. I'm a good swimmer but it still made me feel nervous and I hoped we'd get there and back before the storm

Prisilio had mentioned turned up. A few nights back, the manager at Limbo had told us about the last storm that had passed over.

"Washed away half of the bungalows and cabins," he'd said with a frown. "We don't get many tropical storms here and there aren't ever hurricanes, but occasionally a storm passes by that can be rough. Really rough."

Putting it to the back of my mind I concentrated on the horizon, searching for Bruno's boat. A light misty rain had started falling and my vision was becoming blurred but blinking, I just about made it out in the distance – a dark bobbing pinpoint against a darker ocean backdrop. We hadn't lost him yet.

The outboard motor soldiered on, and Prisilio threw us a couple of plastic macs. I wasn't sure they'd make much of a difference against the rain with the wind as it was but, I managed to get it on just the same.

Thirty minutes in, the Zapatillas Islands were approaching on the horizon and we'd lost sight of Bruno. Prisilio cut the engine right back and we cruised past the first, heading for the calmer waters of Zapatilla number two. The motor now completely off to make a silent approach, the boat gently nudged onto the shallow beach and we jumped out. Down the way, we spotted Bruno's boat once again, a dark silhouette against the sand, and the black outline of a solitary figure to the right.

"My nephew. No worry if he sees us. I told him we coming. He wants to know, what this about. He no like these visits at night," Prisilio said, glancing around "He say a curse on this island. A pirate, buried treasure and murdered people here many year ago. Say he heard them spirits talking last night. He no come back tomorrow. Maybe never again. He afraid of the curse. He not the first." In spite of the warm tropical night, a shiver went down my spine.

"I was good friend once with one of them rangers," he went on, pointing at the cabin, up the beach. "He on here for months; on this island, alone, at night. Say he heard a woman. Round here she called Letty. Legend is she Morgan's woman. He raped her, murdered her, then buried her with his treasure. That she still on this island, talking at night, a strange language."

If Bastimentos Island felt out in the wilds, the Zapatillas Islands felt like they were about to drop off the edge of the world. The wind was really picking up and the palms were starting to sway making a terrific sound in the canopy above. Rain was also starting to fall more heavily now, a pitter-pattering on our plastic macs. The reef to the left was looking rough, waves were starting to swell and crash. The only construction on the island was the small ranger cabin to the right, a shack made of wood and palms, on stilts and set back into the jungle. It didn't look that robust and was in darkness. No light. No ranger. Turtle season hadn't started just yet I reminded myself, as it sunk in that we were completely alone, isolated on this far away windswept archipelago. What on earth could Bruno be doing here in the middle of the night? I couldn't imagine, but I sure wanted to find out.

Prisilio picked up a flashlight from the bottom of the boat. Switching it on, he pointed to the top of the beach, to a path between the trees that I could only just make it out with the beam from the light.

"See that there, that's where he goes. Your man. Path cuts through the island - to the ocean side. It's even wilder there: no lagoon. My nephew say he go along that path every night. Is the tourist trail in the day. But be careful. You follow the trail. There are swamps in the middle of the island – so stay on path." It was pretty dark on that beach with just the flashlight, but he must've seen the look on my face. "The island is small, if you stay on the trail - all OK. I wait here - with my nephew…"

I didn't like the sound of 'swamp,' but we headed up the narrow beach the same, and switching on our second flashlight, we got a good look at the path in front of us. It was made of wooden slats and looked in pretty good shape, but here and there, there were holes, slats missing, and parts were covered with green moss and algae too. *Easy to break an ankle on that,* I thought to myself as we started off, Marco in the lead.

Soon we were winding through the ever-thickening canopy, the sound of the ocean became a soft backdrop as the jungle enveloped us. It seemed like the forest was alive. Moths and insects attracted to the light of our torches buzzed around, frantic for the impromptu light sources. Strange calls, birds or monkeys, sounded off somewhere out there in the dark. My heart was thumping in my chest like an overactive piston and I knew that nothing short of getting of this island in one piece would calm it down. Prisilio's ghost stories hadn't helped and had put me even more on edge. And most important of all, for the first time I wondered if we were in any real danger, not from ghosts but from Bruno. After all, only god knew how he might react if we came face to face out here? Would he be shocked, angry, even violent? I admit, walking along that wooden path, I wanted so badly to find out, at the same time I didn't want to know at all.

"Hey, Marco," I whispered from behind. "What if Bruno is nearby and sees our torches?"

"I know," he said, not turning back, concentrating as we walked on the path ahead, "But what can we do? We wouldn't see the path if we turned them off." He had a point.

Advancing on the narrow, slippery wooden path, winding through the jungle my flashlight suddenly picked up water, to the right, to the left, all around. Prisilio had been right. The elevated, wooden path was taking us through a dense swamp. Like something out of a strange dream, tangled, creeping mangrove roots wound around the path like hundreds of spindly fingers reaching up from the water and mud. Despite the humidity, I shivered again.

Then, through the trees the flash of a light. Was that a sound? Coming to a halt, Marco indicated to the left; A separate trail, going off, no wooden slats this time, just a simple, worn muddy trail through a gap hacked out from dense trees and creepers. This was not the tourist trail: it was a different kind of trail and freshly cut.

The light ahead was moving slightly. I could hear the voice again - then another. Two at least. Trying not to make a sound and without speaking himself Marco signaled. He'd seen something up ahead. We needed to go very quietly, very slowly now. Then, out of the blue, the trail ended, and we were on the edge of a clearing, and…there he was. Bruno.

The clearing was lit with two lamps and a generator was humming. Bruno was down a hole, it looked like a pit perhaps a meter deep.

A shovel lay on the side and he was passing something up to a man who was crouching down with his back to us. The man, bending over, was placing the small handful of muddy things into a backpack. Another three, looked already full, and were on the side of the clearing.

And then, I just couldn't believe my eyes. The shock of it, the sudden realization, the joy and the anger, all at once, the man with the backpacks turned, and the brightest lamp lit up his face. I caught a breath.

Spencer.

Marco, unable to contain the shock, jumped back, the sound of some snapping branches was loud, the sound of the reef a long way away, the nocturnal nightlife less vivid here.

Spencer spun round, was on his feet, glaring, searching in the jungle, wiping his forehead with his dirty shirt arm, he picked up a flashlight and scanned it around.

The forest cover was surprisingly thin, we realized in a flash.

"What the hell have we here?" he said coming over. His eyes locking with mine, realizing, for a moment surprise flashing across his face.

"What the…? Melody Meeks? Is that really you!? Marco, my friend! Long time no see! Fancy bumping into you out here? Care to join?" he said, regaining composure in a second, indicating to the clearing with his flashlight.

More than a little in shock we emerged, stumbled out of the shadows, into the light of the lamps.

"Well, well, well," he said, almost grinning now. "Care to explain? I don't guess you two just happen to be out here on holiday looking for some local nightlife. You might want to hang out in Bocas for that."

Marco spoke first stepping forward. "Spencer, I can't believe it. Is that really you?" He was shaking. I could see the shock of seeing his dead friend right in front of him, alive and kicking, was almost too much to take in. Emotion getting the better of him he dashed forward, gave Spencer a hug, pulled back and studied his face, still disbelieving.

"I, I just can't believe it. My god. You're alive!! What the hell's going on? I was at your funeral just a few weeks back!" he blurted, stating the painfully obvious. "I mean, thank god you're alive! '*Cazzo.*' What happened? Did you tell your mum, sister, everyone? They all think you're dead. We must tell them! We thought Bruno was up to something – sorry Bruno," he glanced over, "but we had no idea – that, that you're, you're alive!!!"

"No, I haven't told anyone," said Spencer, wiping his brow again, taking a step back from Marco, taking him in. "And I'm not going to," he continued, eyeing us, suspiciously.

"Not going to? But, but you must!" Marco took a step forward, again. "Hey, let me give you another hug, I just can't believe your alive, friend!" He took Spencer and gave him a bigger bear hug, but after a second, he pulled back. Spencer wasn't hugging him back but instead was stiff, stiff like a board, arms motionless by this side.

"Wait," said Marco, "What did you say, you're not going to tell your mum, your sister, friends that you're OK, that you're alive? I mean...they must know. They're all in a terrible state…"

Spencer cut in. "No, I'm not Marco. Christ. I can't believe you guys - turning up here. For fucks sake." Then turning to Bruno "You fool. Can't you see what you've done? I wondered if I should trust you. You've let them trail you out here, you blasted idiot."

"What are you talking about?" Marco, said, taking a step back this time.

"Don't you get it?" Spencer said turning back, a look of distain, anger, creeping insidiously over his face. "Spencer's dead. He's not coming back. Ever."

We stood a few seconds in silence. The realization sunk in. He carried on, but I'd already got, it. I'd already started to put the pieces together and I didn't like the picture they were creating. I didn't like it one bit.

"Why should I? Go back I mean. We planned it like this. Do you think I'm stupid? And my mum, my sister? Who cares! They've never meant anything to me. You really want to know the truth? Well the truth is I can't stand them."

"How can you say that?" Marco was looking aghast. "Never coming back?"

"No Marco, never coming back. Are you so stupid? Don't you get it? Even here, now, seeing this?" He gestured to the pit, the mud the backpacks on the side.

Bruno had been quiet until then. He'd pulled himself out of the pit, had been standing back. But he came forward now. "We should tell them Spencer. They're in on this now whether you like it or not," he said, looking tried in the lamp light and much older than his sixty-one years. Spencer studied our faces, glanced around like he was sizing up the situation, mulling over his options. He focused his gaze on Bruno, then turned back to us. A hard look had taken over his face. A cold dread washed over me.

"Look, it's the find of the century," said Spencer – gesturing to the bags. "On the dive this summer we found Sir Henry Morgan's pendant. It's worth a fortune alone. Millions. Bruno sold it this week. A private Chinese collector of pirate artifacts. But he doesn't know that there was a map inside it. And we removed it before we sold it. We can get a better price selling the items separately. He only wanted the pendent anyway. Totally amazing that the pendant had remained watertight all those years. It took me a while to find the gold, out here I mean. I've been living in the ranger cabin back at the beach, but I couldn't dig in the daytime – this place is swarming with tourists," he said with a disdainful look on his face. "We're close to the nature trail here, so I had to lay low and could only dig only at night. I hit the jackpot last week. Bruno's been helping carry it off the island: bags of gold coins. They're heavy and I couldn't have done it without Bruno."

Then I thought I was seeing things. Spencer put his arm round Bruno, pulled him close, gave him a kiss on the cheek. Spencer saw my face.

"Oh, Melody darling," he said, letting Bruno go, coming over. "Still hooked on me after all this time? Poor you." He was scornful now. I'd never seen Spencer like this. What was happening? Where was the Spencer from Cambridge?

"You never figured me out did you, sweetie pie? Didn't you get it? That I can swing both ways? Didn't you realize, while I was shagging you in Cambridge, I was getting it elsewhere too, wherever I could? Girls, boys… Remember the night we came back from the Cambridge Arms Pub, had sex in the kitchen, then I said I needed some air, wanted to pop out and get some cigarettes?" My mind was turning over events, back all those years, to that night. Somehow, I pinpointed it. Yes, it was coming back to me now. We'd been so horny. As soon as we'd got to his rooms, we'd been down on the kitchen floor, stripping each other, making love.

"Well, darling," Spencer continued, "I didn't go out for cigarettes. You were just an appetizer. I went back to the Cambridge Arms and had sex with the bar man – remember, blond, blue eyes, tattoos on this right arm – very cute. I did it all the time, but you were so stupid you never guessed," he added, looking smug and full of distain all at the same time.

My guts fell away inside. Spencer. Bisexual. A cheat. Not charming but cold and calculating. A liar.

"But your mum, your sister, you should've seen them at the funeral, Spencer. How can you do that to them?" said Marco, jumping in. Pleading.

"Why not?" he said, pulling a packet of cigarettes out of his back pocket, taking a few moments to light it before carrying on, the smoke wafting off in the darkness of the surrounding jungle. "I'm adopted. They mean nothing to me. I've always hated my sister and my mum, well, she never really loved me. Always eyes for Helen. My dad was OK, I guess, but then he died. I blamed her. She was always feeding him cakes, shitty food. He had a heart attack, you know." He dragged on his cigarette again, blew out the smoke, and fixed on me. "Bruno and I, well, we've been an item for a while, haven't we old Bru? But now I see you here Melody, well…you're looking good. Maybe we can get you in on this too. Marco, well, I know you've only got eyes for, what's she called, Valentina? But Melody, maybe I've had enough cock for a while…and I could do with some pussy now."

He came over then, slowly, and took my chin between his fingers. His eyes were glassy, he fixed me with a stern but wild-eyed look. I knew what I had to do. I knew right then that this was a matter of survival. I could feel his strength, just in the way he was holding my chin. He was close, menacing, breathing down my neck. I wanted to vomit in fear. Was this really Spencer? It didn't seem real. But it was.

Bruno was suddenly by his side. "Spencer, what do you mean? You know, you're my life. I can't imagine …."

"Shut up, old man…" Spencer shouted spinning round. "You're the one who led them here, you fucking idiot."

And then I saw it, He had a gun. Small, in the belt, hooked into the back of his jeans. And catching Marco's eye, I knew he'd seen it too.

Suddenly there was a rustling sound and out of the forest Prisilio appeared.

"Who the hell are you?" shouted Spencer, spinning back. I could sense his anger was building, his hand was resting on the gun in his belt at the back. I could see he was volatile, cornered, and dangerous.

"It's OK," I said, trying to sound calm, stepping over to Spencer's side of the clearing, next to him. "He's with us. What is it Prisilio?"

Prisilio glanced around, taking it all in. "The storm. Is coming. Need to go - to Bastimentos. If no go now, very dangerous stay here."

There was silence for a moment. Spencer was glaring around.

"OK, look everyone," I jumped in "This guy is right. Listen to the trees. The storms almost on us. We have to get out of here now. If we don't, we might be stuck on here for days or even worse risk drowning on the way back or getting washed away here. Those boats are low in the water – they won't stand much of a swell." It was true. The sound of the trees was alarming. Since we'd arrived in the clearing, we'd all been distracted, but the trees were swaying violently above us now, the rain had started to penetrate the canopy too. Large drops were sounding all around.

"These are the last bags, Bruno, right? There's nothing more down there – are you sure?" Spencer asked, circling back to the hole with the flashlight.

"Yes, nothing, that's it."

"OK, let's get off this island, and we'll figure what to do with these three over in Bastimentos. And no funny business," he said, patting the gun.

Taking a backpack each, we headed back along the trail. Bruno took the lead, Spencer the rear. I kept thinking of the gun and that Spencer had tapped it. He knew we'd seen it. It was a threat plain and simple.

Within minutes we emerged at the beach.

"Where's my boat?" Shouted Spencer, wild eyed – scanning the beach. It was gone.

"I told my nephew – go," jumped in Prisilio. "His boat is small. Or he no make it in the storm."

There was no choice in the matter now, we were all in the same boat, literally.

The rain was coming at us sidewise and the palms at the back of the beach were being pulled back and forth by the wind. Looking out to sea I could see that the waves were much choppier, more agitated than before.

We clambered onto the boat and Spencer passed up the four small, muddy backpacks. Then with Prisilio at the stern and engine kicked into life and we were soon powering out of the lagoon and into a choppy sea. Looking back, Zapatillas looked even more deserted and windswept in the storm. But then a doubt. What was that? Through the swell and rain and a flash of white lightning, I saw a figure. Yes, someone at the top of the beach, emerging from the jungle. A small dark figure. Was it Prisilio's nephew? Had we left him behind after all? I squinted, rubbed the rain from my face. Yes, surely that was a figure, small waif life. Not a man: it had the form of a woman. I was about to shout to Prisilio. We needed to head back. Someone was stranded on the island. But then looking again the figure was gone. Perhaps it had been a trick of the light. Looking up at Prisilio, he was fixing me with an eye, a stare I'd never seen.

"I know…what you saw. We no going back. She has to stay there, that her home." He shouted over the sound of the waves and wind. I didn't understand and was about to ask what on earth he was talking about, but a jolt of the boat made me catch my breath and I had to grab onto the side at risk of going right over; and the moment was gone.

I tried to wrap the now sodden plastic mac around me, but it was hopeless in the wind. We were all totally drenched; a mix of rain and sea water, and still thirty minutes to go. I was trying to cling onto the side of the boat when suddenly Spencer was beside me, shoving himself in between me and Marco, pushing Marco to the bench in front.

"Melody. Come with me," he shouted over the outboard motor his face inches from mine. "I'm planning to head down to South America once we've sold this gold. What with this and the money we made from the pendant I'll never have to work again. If you come with me, we'll live like a king and queen. You can have whatever you want. A big house. A yacht. What have you got to lose?"

I couldn't believe what I was hearing. Here was the man who had faked his own death, admitted to sleeping with Bruno, now suggesting I up sticks and head off to South America. I was about to open my mouth but caught a glance of the gun now in his belt at the front. Spencer was clearly deranged, and I knew I had to play this carefully.

"Sure," I said, trying to sound convincing. "That could work. But what about Bruno? You said you two were an item now and…"

"Oh, that old fart?" he jumped in laughing above the sound of the outboard. "Melody, wise up. I was just using him. You know, sex just a couple of times a week. That was all I could bare. He's not much of a looker after all, is he? Old and wrinkly. But he's totally mad about me. Shame really but I'm going to ditch him soon. I needed someone to help with all this. Faking the death, a credible witness, someone to find a buyer for the pendant, while I took myself off the radar for a while. And it worked." He was grinning now. I thought I'd gone insane.

"But I don't get it," I carried on, grabbing the side of the boat as a particularly large wave smashed into the side and sprayed us with white, foamy saltwater. Spencer leaned in more, pinning me against the side. It was starting to hurt. "Why the faking the death thing in the start? If you found the pendant and wanted to sell it, why go through this elaborate charade?"

"Oh Melody," he laughed. "Always so innocent, so naive. You haven't changed a bit. And a journalist, too? Come on. Clearly still not better than that waste of a mother. Don't you know anything about international laws on treasure? Haven't you done your research? Don't you understand what we found here? The significance of this? The pieces are so unique, so valuable. If we'd handed them to the Panamanian authorities, they would have tried to claim it was theirs, the British, the Spanish and the Peruvians too. See, good old Sir Henry was from Wales, and he stole the pendant and the gold from the Spanish, and we found it in Panama waters, although it was stolen from Peru by the Spanish in the first place. The legal dispute over ownership would have gone on for years, and we might have been able to cut a deal in the end but who knows, maybe nothing. Maybe a few hundred thousand and the things in a museum somewhere gathering dust. No, no, no," he said, looking at me intently and then staring off into the ocean, as if searching for something. "This was the only way. And you know, now I see you again after all these years, I'm wondering why we don't get back together. It's perfect!!! From where I stand there's perhaps just one thing in the way…Marco. We need to get rid of him…"

In a flash he was standing up in the swaying boat. Leaning forward he grabbed Marco. Then he was wrestling with him. To my horror I realized, dear god, he was trying to throw him over the side of boat! Prisilio could see what was happening but was struggling to keep the boat on course, the waves were coming from the side now and, while we were almost at the reef, calmer waters in sight, we still had a fair stretch go. Even worse, if we went off course and hit the reef, the boat could capsize, even be split into smithereens.

They were both on their feet now. The boat, unstable in the water already, was rocking from side to side, almost capsizing. I tried to pull Spencer from Marco, but he violently pushed me off and with a thump I fell back, cracking my head on the side of the boat. Then suddenly, crash, over they went, into the sea.

"Stop, stop the boat!" I shouted, "Prisilio, stop the boat! They've gone over! Marco, Marco!!!"

Prisilio cut the engine back and tried to circle back round to the spot where we could see two head bobbing, still fighting in the foam.

My heart was in my mouth, I don't know how I managed to speak but somehow and from somewhere deep down I kept shouting, "Stop, stop it, Spencer. Marco, Marco!"

Then, splash, someone else was overboard now too. Bruno! What was he thinking? The sea was swelling, the reef creating even more white foam. There could be currents out here, he was sixty-one years old. But then I remembered; he's a seasoned diver, maybe he'll be alright. In fact, with a confident crawl he'd already reached them. Their heads above water one minute then under the next. With the swell of the waves I lost sight, then as a wave receded again I got another view, just Bruno's head showing now. Where were Spencer and Marco? They had gone under! I was frantic.

"Marco, Marco!" I kept shouting.

Then, another swell and two heads! Bruno was dragging someone, Spencer to the boat. Oh my god. Marco! He must have gone under. The tears were streaming down my face by now, mixed with rain and the saltwater of the sea, the panic and the terror and the thought of Marco drowning, under the waves. I couldn't bear the thought that he was sinking down in the bottom, caught underneath in a current, trapped on the reef, drowning.

"Marco! Marco!" I shouted again, hopelessly, clinging to the side of the boat, desperate and then…

"Marco!" Bruno was bringing him up. He'd saved Marco, not Spencer. The relief was overwhelming. The joy of seeing him, limp but with life, collapsed in the bottom of the boat. In a flash Bruno was back in the sea, searching, but the swell was getting stronger, Spencer was nowhere in sight.

Prisilio pulled out a flashlight and we searched for a good thirty minutes but eventually gave up.

Spencer was gone.

Chapter Eighteen

Prisilio set the boat on track back to Bastimentos and before long we'd passed the reef and had entered the calmer waters of the lagoon. Tired, shocked, and beaten, we headed for shore. Climbing out of the boat we jumped down and collapsed, like wet rags on the sand. The rain was still beating down, the wind pummeling us from the ocean, but it didn't matter now. We were alive. Spencer was dead.

Bruno staggered down the beach a little way, but out of shear exhaustion, unable to go further, his spindly legs gave way and he collapsed on the spot in the sand. I don't know how long we all stayed like that, catching our breath, taking in the situation, reflecting. It was surely just a few minutes, but it felt like an hour.

Eventually, Prisilio came over with the bags, dropping them on the sand: Four drenched, muddy backpacks stuffed with something of immense worth, from a bygone age. Then Bruno dragging himself off the sand stood up. He reached down to one of the packs and pulled something out.

"Take this," he said, passing it to Prisilio. "Something to say, well, thanks. Just don't tell anyone I gave it to you. And here's one for your nephew too."

Prisilio looked down in his palm where he held what looked like a torn, ragged pieced of grey cotton. Then I caught a glimpse. A piece of gold. Round, heavily beveled, covered in dark sticky mud, but there was no mistaking it. It was a coin, two of them.

"No. Cursed," he said passing them back.

Then, without another word, just a nod. Prisilio headed off up the beach and was gone.

"What now?" came Marco from my right. We stood in silence for a while. Thinking. Trying to comprehend what had just happened. I needed a drink. A stiff one.

"You'd better come back to my cabin. I need a rum," Bruno said, gesturing, as if reading my mind. "It's the last one on the end. We can talk."

I wasn't sure what there was to talk about right then but, picking myself up, we both followed in silence as he picked up two of the bags and led the way.

Bruno's cabin was wooden and single story. A few steps up led to a simple bedroom and small bathroom on the right. Some low-level wooden chairs and a coffee table functioned as a small sitting area. It looked like he'd settled right in, there was washing on a line and stuff everywhere.

Messy, I thought, dropping the backpack I'd been carrying in the corner with the others. *Just like his place back in Rome.*

He switched on a small lamp by the bed. It cast a dark amber light around the room, disturbing a lizard up above that scuttled away out of sight into a dark crevice.

On the right there was a cabinet, with a bottle of Panamanian Abuelo Rum and some glasses. Taking three in one hand and the bottle in the other, he came over and indicated to the wooden chairs. We sat down in silence. The reef sounded loud from here. The storm didn't seem to be passing after all. The rain started coming down again hard, large drops bouncing off the leaves and foliage which circled the small, simple wooden terrace. After pulling over a heavy, green tarpaulin rain curtain to protect us a little from the now driving rain, he poured three generous measures of rum and passed them around. It was an awkward gathering. Where to start?

"Well," Marco broke the silence, "I suppose we'd better call the police. The sooner the better. We need to report Spencer's death."

Bruno quietly put down his rum. "Report his death? Call the police?" He was almost laughing, but I knew it was ironic. "Marco, he's already dead, remember? And the police – they're way over in Bastimentos. With this storm, who knows when we can inform them and when they'll get here? We might be stuck here for days. And how are you going to explain all this to them? It all looks so suspicious. Do you really want to get into conversations about a suspicious death, someone who's already supposed to be dead, with the Panamanian police?"

The blood drained from Marco's face. I could see he was weighting it up. Almost panicking. I didn't feel so calm myself. But Bruno was right. Spencer was already reported dead. And Bruno and Spencer had already been involved with the police over here – bribing them. Bruno would get convicted for sure; at the very least for stealing important historical artifacts and at the other end of the spectrum, bribery and fraud. We would all be implicated, even under suspicion of murder. Calling the police didn't seem like an option, at least not from where I was sitting.

"I agree with Bruno," I sighed at last, straight faced, turning to Marco.

"From whichever way you look at it, it's a mess. Too complicated. They'll never believe it. They'll think we've cooked up some bizarre story to cover up us killing Spencer." His name made me wince, realizing now that the man I once loved was a pathological liar, a player, a fake and potentially a sociopath. But nobody deserved to die. Not like that. Not even Spencer.

Bruno turned away, and after a second, I could see from side on he was crying. His shoulders hunched over, bony and old in his damp, muddy shirt, shaking with an outpouring of emotion. It was awkward to watch, but I couldn't help returning to the fact that Bruno had been in this with Spencer. We were silent for a moment or two.

"So, Bruno. What's the deal here then?" I pressed on, while Bruno tried to collect himself. "Why did you help Spencer? If we did call the police, you'd be the one most up to your neck in it. There are witnesses, remember? I mean people who can talk about you digging those things up, stealing them. Prisilio's nephew for one. Both him and Prisilio can tell the police all about it, including what happened tonight."

Turning back, wiping his eyes with the back of his hand, he took a large gulp of rum and poured himself another glass. "I was in love with him. He promised me a new life, a new start where I could finally be who I am."

"What do you mean?" broke in Marco, "Who you are? I don't get it. You were married to Maria. You told me you loved Maria. That she was your life. Now you're saying you were in love with Spencer?"

"When I was young, it wasn't easy to be gay," his voice breaking, his hand shaking as he took another sip. "You can imagine. Or maybe you can't. It was Italy in the late seventies. The pressure, from my family, the church, society's norms. Maria, well I met her at school, she was pretty, she was lovely, I thought I could forget about men, make myself be straight. I tried. We muddled along for a while, but then well I had to come clean." He paused. "We never had any children. She wanted them, I just couldn't …well, you know…anymore. I broke her heart, but she loved me anyway. She would never leave me. And I loved her too. I was only unfaithful to her a few times. It was purely lust, you see…" He took another sip of the rum, his hand still visibly shaking, then went on

"Then she got ill. It was liver cancer. I couldn't lose her. Despite it all she was the world to me. I'd learned to live with very little sex and well by then I was in my late fifties – I didn't care so much anyway. We tried every treatment we could. This hospital, that hospital, nothing seemed to be working. Then I found out about a new treatment in the US, a doctor. He performed amazing operations, they said. Could save lives. Took the liver right out, cleaned it, cut out the tumors put it back, survival rates weren't great, but … well what do you do when you're desperate." Marco looked grim, nodding perhaps hearing the exact details of Maria's treatment for the first time.

"Yes, I remember a bit about that," he nodded, "You mentioned once that you'd gone off to The States for a while, right? But what does this have to do with Spencer?"

Bruno took another swig of rum and went on. "Well the treatment was ridiculously expensive. I didn't have the money. I re-mortgaged the flat, borrowed from the bank." He stood up and walked to the cabin edge. The rain curtain, a little pulled back now, gave us a glimpse onto a turbulent sea. Turning around he looked at us, his eyes beseeching for understanding.

"I never told her, about the debt. But I ratcheted up half a million over and above the apartment." The pieces were starting to fit. Bruno went on. "Then she died. For two, three years I was lost. I was in debt up to my eyes and, well I even thought about killing myself. Then Spencer showed up. He was young, he was charming. We went on diving holidays together. He paid for me. He seemed interested in me. I, well, I fell for him. Then we found the Morgan site at Easter on a dive. It was incredible. Then when we came back this summer, we hit the jackpot and found the pendant. We immediately knew it was worth tens of millions alone if not more, but we knew if we handed it into the authorities the case would take years. We didn't know what we'd get, if anything, but probably not enough. Then we opened the locket and found the map. We knew there was even more treasure buried on Zapatillas. The map was surprising accurate. It was remarkable! So intact after all those years. Quite a miracle. We knew that the buried treasure would be worth a lot too. So then together we planned it all out. Spencer wanted to sell the stuff on the black market. Fake his own death. He wanted to start a new life, never come back. He told me he hated his family, that we could do it together. So, after we faked his death he came here, to Zapatillas. Spencer found it, the treasure I mean. He started digging it up and we planned to get if off the island and sell it on the black market too, like the pendant. Bit by bit as we needed it. We got buyers lined up. Mainly in China. It was easy, you know. I have so many contacts in archaeology. You'd be surprised how many people go crazy for this stuff. I mean we struck it lucky. Luckier than we could've imagined." He was looking at us now intently, his eyes bright with the reality of the find.

"You know, pirates hardly ever buried treasure. It was far too dangerous." He went on. "They knew it was vulnerable. We found bodies, skeletons down there with the treasure. Looks like he'd killed some of the crew to keep it safe, I mean keep its location secret. Incredible…" he mused for a moment lost in thought.

"So, you see. I take the blame too." He went on, coming back with a jolt to the present day. "Just that well, Spencer told me he was in love with me, that if we did this thing together, I'd be rich. I'd pay off my debts, sell up and I could meet him in South America. We'd spend the first years on a yacht, keeping low, out of sight. Sail around the Caribbean, down to South America. Then we'd come back to Panama, set up home, live happily ever after." Suddenly his face darkened. "What a joke. How could I be so naïve? Tonight, I saw he didn't love me at all. It was all a con. He was using me…"

We were silent. For an instant I felt sorry for him – for the first time.

"Bruno, what happened on the boat?" I asked more gently now, "You know, in the water? How did Spencer drown?"

Bruno looked at me a good while. The tears welled in his eyes again. "You saw what happened." He said after a long pause.

"I didn't, and I don't understand. Spencer was a strong swimmer. How could he drown like that?"

Marco stood up. "Melody, some things are best left, as they are, if you know what I mean." He glanced at Bruno.

"I want to know." I said, fixing Marco.

"OK. If you insist." Marco said with a frown. He paused, then he went on. "Spencer was pushing me under. I had to do something. I pushed him away, twice, but he kept coming back, trying to push me down. I was under, taking in water. Drowning. I had to defend myself… I, I punched him in the face. He went under. Then Bruno was there, pulling me to the boat…."

I studied Marco face. He was distraught, recounting it now. He'd had to defend himself. He wasn't to blame. But Bruno had made a choice. Spencer or Marco...And he'd saved Marco.

I wanted to cry, to weep, to grab Bruno, hug him and thank him for the rest of the night – but for some reason I didn't. I just sat there both grateful and numb all at the same time, still shocked for the turn of events and that when it had come down to it I cared that Marco had survived over the man I thought had been the love of my life. We were silent for a good while. Then an overwhelming exhaustion welled up.

"I'm off to bed." I said standing up, almost dizzy now. "I've heard enough for tonight. I, I need time to think. It's, it's been a shock, I, I don't know… I need to sleep…" I wanted to collapse, lie in a bed for a week, sleep and never wake up.

"Coming with you," said Marco, jumping up, still visibly shaken at the recounting of the tragedy that was only just minutes behind us. He looked different, for a moment I couldn't work it out. Then I realized. No glasses. He must've lost them on the boat.

"But let's meet tomorrow, Bruno." I said, turning to face him. "You've done a terrible thing, being party to Spencer's fraud, his deceit and this, well criminal activity, but I think I can understand, to a small degree. We've all been duped by Spencer one way or another. And you saved Marco's life. In any case, it looks like nobody's getting off this island tonight or possibly tomorrow morning for that matter too. I need to think. Think what to do. What I want to do. Let's meet and, let's try and figure this out. OK?"

"OK," he said, the tears streaming down his cheeks now, a beat up, washed out, broken, old man.

Chapter Nineteen

We were stuck on the island for another day. No boats in or out – tides still high, the storm passing over, low, brooding, and oppressive. But it wasn't all bad. After breakfast I left Marco in the main reception on the hotel computer. I needed some time on my own, so I told him I was taking a walk.

"In this rain?" he asked, looking across, surprised. Given, it was pouring down outside I could see why - but I also wanted to see Bruno again. I explained and he looked resigned but understanding.

"OK," he nodded, "I'll book our flights back to Panama City for tomorrow. And I'll see if I can get our flights back to Rome a day or so early too. If you want to leave me the details, like the booking reference number, I can try and do yours too if you like?"

"Don't worry about mine," I told him grabbing an umbrella. "I'm going to try and change it later myself. See if I can go directly to London."

For a second, he looked surprised, deflated even. "I see," he said, thoughtful, his mouth half open, something; a thought or feeling from inside, unsure, almost ready to come out but not quite. Then an imperceptible shake of the head and he straightened his back, as if in resolve against something I couldn't understand.

"I'll just sort out my own, then. I, err, well, no worries…"

Walking down the beach in the rain under one of the hotel's bright yellow umbrellas felt strangely comforting. By the time I'd packed my bags ready for the forthcoming trip home and got out, the wind had passed and for a moment a barely perceptible strip of blue sky appeared on the horizon before clouds nudged it out of view again. But in an odd way I almost liked the heavy, grey skies. Perhaps the grey made me feel more at home, the colors more attuned to a London afternoon rather than the tropics.

A short way along the beach I found Prisilio with his boat. A scratching sound reached me before I could figure out what he was doing, bent over, working hard on the left side hull. Getting closer I could see, he was sanding it down and had a pot of sky-blue paint on the sand, ready for a new coat. Clearly, he was doing some more repairs. As I passed, he glanced up, nodded a hello. He was still wearing his Ray Bans, despite the sun being nowhere in sight nor likely to be any time soon. Then, pausing, he shouted over. "I think you see her."

I stopped and turned around. "Saw who?"

"Morgan's woman – Letty, they call her round here."

For a second, I wanted to laugh, half ridicule the notion, but for some reason I didn't. I kind of knew he was right.

"Yeah, maybe I did," I nodded. "Maybe I did."

Bruno was packing his stuff. The four little backpacks were gone, two larger brand-new ones having appeared, buckled up as if ready to go.

"Ciao," he said as I climbed the steps to his cabin. "Rum? Or too early?"

"Sure," I said, grateful for the invitation. "Not too early."

He poured two Rums in short, heavy shot glasses and we sat down on the same low wooden chairs. This time the rain curtain was pulled well back, and we had an uninterrupted view of the sea, the reef and Zapatillas islands – low, a strip of vibrant green on the horizon. The rain was coming on harder now but not driving down quite like the night before, instead gentler.

We drank our rum in silence for a while then he turned to me. "So, what are you planning to do? You didn't really say last night. Go to the police here? In Italy? I can't say I'd blame you." He studied my face. I couldn't help but see how worn he looked. Tired.

"We talked about it this morning, Marco and I," I said, looking back out to the horizon, unable to look him full on for very long. "And well, we're not going to do anything. You're free to go. They'll be nobody on your tail. On account of us I mean."

Turning back, I studied him again. The relief was clear. His shoulders visibly dipped, he looked away, not saying anything, then just poured another two glasses of rum – one for him and one for me. It wasn't Captain Morgan's, but the half bottle of Abuelo from the night before. It didn't matter. Any type it would do.

We sat in silence for a few moments, then without glancing over, looking out on the horizon, he spoke up again.

"*Grazie.* I can't tell you how much I, how much I appreciate it. I know I've done a terrible thing. So, tell me. What do you want? I mean, do you want a cut?" He turned around to me then, his eyes suddenly searching.

"Oh, nothing, thanks if the treasure's what you mean. Just take yourself off. Disappear. Enjoy the rest of your life. You see, I think we've both fallen victim of Spencer. Many people have been fooled by him in the past. I think we both fell for his lies. You know I've been thinking this morning about all the lies he's told over the years. At least while I knew him at Cambridge. I don't think half of what he said was based in any resemblance of the truth. And, well, I for one just didn't see it then. I see it now though. He was a con artist. We're both victims. And well, look, I don't want you to end up in jail. What good will that do? And…after all… you saved Marco's life. You didn't have to. You could've saved Spencer. Marco could've drowned. But you didn't. So, you see, we're both just grateful to you. For that. Consider this our way of saying… thanks. But, just one thing. Tell me. Was Spencer's sister, well, was she in on it too? I'm just curious…"

Bruno poured himself a third rum, offering one to me too but I shook my head this time. "Spencer promised her a chunk of money. You see, we needed someone to make his death convincing. There are always more questions asked, you know, without a body. If nothing else, the process is much longer, drawn out. As it happened however, an American tourist drowned after we came up with the idea, just the day before we had planned it all, while surfing. We found out quite by chance from a fisherman.

He looked quite a lot like Spencer too, tall, blond, blue eyes. Spencer bribed the local police. Then they told the American's family that the man was lost, swept out to sea. All we had to do then was label the American's body as if he were Spencer. Of course, they also had to pay off the guys in the mortuary over in Bocas too. The American guy's family weren't here, his friends had moved on. It was surprisingly easy to do, and well, you know Spencer. He could convince anyone to do anything and with a bit of asking around, he'd found out that the police over in Bocas were easily bribed. There've been some odd cases around here recently, I mean in Bocas. Even a mass murderer, other things too. They're pretty useless and corruptible so it seems, and we gave them a good chunk of money. Then Spencer agreed it all with his sister. What I mean is we'd both identified the body. I did it here and she did it back in Rome. She had to convince her mother not to see him – but that wasn't hard. She knew her mother wouldn't want to, being the squeamish type and in any case, the body had decomposed quite a bit by then. I don't know if anyone taking a look would've known it wasn't Spencer. The American guy's face was pretty bashed up too – It'd been knocked around a reef for a day before they pulled him out."

"But why did she do it?" I asked, astonished and appalled all at once.

"Apparently she was desperate. She'd married well but her husband had lost all his money in a rogue trading deal. He might even go to jail and they were going to lose their house. Oh, and she never cared for Spencer, so when he proposed the idea, well she jumped at it. And the thought of never seeing him again, let's say it didn't seem to bother her, not for five minutes."

"I see." I nodded, understanding more now. It explained her not answering my calls. I'd tried a couple of times since the funeral, but she'd never picked up. I'd put it down to a whole host of reasons but never dreamed of this. And thinking back, somehow it all seemed to make sense. I knew now that those tears in Rome had been of the crocodile kind. I'd had a funny feeling about her at the time but now it all tied up.

"So, what next, Bruno? I mean, I don't need to do know the detail, but, well, never going back to Italy?"

"I'll sell my apartment in Rome, pay off the medical debts. There won't any money left over from that. The bank owns it now. Then start a new life. I want a fresh start away from Rome. I've already seen a place I want to buy here, and I put a deposit down on a boat last month. Of course, I'm not the one who's supposed to be dead, so I can come and go as I please. Maybe I'll go back to Italy too someday… but not for a while. Too many bad memories. I should have enough once I sell the rest of this stuff," he said, indicating to the backpacks, "to have a very good retirement. Never work again. Thanks to you…"

Back in my cabin that night, I lay in bed, under the mosquito net, the fan slowly circling the air above in no discernible direction. I thought about Bruno's offer, of a cut. I hadn't considered it for a second. I wanted to stay clean, not be dragged into any of it. I would've always been ashamed, afraid, looking over my shoulder. And not only but the stuff would be sold on the black market whereas it should've been in a museum. That was one of the hardest things to square about Bruno and letting him go like that. That the treasure wouldn't be turned in, couldn't be enjoyed by the public, but would be locked away out of sight in the private collection of some rich guy in China. It seemed such a shame.

Turning off the light, with the darkness of the jungle and the sounds of the night-time all around, London was beckoning.

Chalk Farm, London

Now

The rain has stopped, finally. It's been raining on and off all day. It's quiet now. The city is almost sleeping, if it ever really does. The radiator is on, the sound of tubes cracking as they expand with the heat, and for the first time this autumn I feel its warmth through my blanket. It feels cozy, it feels comforting.

Have I said before how much I love sitting in this kitchen, at the table by the window, laptop open, garden down below?

I'm lucky. While I have no outside space of my own, no terrace, nor the green fingers to go with it, Samantha, who owns the ground floor flat, loves to garden. She was out there during a gap in the rain in the cold, gloves on, pruning, cutting back for the winter. It makes my view all the better come spring when her efforts pay off and the plants burst into life and color once again. Earlier today I could see her planting bulbs. When we met on the stairs last month, both on our way back from the local Sainsbury's, she'd told me she was taking a trip to Holland, Amsterdam. No doubt she brought some bulbs back. I hope they're yellow. Bright and cheery like a yellow umbrella on a faraway tropical beach in the rain.

If you were to take a short walk to my bedroom – it's just off the hall on the left - and peek inside, you'd see another bright yellow thing. A small suitcase. I bought it just the other day. You'd also see that, apart from the color (which I love - I mean, who else has a yellow suitcase? Did you ever see one? I haven't) it's open and semi packed. Yes. I'm off on another adventure.

And I wasn't expecting it, not at all. But isn't that the wonderful thing. I mean about life? The unexpected?

The Facebook feature was a hit. Mac gave me a six-month feature contract. Scrapped *Melody Talkin'*. I was elated. *Enough of Melody Talkin'* I thought. She's been gabbing away long enough. So, things were looking up.

And then one Thursday, the news. *Zenith* was bust. Closing down. Goodbye *Zenith*. For good. So much for Mac and his grand plans. He hadn't even gotten started and as a result, neither had I.

I've been doing all kinds of bits and pieces since then. It's not been easy but I'm getting by. *Melody Talkin'* was resurrected in '*City Vibes'* a freebie commuter newspaper. It wasn't the plan, but the good news is it's a daily, so I have a half page every day and it pays the bills.

It's been a year now. And that's when the first envelope arrived forwarded to me via Limbo Hotel, Bastimentos Island:

Dear Melody,

Greetings from Panama.

Please accept this small coin as a token of my appreciation.

I'm sure Sir Henry would've wanted you to have it.

You might like to know that for the rest, for the major part, I handed it over anonymously to the Panamanian authorities along with the coordinates of the wreck and the excavation site on Zapatillas. You were right – the archaeologist in me just couldn't see this amazing treasure sold on the black market. I struggled with it for a year – but it's too incredible, too rare. The world needs to see it rather than be kept in the vault of some private rich collector in China or who knows where. It needs to be in a museum for everyone to enjoy. So, I kept a little of the less interesting pieces and handed in the rest.

If the Panamanian newspapers are reporting correctly, the authorities were extremely surprised and delighted. They are already talking about opening a new museum exhibit where the public will be able to enjoy Sir Henry's amazing gold. It will likely be on the site of Panama Viejo – the site of the original Panama City and which Morgan sacked. Quite poetic really. I'm glad it's found a home – although the Spanish and Peruvians might have something to say about it. By the time you read this letter (I do hope it finds you. Hotel Limbo agreed to forward it to you)) it will very soon most likely be making international news – so you might like to follow the unfolding story in the press.

Arrivederci.

Bruno.

Soon after the second envelope arrived. It was classy, cream envelope with the logo of 'Aventino Hotels' in a delicate grey type on the top, left hand corner. Over coffee and toast I opened it quite carelessly to be frank. A promotion I thought, some kind of special offer: A spring deal, a romantic Valentines break for two with breakfast included, perhaps a coupon with 15% off. I wasn't planning a trip to Rome but was interested. Maybe later in the year, once I found the courage to go back. But instead a handwritten note fell out and another envelope inside. The note had been carefully folded and said:

Dear Ms. Meeks,

We are forwarding to you the enclosed envelope which is addressed to you. Our sincere apologies – we found the envelope last week when we were renovating the reception area. It appears that this envelope had been left for you at some point last summer in your pigeonhole and we failed to pass it to you. To explain, unbeknown to us, there was a gap at the back, and it fell down the back of the unit. Once again, our sincere apologies for any inconvenience this oversight may have caused.

Yours sincerely
Gianni Rossetti

Assistant Hotel Manager – Hotel Villa San Pio, Rome.

For an instant I was bemused. Then a wave of a memory washed over me.

Marco.

More carefully and sitting up now I opened second the envelope. It read:

My Dearest Melody,

Sorry for this badly written note, forgive me, but I must try and express to you what I feel, deep down in the core of me.

The first time I saw you, at the church, I knew that I loved you. Not just a surface love, but a love deep down in the very bottom of me.

You are everything and the only thing I want in the world.

I am so sorry for what happened the other night – that I had to tell you the very next day that I was not free to be with you – that I had a girlfriend. But you should know, that night was the best night of my life. Whatever happens I will never forget it.

You see, I'm not free right now. I tried to explain in the bar, but you kept closing me down. But I wanted very much to explain. I wanted you to understand. I thought about it last night and thought that the best way to explain is to write it to you. You see my girlfriend Valentina's mother is dying. She only has a few weeks or months to live. I tried to make it work with Valentina for some time. But I know it's over between us. I've known it for months, but I can't leave her - not just now. It would be too cruel. We met at school and she relies on me so much. I can't break her heart while her mother is dying! But in time, I want you to know, that I will find a way, to say goodbye. You must know that I want, need to spend the rest of my life with just one person – you.

But I see that you are still in love with Spencer. I see what happens when you hear his name. I see that although he is dead your heart is still with him and I want to respect this – even though it kills me every time I think of it.

So please, don't give up on me - I find it hard to express my feelings sometimes - that's why I'm writing this to you now.

I hope if you read this you will understand, give me a chance at some time in the future.

Melody. If you read this, now, in the future, whenever you do, if you ever feel just for five minutes that you might feel something for me – that you are over Spencer. Please come find me.

I'll be dreaming and waiting for you.

All my love,

Marco

So, my bag is packed, my flight to Rome is booked. I'm ready for a different kind of adventure. Who knows what I will find and where it will lead me? I hope that Marco is still at Sapienza University, pouring over his journals, embarking on his longed-for study of Nero's Golden House, that I can find him there… and if not, then I'll have another hunt on my hands. Maybe it will come to nothing – even if I find him. Maybe it will be everything.

You see, when *Zenith* closed, Marco had no way to find me, to get in touch this last year. I realized that I never gave him my home address. My phone was stolen from my bag (a drunken girl's night out in a pub in Covent Garden) and I have a new number now. Maybe he's tried to find me these last months. Maybe not. Nothing in this life is certain. I've learnt that the hard way. The only thing for sure, on this next adventure, is that there'll be no pirates, no map, no Facebook feature. But I am hoping to find some treasure, the biggest one of all. Love.

EPILOGUE

Jamaica
Five miles inland from Port Royal
1676 ca.

Word soon got around the plantation. Sir Henry didn't have long, and the slaves were restless. Less sugar cane was being cut, more talk around the cooking fires by night. They didn't care for their master greatly, but uncertainty was perhaps a crueler overlord and Morgan had been fair compared to some. The beatings and whippings on the next plantation were known across the island and by comparisons of the day, Sir Henry was a good, even kind master. No male heirs were the nub making the future an uncertain beast and by all accounts Lady Mary was done with plantation life, already planning a return to Wales. If so, the plantation would be sold to who knows who, the slaves kept or sent who knows where.

Many a doctor had visited Morgan's dark stale bed chamber these last weeks. The sun, kept at bay by heavy wooden shutters, did it's best to poke a finger in, but any rays that made it through, mostly when the sun was overhead at mid-day, were soon thwarted by the heavy, ruby colored drapes which the Lady insisted be kept drawn at all times.

"The light, he doesn't like the light," she reminded the many doctors who were brought over by horse and cart from Port Royal each day and who always arrived with an array of potions, powders, ligaments and leaches. The Lady had told the maid to set up a small wooden table and a washstand, to the right of the bed, and in the gloom, they took turns grinding, mixing and pummeling an array of varied, mainly unknown ingredients. They administered compresses and let blood. They gave him boiled potions and broths. But even the most highly trained medics of the day couldn't deny the decline was well and truly set in, his days numbered in few. Fact was that life on the seas was hard on any a man and it had taken its toll on Morgan like any other. Yes, a private, more comfortable cabin, first in line for fresh food when the ships cooks had the ingredients, not the same as the hardships of the common crew, but still... bones bent and gnarled, infected wounds and soars, malaria and one leg full of gout from too much rum and grog. He coughed and wheezed, the cigars and hard tobacco had lined his lungs many a year past. Then there was the new influx of slaves which complicated the ongoing quest for a diagnosis. They'd seemed healthy on arrival compared to the last consignment, fresh off the boat from Port –au-Prince. But then the yellow fever had taken five and, in the candlelight, Mary was convinced that Morgan had a yellowing tinge to the tips of his fingers and the white of his eyes, more than the many years of tobacco smoking would color in.

From time to time he roused and managed to take in a little water, some medicine, before slumping on the bed, hot and sweating one minute, cold and shivering the next. And then, sometimes half delirious, sometimes more cognitive than to be expected, he grabbed Mary's hand murmuring, ranting, always the same:

"The Satisfaction!"

He'd never gotten over the loss of this ship – his finest, his favorite. The month The Satisfaction had gone down, the tales had gone around Port Royal like a wildfire. The Satisfaction, sunk off Bocas del Toro! Marquez! Just a few survivors, the captain one of them! Treasure, lost. Gone for good!

"Marquez, damn him, damn him to hell."

Mary leaned in to hear, his voice a whisper now. The doctor bent over and took his pulse. It was weak, barely to be felt.

"Blasted Marquez. Waited, outside the cove. Just one cannon shot. The Satisfaction! Wicks! Roberts!"

"Henry, don't trouble yourself about The Satisfaction – so long ago..."

"She went down too quickly!! Men, sharks. The pendant, the key – the, the treasure... need to go back, find it...we need to get it. Our plantation house - So beautiful. We need to build it before the rains start. Gold... more wealth than you can...Marquez..."

"Darling, don't trouble yourself...I promise you. Just get well." She squeezed his hand. It was going limp. She could feel his grasp on this early February evening slipping out of hers.

"We'll find it, one day, very soon my darling," she said. "Don't fret yourself. I promise."

Author Bio

Suzanne Hope grew up in Heysham Village, Lancashire in the UK and studied history before launching a career in Fundraising and Marketing. Through her work for international organizations she has lived in London, Rome, Geneva, Bangkok and also spent two years in Panama in Central America where she became fascinated with pirate history - and ***The Treasure Seeker*** was born. She is now living in Brooklyn, New York with her husband Francesco and two cats Mimi and Bunny. ***The Treasure Seeker*** is Suzanne's 2nd novel and the first in the new *Melody Meek Mysteries* series. She is also the author of 'The Bookshop of Panama'.

You can find out more about Suzanne and her books at www.suzannehope.com

Made in the USA
Middletown, DE
07 February 2021